C000121180

DIVISION

[THE CROWS OVER CROSS HILL]

JOHN BOWIE

RED DOG
UK

Published by RED DOG PRESS 2021

First Edition

Paperback ISBN 978-1-914480-12-6
Ebook ISBN 978-1-914480-13-3

www.reddogpress.co.uk

For those that didn't make it out.

[division]
/dɪˈvɪʒ(ə)n/

1. The action of separating something into parts or the process of being separated.
2. Difference or disagreement between two or more groups, typically producing tension.

'There are things that have to be forgotten if you want to go on living.'
— *Jim Thompson, The Killer Inside Me*

PROLOGUE

A WALK IN THE DUNES

A FAMILIAR SEA fret, carried on the evening's breeze, gently kissed her face as the air, dunes and waves offered up their daily tourniquet release, to soothe Mia Thompson's lifetime of pent-up regrets. Only this time was different, her solace was interrupted, she'd found death in the dunes. She realised it wasn't a sand covered rock as the mound depressed under the weight of her heel. Her whole foot went in, forcing out a rancid, angry rasp of air that escaped a body which had lay undiscovered for days, maybe longer.

Resigned to nature's caress.

It was a corpse wrapped in a blanket of sand, seaweed, driftwood and bottle tops. Washed up, hidden or discarded but not fully forgotten. It reeked, and was fresh enough to be missed. The body's imagined story flashed before her eyes: loves lost, futures out of reach and dissolving into the beach. Joining with the granules of ground down pieces of rock, stones and matter, all with their own stories to tell. The body had found its eternity in the sands. And if its life was like Mia's, its zenith lay there with the damp seaweed.

She'd walked Marlie over those dunes early most mornings and sometimes in the evening. Like that evening, as the moon married the sea, sand dunes and silhouettes of sharp grasses crested the brow of each hill as her little black cocker spaniel ran wild, free and manic. Joyfully playing, as her mind wrestled feelings of being trapped, unloved and stuck in life's relentless grey malaise. She was beaten down by a resentful partner. The same one who picked her up each morning, only to repeat the cycle by closing time, when he was booted back out onto the street.

Each evening brought her escapism, as greying hues with sepia splashes from retiring skies became her very own classic movie—a special evening performance, under the moon's spotlight and the sea's potent, visceral direction. The dunes and beach her big screen.

That night, when she'd driven down the old potholed country lane to the back of the beach, her head was filled with idle dark ruminations, as always. She ignored them as long as she could, then she needed out into nature. To cleanse the soul ready to be muddied again, by him. Otherwise it would overflow and she was scared where that could lead. The questions always came in order:

Was anyone ever happy?

By the time she slowly parked, opened the door and sat for a while with the steam from her breath hanging mid-air, the spaniel was frenzied with excitement. An excitement she was now immune to. But travelled the motions, vacant. Like a laden coffin through a Vegas strip with the lights of other people's vibrance and life bouncing off the lid.

Why am I still here?
What was ever the point?

By the time the dog had run off ahead, her feet had trod, crunched and tamed the flats leading up to the main central dune ahead, as her feet parted the ground that was filled with tiny white, blue and yellow flowers. The footpath leading up to the mass of dunes was her red carpet and, by then, the purge had usually begun.

This time wasn't usual, at first. The crest of dunes and sand growing darker with night's encroach, beckoning her to the water's edge, as nature responded to her questions with demonstrations of hope and continuation in her scents, sounds and textures. Regardless of her inability to always appreciate them, she knew they were always there to perform for her. Sometimes, this was all she needed. To feel part of the jigsaw.

The sea welcomed her most of all. But its deep dark blanket always made her wary of how much to welcome it in return. Knowing one day, soon, she'd take the full embrace.

Go all the way in.

The sea listened. It was a woman, of course. Never a man. It never responded fully. Often that's all she ever wanted: someone to listen, just a bit… She didn't want to go all the way in. Not today.

Maybe this was it… this corpse… a first reply? A sign. An echo of things to come and a resonating stench of the things that are. Echoes of a future. Dreams of future memories.

These walks were essential, to keep going on. The sea's motion brought a mind's massage, to take it all away, as her feet moved over the sands towards a wisp of cold sea fret that pecked her cheeks each day at the shoreline. The sea often felt like an ageing, or dying, relative with more sympathy for her to go on, than for themselves knocking on Death's door.

What else was there to do?

She was scared of the true answer to that one.

She'd finish with curses for *him: Fuck it. Fuck you. Fuck him.*

Eventually, she always did. Go on. Returning to the car, with her beloved dog, Marlie.

As close to real love as it got. Never going all the way into the waves. Marlie wouldn't let her. For the dog, there was always another bit of seaweed and sinew to chew on, or a dead seal carcass to roll in, before returning to the back seat of the old yellow VW Golf. A hundred thousand miles on the clock and the VW had never left the county. The old girl could practically drive herself to the beach. As could Marlie. A tattered tartan blanket in the back for Marlie brought a familiar comforting wrap after the chilling wind set the bite of the sea to sand-matted fur. There was nothing for Mia. She embraced the chills willingly each time. A reminder she was alive. Before her home life brought numbness and it started all over again, and she wished she wasn't, alive.

Why doesn't he listen. Only talk, lash out, hit out?

That night a blood-red sunset cast its mirror image over the waves as a distant lighthouse cut through the surface of the sea. White horses battled relentless rolling crests that attacked the battered shoreline as lines of incinerated wooden sea breaks, sea blown victims pointed out to the horizon. A line of weed and carcasses gathered; rejects of the waters. A line of dead between land and sea. Two-meter cubed tank blocks, old war scars, stood sentry at the base of the dunes in a row. Rolled and skewed by the moving sands. A testament to the coastlines constant threat of attack over the ages. Under the sands lay more relics from squads' endless firing practice in anticipation of the invasion that never came. Rifle shells in graves with sea shells.

Unseen, beneath the dunes, those buried WWII bullets, where soldiers took practice, joined with Viking shields, Palaeolithic flint arrowheads and Celtic pots. Surface signs are there too with a constant supply of sand-coated carcasses, bones and other washed-up evidence of life's insatiable ebb and flow.

This time, it wasn't a dead seal for Marlie to roll in.

She jumped further away from the lump in the sand, stumbled and fell. Realising what she was on top of. The now unmistakable body's form made clear in the moon's cast.

She gagged but wasn't sick. Not at first. Then it came, the acid, tears. Only this time it was for someone else. And it had come on suddenly, rather than the usual build up in anticipation of *him* coming home drunk again from the pub.

Fuck she wished the lump was him.

Baring witness to a tragedy, her own still dominated her pity. The sand moved and a once human hand dropped out of the sandy, body-shaped lump. She gagged again. With the corpse's sandy-shiver came an exposed forearm—bone and flesh like driftwood; beaten and battered by sea and sands. Sandflies and tiny creatures of the shore moved towards, over and into their brittle prize: the tissue that hung on, just. Before an inevitably larger hungry scavenger, a seagull, crab or the waters would hope to detach all that remained to submit it to the tides. Disposing of the being's whole, fusing its remnants with the greater mass and nature's continuation.

She looked in her pockets for two coins. To put on the eyes if hers were to meet them. Without thought, instinct told her the boatman would need them if there was a chance this sorry lost soul would make it to the grace of an afterlife.

No coins. Nothing.

She imagined *him* spending whatever he'd found in her purse on the last round of the night, he wouldn't ask her how the day and night had been. He wouldn't care to ask why she looked more shell-shocked than usual and smelled of a new death. Rather than the one he'd kicked from her. He'd batter her and fuck her, sore, and it would start over again the next day.

She wished she'd put him there in that mound to be chewed up and rolled around in the beaches shit and detritus. When he lay there, she'd keep the coins.

As she stared, a small crab emerged from the flesh. Then small maggot-like-creatures, things essential to the later cycle of life, Death's workers, moving in and out of the corpse in an increased frenzy. Life exploding from death.

Pop. Spit. Pop.

Something flew and jumped with another rasp of air. She felt something hit her face, her lips. She tasted death first-hand. It tasted like burnt bacon. Tomorrow she'd be vegetarian. She heaved but there was nothing to come. Her stomach muscles ached, cramping from the continued effort.

Stillness returned. No waves or birds. Nature stopped in respect of the corpse for a moment's silence. The respite soon broke, before she could catch her breath again. The animation returned as there was motion overhead with gulls eagerly eyeing their next meal. Black birds gathered as well, standing to attention on the brow of the dunes nearby. A murder of crows to mourn a passing soul. A chorus of respect came in their voice and song. But she was hardly tuned in to hear.

Marlie stopped staring from a distance and ran up, excited, tongue out and ears flapping behind in the wind... About to dive in as usual. To roll deep, mark a spot and steal another dead scent to wear with pride. She relished it. Loved it. Her dog friends would read the news on her, every last rub of the week, from badger shit, fish guts to dead birds. All worn with pride on her shiny coat as she basked in the smells like they were expensive French cologne.

Suddenly the dog stopped, sand kicked in the air from its breaking legs. It was stilled by true lifelessness. Made uneasy by this unusual form where there once was animation in a fallen master. She wanted to join the crows in respect but also wanted to be near and comfort Mia. It's what she lived for. If only Mia fully knew. She loved Mia and always would.

The spaniel tried to creep, crawled a little closer, but something dark and unseen prevented Marlie from getting any closer. She had frozen, as if hitting an invisible wall two meters from the now part-covered body, as the heap now released a new round of stale odours. Further exposed fresh elements meant to attack and accelerate its decomposition.

Marlie whimpered. Shaking as if feeling the North sea's chill for the first time and the winds failed to dry her fur.

All the birds now circled overhead, growing in numbers. A banquet awaiting. The crows had taken flight, joining Death's tainted symphony. A black and white murmuration to a stranger's passing. This dance of the skies was more frequent than most people in the coastal village, or visitors, knew about. Over recent weeks it had become even more common.

She got out her phone. Dialled the police. For once the call wasn't for her, to report her partner, or find his whereabouts. This call was for her discovery: the body lying in the sand at her feet.

There's always someone worse off.

This body wouldn't wash away its worries now. They had already been purged, battered and ripped away with a last breath. Like life from the empty shells and fish in a daily-changing collage of kelp and seagrass in the shore's wrack zone.

She desperately wished he was part of it.

THE YOUNG OFFICER looked at the lump, then back to Mia. Just nodded. An older WPC joined them alongside. They all wished it was him in there but knew it wasn't.

'Thanks for calling it in. Do you need a lift back? Okay to drive Mia?'

'I'm okay.' As she spoke the sands shifted from the upper part as a face, shrunken back lips and yellowing teeth like an Egyptian mummy were out in the air.

'Fuck,' the young officer cried, ran off to the shore line, and was sick over and over. The gulls cawed, eyeing up another meal gifted to them. The crows didn't move. Back in position on a line. A funeral mass, nodding in respect.

Mia and the WPC hadn't moved. This time Mia wasn't sick and the female officer had done her time in the big cities, and didn't react either.

'Shame,' the officer said.

Mia knew what she meant. 'Maybe one day... he'll just leave.'

'Maybe,' the WPC said, looking at the corpse. 'Maybe he will.' And she put an arm around Mia.

1

ALNMOUTH

JOHN BLACK SAW the all too familiar blue flashing lights in the distance from his train. This time cutting through hills and coastal lanes, rather than the industrial urban cityscape he'd just left behind but had grown used to recently.

The red lights streamed like veins through the country lanes, as the sun battled heavy clouds to set the day over the estuary and beach; a visual battle between man and nature. A fight nature would always win.

The police cars and ambulances rushed to what was normally a dead space of a village on the North Sea. A place John had spent most of his formative drinking years with Pete and Naresh. It was a place that could have been home. And Pete and Naresh could have been friends. But women, personal wars and drink had changed them all. John more than most, with the added layers of 'real warfare'.

His head vibrated against the carriage window as his hands shook on the small fold-out table and the train slowed in approach to his stop. His brain settled from the motion. Fluids settling in his skull.

When he last left there was silence on an empty platform. With his return, came chaos, sirens, and flashing lights. This wasn't what he'd hoped for. In the city, it was expected and he had both sides of the law onside. On the coast, in this little village and its rural conurbations, he had nothing. He was just another unwanted homecomer to rub the noses of the trapped zombies that inhabited the holes of his upbringing. He'd walk salt into all their wounds with each reopened door.

He'd anticipated nothing waiting for him but resentment, and a funeral; deader than most.

He assumed now that the police had heard of his arrival, and had decided to provide a welcome party—but they were going in the wrong direction for that—away from the tiny hut and a footbridge of a station.

That's how he'd felt himself the entire journey since his train had left Manchester:

Headed in the wrong direction.

Away from her.. and going homewards. But not home.

His hands shook again and his fists clenched. Veins and tendons burned. In a flash he wished he drank like he used to. All the time. To obliteration. To dull the senses. Something told him it would return; the thirst. If not before, then at the funeral and certainly by the wake. Northumbrians, the Scots and the Irish had a way of attacking death. His family had the blood of all three. Someone would have let the publicans know to stock up. Or, there'd be hell on the streets.

More than this, he needed to drown the sorrows of leaving his true love behind.

There was too much weight in the love of a woman he'd nearly got killed, and could do again. It nagged and hurt, and he knew the feeling would never go. Even if he doused it in whisky and drank the area dry. It would remain, even if they did ever find a way to be together. That's what it meant, to love her, for him. Always pained to protect and care for her more than himself. It's why he'd cut his drinking. He needed to be sharper than before. And it's why he planned to start up again, to forget why...

Normally, he'd avoid a family funeral or any other gathering. But he was using it to create that distance; from her, from his enemies, for her sake. He told his brother he'd show presence, take one for the team. And John loved her, Cherry, too much to be near her right now. So he went North. To these borderlands of Northumberland.

Maybe John should have gone home before then, whilst he still had one. He hadn't. Devoid of any connection, this time disconnection was to draw him back... A death, duty, and the family funeral. His own mother.

Damn his fucking brother for not sharing the load.

He created the distance from Cherry, using family. Heavy in irony and not easy to get on the train, but it was done. He was there.

For Cherry. For me, he thought.

Love. Together forever.

Even though apart.

There, it came: the thirst. A need to wash down all the regret and baggage.

Ambulances joined the stream of emergency services outside going the other way. They were for another body, a death. A funeral where he wouldn't be expected.

PETE AND NARESH turned up to meet his train. They sat in unsaid apprehension. Both too proud to show nerves.

He was just a man.

Soldier: fuck that.

Writer: who gives a shit.

He is... just... a man.

Worse than that. He left, made something of himself, and then thought to come back again.

The world and John had changed since they had last met, spoke, drank together. John'd been chewed up by wars, spat out by gangs in Manchester and Bristol and had come out of it all— neither one side or the other, he was something else now. No worse. He was writing about it. Whereas Pete and Naresh's existence had remained a closed-off treadmill of their own making. Lacking confidence, trapped in the confines of the suppressed self-belief of the ancient town walls of Alnwick. The castle and its walls had kept it, them, and everything, locked down for centuries.

John's train fully stopped: Alnmouth. It was the nearest station to his hometown of Alnwick, just over three miles away. Alnwick remained disconnected from the mainline veins of public transport that could lift it from its medieval stronghold past and being a fixed, dormant cultural desert.

JOHN'S AGENT STILL had her hooks in him, as did his therapist. The agent would call to remind John to write. To remind him it mattered to her. His therapist used to call to remind him it mattered to him. She didn't need to anymore, and knew it, her words echoed around his head as much as Cherry's.

Write it out.

Don't let it linger.

Everyone suffers. Carries a load.

Externalise it. Expunge it. Dissolve it by realising it on the page. Burn it if you have to.

The writer's thing his agent insisted he go to on the way up North was short-lived. She knew that, in order to survive, he needed to pursue the healthy vocation that separated him from past traumas, so pushed him to attend, despite his resistance not to.

'Do a writers' thing on the way up. It'll be good for you... and us,' she'd said. 'Who knows, you might even meet a real agent rather than me. You could do with a break. And I could do with being bought out.'

'I hate writers' things. I fucking hate writers. And me most of all, for turning into one. I was happier when I drank every day and relived my mistakes in my head. Now, I have to set them in stone and write them down.'

He did what he was told—M. Pamplemousse knows best, of course. What ex-stripper, burlesque titty-twister that now runs a biker's bar, and literary agent wouldn't. The door to her bar was made of human skin and blood. And her tits, at fifty, were like canons; shooting for the stars. She wasn't to be argued or fucked with. The bikers knew that. John knew it most of all.

At the Crime Spree Conference in Birmingham, he'd walked straight in and up to the bar. It was six-deep with Wordsworths, Wildes and Hemmingway-wannabe-pricks. Peacocks prancing, desperate to be asked what they were working on. To allude to being the next big thing, undiscovered; of course. Giant posters adorned the walls and projections to screens about the hall: best seller here, coming soon there, must read over there. It made him sick.

These people wrote for entertainment. For him it was a mechanical, a momentum. It was both necessary and a bloodletting. And they were all tainted leaches to him. In it for the money, fame and fortune.

For him it was to breathe, exist and be.

'How's the book going?' the person next to him said at the bar, touching an over preened red goatee beard. John nearly threw a punch, anxious to the point of already having noted all escape routes and toilet locations. The bar, unfortunately, was a necessary evil. To put out the flames you had to wade through the tiers of perching wankers.

He turned, walked straight back out and into the O'Shea's Irish pub next door, ordered a Guinness with double Jameson's. Downed them. Then, left to re-join his train up North, Alnmouth village station and then to Alnwick town where he was booked into the White Swan Hotel. A world apart from these people. It was its own literary hell.

AS HE ALIGHTED the train and saw Pete and Naresh waiting. They looked nervous.

He'd written more than he'd drank lately; steering away from trouble after Cherry was hurt. And these two had only one way of going at it, full tilt or nothing at all. And they'd never done 'nothing at all' when it came to drinking. It was the only way to them and how better to sedate their predicaments whilst supporting the local economy.

He could see it in their eyes, his increased abstinence was about to be challenged.

Drink... and trouble would follow.

'Sirens stick to you like a stink to shite,' Pete said. His aggressive humour masked insecurities. Feeling the lesser man most of the time. In front of John, even without fully knowing anything about what scars he had, he was definitely doubting himself. He looked away before the eye contact revealed this.

'Nothing goes on here. You grace us with your fucking presence. And the place lights up with blue flashing lights everywhere. Welcome back, JB. Try not to kill anyone whilst you're here, eh?' Naresh added. It was a joke, poorly delivered. Naresh wore the malaise of an aged clown sweeping the stage after an empty show.

Only John knew the truth or gravity in what Naresh had said. John would try, not to kill anyone. Try.

They stood a while in silence, weighing John up. He put his bag down and let them. He tried to remember if they were actually friends, or just people he used to drink with before he realised it worked better for him alone. And they looked and tried to figure out what happened to him, the years, and if he was always this fucking weird.

He was. Just there was more of it now.

Pete eventually said: 'We're still barred from The Sun and The Schooner. They didn't like Naresh's confusion between the fish pond and urinal last time. And you're banned from there and everywhere else... Guess they just never liked your face, John.' The silence was broken, Pete had made the mission clear: get fucked and catch up. A true agenda would follow the pints. As the pints would become the agenda.

'The Sun it is,' John said. 'Like they give a shit. They need the money,' he conceded, there was no other way here. He either got on with it or boarded the next train back and skipped the funeral. It was tempting. He needed a drink.

...and trouble was sure to follow.

2

13:15 TO PADDINGTON

NINA WAS OUT, but despite her new freedoms, having been used for years as other people's sex-type-thing in prison, she was trapped by the scent of them all that indelibly stuck to her skin and those memories, like tar. The smell of the last guard was still strong. Like rotting fish and shit: in her, on her. She doubted it would ever come off, but she knew how to try.

She needed true release. She needed to take, rather than be taken.

Since leaving HM Prison Styal hours before, she still felt physically trapped in there. She was sure the memories would never shift but meant to lubricate them before overwriting them with her own design. She'd spent an afternoon drinking in the Bishop and Bear above the concourse of London's Paddington station looking at the mobile phone in front of her. It was a potential to be tapped; Pandora's box, maybe. A candy stash with a hidden shard of glass. A roll of hidden fags under a mattress soiled by the thirty guards rolling out of, and off of her.

Every idea, memory—broken.

She did have it. A way out. Her own design.

John and Nina—King and Queen of the underworld.

Gone.

Johnny Cash was playing his version of a song, but all she heard was the Nine Inch Nails' version. Cash's words to *Hurt* played and echoed about the tiny ceiling speakers and her brain cast its own version. Eventually, his lyrical dulcet tones won her ears over, so much weightier than the busy train concourse below, Cash won out. She couldn't cry. If ever there was a definitive time, for a more conventional release; that was it, and she couldn't. Wouldn't. Never.

She let the moment pass.

She tapped on the phone's screen, toying with websites she'd been told about inside.

'There's loads, pet,' Tammy used to say. 'It's a hole-hungry cock-fest out there. Fanny-stuffing-festival too if you so likey?!'

She didn't, 'so likey'—neither idea really appealed. Nina was a closed book, but had been infiltrated. She'd used her body to get by, and get out. An early release after being the vessel for so many of *theirs*. And now she needed to cleanse the trespassers from her skin.

The last man to visit her in her cell had become something of a regular in the last weeks. He breathed hard at her, drooled whiskey spit and made her wear a wig whilst he did it. He had some fucked up ideas, they all did. It didn't matter, she knew her enemy. The call had come long before she went inside. John Black was meant to be her partner, or die, and he'd long since turned down that first choice.

That fuck could have sealed it, with John. But instead she'd been made to take the whole prison service on.

Drinks came as the mobile bounced around in her finger tips. It was a portal to opportunity, connections and the sealed fate for those to come.

She closed her eyes and saw the glory of it all: lines of bodies, fates sealed. Buried in boxes. Cut up and shut up. Pained before their demise underground, but not so much as to cut the punishment short altogether. She'd been confined and prodded, poked and fucked so hard and for so long—it felt time to inflict the restrictions, penetrations and destruction of the soul onto others now.

'This seat taken?' a pinstripe suit wearing city gent grinned, cocksure and eyed the seat opposite her. But, really only having eyes for her, which had been on her the past half hour from across the bar. He was lucky, and didn't know how close he came to missing his next meeting.

When she looked up, she was unable to contain the evil thoughts spilling over her face and he saw something in those bloodshot eyes he would never forget. It would make him hug his kids extra tight that evening, and make him wait another fortnight before trying to cheat on his wife again. But he would, again.

She dismissed the irritation of the suit's interruption and returned her gaze to the mobile phone's screen. He wasn't worth it. A mere fly to be swatted away. Not even an appetiser. She had a quick look and a scan of some homepages between the lines of triple vodkas that lined up in front of her. The fluid was as flavourless as possible, she needed a fix without the refinement of a flavour sensation to go with it. Nothing she found online looked like it would provide the much needed remedy to go with the vodkas.

She craved. Thirsted. Something close to a guard, close to John. Something close to hell. Or, that she could bend, break and make into it.

'Ding, the next train at platform 13 is the delayed 13.15 from Manchester, Piccadilly,' a tannoy announced over speakers struggling with Dire Straits.

Her desires were unconventional, dark. She'd need to dig deep. Or did she need to just have a more normal hit first. Could she just meet, fuck and move on? Would that do it for now? Something a bit rougher maybe? A hard bang up against the cubical door then donkey punch their fucking lights out as they came—maybe that would do.

The vodka was working but the sites weren't—nothing grabbed her and the clock was ticking. China Bob's train was arriving soon. He'd meander about a bit like a shark in the kid's end, looking at the commuters like they were lunch, but then they'd need to meet up and to get on with the task at hand, and get themselves some wheels and get up North. She fucking hated trains, or being driven at someone else's hands. She had the control back in her life, and it was staying.

She wasn't totally sure what it was she did need from the web search. But kept idly scanning the results over and over. She hoped she'd know it when she saw it, at least something close enough to bend and break into the mould of her desires. There was a niche out there for every sick fuck on the planet. She wasn't all that different. Wants, desires, sucks and fucks. Then leaving before the consequences settle in. There must be a website for that. God help any of the sick fucks she found out there.

Tap, tap, tap:

PlentyofFlesh.com? No.

LightmyFire.com? No.

FuckaUniform.net? No… Hmm...maybe… 'Can I specify a prison warden?... Hmm, no!

FlightsofFancy.net? WTF?! No.

She grew bored. With limited time to fill.

She had someone else to meet. And their train was now arriving very soon. Someone who she shared a common enemy with her. China Bob, AKA Snake Eyes was due on the next train. He'd taken a rap for John Black too. She knew his rep'. Damn, she felt near related to him now. Bonded in pain and torment by John Black's very existence. Snake Eyes would love her for it. China Bob and Nina were the new partnership John had passed on. Now they needed to remove him all together. But first, there'd be a little game played at his expense. Boxing up his keepsakes and burying them alive.

She went into prison because of John Black... She used to be a DJ, a small-time drug dealer and a sex toy to the Manc-gangs she was used and pimped out by. She was so out of it back then, she didn't really get the dealing thing or the consequences: as Nina span those hypnotising black discs, that 'dumb-young-thing' drank too much water after a bad pill and collapsed off the stage in their club.

So, John brought the whole fucking church down about their heads, and those like Nina were led like priests to be burned at the stake for the worship of false gods. Fuck 'em all, if they wanted to get screwed up in some hedonistic cess pit.

'I'm just a fucking DJ,' she'd said in court.

'You're just a DJ that sold bad gear, that killed a young girl,' they'd said.

'Fuck them all,' she'd said to no one in particular. But, meaning everyone. All of them.

Nina thought, John'd had some crisis of confidence at the time, an attack of morals, and forgot whose side he was really on. Who gives a flying fuck—he took them all down. He took down the gang boss too, and Nina was sure it was her role to naturally follow in his steps. Fill those shoes. That wouldn't happen now, because of that fucker: John Black. She was meant to be transformed, and become Queen Bee over Manchester's gangland. Instead she became the guards' fuck-puppet in prison. John could have made an alliance. Instead he made hell all about himself. And Nina was keen to keep the fires burning.

Delusional. Definitely maybe.

Back inside when she was locked up and eventually sobered up, she was in a small windowless cell, a concrete torture chamber had grown up around her, a dank blanket of grief and despair for path's untaken and regret for choices made under the influence. And all the while, Black was in his cosy Witness Protection, having testified, shared everything. Free to fucking roam.

Devil or cunt. No matter. He would suffer.

Next, she heard that John had kicked her gang boss off a fifteen-story tower block and took over his mantle. Her fucking mantle, not his. She'd worked hard to earn it. She'd never be able to wash that taste from her mouth now. And he'd stolen the right to rule over his empire from her. She'd sucked, fucked and toiled away—it was always meant to be hers.

ALL OF IT. Hers.

Now, with Snake Eyes arriving soon, she was going to take it all back. China Bob's Snake eyes paired beautifully with her reddened eye holes, windows to the transcendent grief to come. She'd heard wind Black was headed North to a funeral... She aimed to make sure of it being *his*.

She waited impatiently for Snake Eyes' train to get in. But was growing less patient at trying the websites to find someone to fill the time slot.

She had her plan, and was sure Bob and his Snake Eyes would be on board to take down John Black. First, she needed this release that insisted on nagging at her. She had a weight of a thousand bad screws to try and rid herself of. Itching at her between the legs they pulled apart. Now she needed to fuck and dispose of someone, on her own terms. It wouldn't save her, or not change a thing, she just wanted it bad.

She looked at the screen and smiled. Bingo.

'IT'S FUCKING GENIUS, I tell you,' Rupert told him, grinning like he'd found a way to print a winning lottery ticket. 'So simple. Seriously. If it wasn't my website idea, and you found it on the web right now, whilst waiting for your train... you wouldn't give it a go? — Bang a bit of strange? I don't believe you.'

'Not for me, Rupert.'

'Bollocks. You'd hop straight on. Blow your load, then be off to catch the next train out of Responsibility-ville. And it'd be, hello... next stop: Happy Emptied Balls-town!'

'For fuck's sake. Who needs another fucking dating site, Rupert?' Ryan snapped and pushed his empty pint glass to make a point it needed filled and he was sick of Rupert's crap. 'Seriously, Rupert. You never heard of fuckyoufuckme.cum or what? People don't even need to meet up anymore. They just strap on these USB crotch attachments and can screw an old drunk in Japan from a bedsit in Basingstoke, if they so please. What's so different here, with your brain child? A stinking brain dump more like...'

'It is shitting genius, I say,' he said. Then, stood to go to the bar for refills. 'This *is* different. 'Long live the new flesh', Ryan!' he said over his shoulder.

'How is it any different from the three million sites preying on horny lonely sad sacks who can't just walk up to someone and say: hello, I'm bored, fancy a fuck?'

'Not everyone's got your brassy balls, Ryan,' he stopped and turned to finish.

'Fact.'

'Besides, it's got a USP.'

'Bollocks.'

'Serious… I can't believe no one's even thought of it before. We'll have the market wrapped up tighter than a nun's crotch.'

'You wanna rut a stranger? Just go talk to one, and get the drinks, NOW!' Ryan pointed a chubby finger at the mid-aged woman at the bar, all in black. Kind of French or Italian in Ryan's head. Actually, probably from Clapham and born in Birmingham. 'I'm serious, before I do any work on it, what makes this site so different?'

'It's target market. Look around, what d' you see Ryan?' he waved his hands, gesturing to the bar.

'A load of bored fuckers, late for, waiting for, or intentionally drinking to miss their bastard trains. And then there's us, isn't there… us stupid bastards sat watching them.'

'Exactly. Imagine it,' he walked back, put the empty glasses down and placed his hands on the table. 'Imagine a site where you have a way to get that fast, no-strings fuck to fill the fifteen minutes you have to wait. Or, you're bored on a delayed train, stuck outside Reading. Ping. Off goes an alert: meet me by the toilet in a minute for a blow job.' He nodded his own approval, then picked up the glasses again and walked back towards the bar.

Ryan glared, then his eyes glazed over as his mind recalibrated from piss-taking mate to business. Then he nodded. The dick head had something. Why not? He got out his laptop from the bag under the table and cracked his knuckles. He had work to do, fast. The only way he ever worked.

'What's the radar thing on your screen,' Rupert said looking at Ryan's laptop as he sat down with fresh pints.

'That, my public-school boy, walk the school leopard and get your dick stuck in a hoover, *friend*…is a 'Find my iPhone' hack off of the Dark Web… You see I've been using it for a footy supporters' app. It simply grabs people's footy teams that they support from their Facebook profiles. Then it has been showing me which pubs the 'away' and 'home' supporters are in... So, when I wanna catch a game I know where to be, and where not to be... Now, if I just,' and his fingers went crazy, attacking the mini laptop's keyboard, 'change this, and then this mother fucker here... and drop this banger...' Crash, his index finger smashed into the keyboard's 'enter' key. 'Now, look!' Ryan was the least conventional looking programmer there was, more an ox of a snowboarder. He worked hard and fast.

'That doesn't look legal.'

'Dark web magic... Who gives a fuck what's legal? It's fucking magic. I'm a maverick. Now are you looking closely, or what? Pay close attention fuck-tard. This is gonna make me rich and you famous.'

Rupert winced. He regretted having to ask Ryan to do stuff, but didn't know anyone else as good, quick, or immoral as him—he was, and would always be the man for Rupert's little pipe dream web projects.

'What am I seeing?' Rupert became excited and scared in equal measure.

'Instead of showing supporters of Chelsea or Sunderland fans. Now what we're seeing here is 'singles', 'actively looking'...and 'within 50ft."

'Holy-fuck-a-monkey!'

'Yes, my slightly dim witted, occasionally-comes-up-with-an-okay-idea friend. More like: Holy fuck a random stranger waiting for the 13.15 to Paddington to get in!' Ryan said, 'Now what do you wanna call this? Pandora's Box?... Meat Me.Cum?... Or some other crass piece of shite from the barrel of tits you keep falling into and coming out sucking your thumb?'

'Ships in the Night... Dot com.'

'Grrr,' Ryan growled and registered the domain. It was a good name, and he hated it.

AS THE LADY walked out the WCs and past Ryan's table she seemed to wipe a red stain from her hands into her black jacket sleeves. Ryan thought nothing of it, as he looked at the headshot and profile description he'd set up for Rupert as a joke on their fresh new website. It shone on Google and he smiled, proud of his work:

'Ex warden seeks ex-con for fast fuck and pay back. I didn't give you an easy ride and don't expect one in return. You've been a naught girl—now let's see just how naughty we can get together.'

Ryan laughed at his own words. He looked again at the stranger, the lady in black walking past, swore she had red eyes… He ignored the possibility anything had gone wrong and went back to laughing at his set up; giggling as cider started to run out of his nostrils.

IT TOOK THEM a day to scrape Ryan's guts off the toilet cubicle walls. Another week to get rid of the smell. It was a while after that the coroner finally got the smile off his face. In the end they had to sever the muscles in his cheeks to create something more befitting a man who'd been gutted like a fish mid-orgasm.

Nina met China Bob. She knew instantly his beautiful snake eyes were the perfect match after all. She had another fish to gut. They were headed up North, by car—she wouldn't ever be driven again.

Outside the station, the taxi rank was being held up by a fat loud Yank loading up the back of his 4x4 silver Range Rover with expensive luggage.

'All right, all right,' he said waving his arms at the waiting taxis. 'I'll be a minute. What's all the rush? You limey fucks are late for catching us up anyhow. What's another second gonna do? Evolve you into a rich state where you don't need to borrow from us anymore. Shut the fuck up.'

Nina looked into Bob's snake eyes. Her look didn't say anything, the eyes were empty and her lips didn't move. But he knew. Like a shadow moving across the side of a building, he bundled the yank into the boot, in a fleeting instant, like he was one of his own bags. No one in the queue was sure it had actually happened; it was so quick. In a flash of metal something came from his pocket and silenced the brash noises before they restarted. And with it Snake Eyes and Nina were bound together. Partnership sealed.

Nina was already in the driver's seat. She nodded slightly. China Bob sat in the passenger side.

This is going to work, she thought. Like her last killer-fuck. It was perfect.

Then she cried a little. Released. Fortunately, it was the far side eye and she quickly wiped it away before he noticed and it became real.

3

HOLY ISLAND

RUSSELL MYERS PAINTED the same patch on his coble boat every day. Over and over again. It didn't make him *happy*, but it did make *him*. Without it as a substitute, he had nothing left. The waters would crash on the rocks around the island in tune with each of his laborious strokes, as his hand holding the brush brought up memories. By the time the tides allowed the road causeway to be driveable, and let visitors onto the small island, he'd aim to be back indoors cleaning the brushes. His actions reset; he'd be ready to start up the next day.

It was the same ritual each morning; coffee on the stove boiling on an old gas cooker as he looked out the small cottage window at that island causeway. Clear of sea water for a few hours, then the sea would wash over and shut it off from the mainland. And he could breathe a sigh of relief that the waters shut them, the tourists, out a little longer. As the kettle started to whistle Russell would pick up the two small tins of paint, a medium and small brush and put them on the counter. Then he'd pour the water onto the four teaspoons of instant granules in an old tin cup and head out to his boat.

'Four spoons made it almost like real coffee,' *she* used to say to him.

Although the boat now lay beached and weathered, that patch always looked freshly painted on her. He tended to that section of the boat like it was a loved one's grave, and the paint strokes were fresh flowers. It gleamed white with a deep navy text:

Lilly-Anne

It was the same every day, ever since she had died. The love of his life, taken too soon. Is there any other way than 'too soon' for the one that's left behind? They had no children, by choice. Neither of them really liked people very much, stayed civil enough around them when the need arose. When they'd moved to Holy Island it was a hidden landmark, known to a few outside of the area and a few more on the search for religious trails. By the later years every man, dog and his ugly sister visited the place.

'They'll take the holy outta the place,' she used to say.

It was a small miracle they'd met each other and it had worked out like it did. Both of them were singular isolationists, and they were brought together by a sympathetic cosmos willing them some love and happiness. It had been filled with such things, that love and happiness, until the light in her was taken away, in a flick of the switch. Like all of a sudden they were out of favour with the powers that had brought them together.

He was embittered, they both were, near the end. Turned away from God.

They were furious at the irony of the name of the island they'd made a home of: Holy Island. They'd always thought Northumbrians were hardy stoic clans of people, unfazed by the elements, hardships and battles. Then *it* came. The attack of the annoying, invisible foe floating about her veins and eventually killing her. It was too much for them to bear. And it broke their faith.

'No one's ever really happy,' she started saying.

'We had our time,' he would reply.

And she would smile, remembering how simple it had been. But wishing they'd ventured further, out of the county, far off into Scotland instead, maybe—found a real hideaway. It was too late by then. They'd had their time.

Russell stayed on the island to be near the memories, he tended to them like wilting flowers, sure to fade with him as his own health deteriorated. He wanted to stay there until it was his time to meet her again. He no longer believed that would be at God's doing, temple-blessed or otherwise. But instead, now he saw their place in the stars, sea and sand. The pagan routes of the lands were all that remained for him. When the priory's hold and Christian namesake had been taken from him by her death he saw only the boat, the sea and the birds waiting to eventually mourn his passing as well.

He looked up whilst putting the finishing touch to *Lilly-Anne to* see a grey Range Rover racing across the causeway. Water shot up from its sides, in a display of brash disrespect, like it was a missile shot from a battleship, skimming the waves aiming to destroy the island.

Another middle-class no-good-son-of-a… he thought.

'Easy, my love,' the voice of his wife stopped him cursing.

'Sorry dear,' he whispered. 'Another tourist after the touch of a saint at the fallen priory. Or a crab sandwich.'

'You're right, fucking twats,' her voice cut in with her own curse. The she-devil on his shoulder. He smiled. In that moment, she lived again and their two souls touched, and parted on the wind. His eyes welled up and he smiled.

'I miss you,' he muttered and touched the name on the boat. The wet paint sticking to his fingers.

'I hated the water, and you spending so much time on it in that damn boat,' her voice in his head said.

He saw her smile. Never serious. She used to love him when he left to go fishing and even more when he returned.

He rubbed the brush on his shirt, the same patch he always did, now hardened stiff, and drank what was left of his coffee wishing he'd put a fifth scoop in.

'Four's not enough to make it taste real. Needs another,' he used to tell her. But always made it her way.

The visitors in the Range Rover weren't tourists. Not like that anyway. These two came to collect on a blood debt and were just warming up. They'd come to stretch their muscles and sharpen their teeth before the main course began.

NINA FRASER DROVE the Range Rover hard down the old island's causeway with little concern as her passenger slept. As far as she was concerned, she was the Devil, here to purge the island of any holy remnants in its priory, the rubble and rocks. The car she drove was a missile, carrying a full load of hate.

The tidal lump of Lindisfarne, or Holy Island, was a psychological irritation to her and since she was in the area, on *business*, decided to pay it a little visit. She had more than a few crosses to bear and would bury one or two of them here on that sorry rock.

She sat, engine still running, with the door open, gazing out at sea.

Puffins flew overhead and there were probably seals nearby. She cared very little. Other irritations. She had a growing nagging impatience for blood. Her mind churned at her making, grating away and the pains inflicted on her inside, the degradation, the humiliations leading up to that point in time where she sat on that holiest of islands.

She wasn't long enough released from prison to really see the outside world as it was for other people. She was blinkered by bad experiences; all she saw were memories best forgotten by most people. But she wasn't most people. She revelled, rolled and covered herself in them—and buried all normal responses. She fed off the things that would break normal people.

In prison, by the time the twentieth guard had visited her in her cell, she had buried what was left of her more conventional emotions. When they eventually grew bored, they let the other inmates have a go—a lot of lesbians, and experimenters, looking for an anger outlet and blame target. And she gave them that. She saw money changing hands in the queue outside her cell, as she lay limp and numb. Her mind long since travelled and parked up in a closed off garage, divorced from her body's defacement inside and out. Queue jumpers would pay, wanting a fresher ride. All it cost was a fag or two to get closer to her before the next in line. No one looked kindly on her, with a reputation for having spiked underaged girls' drinks in the club she worked. The Chinese whispers embellished her sins and with it her added punishment and degradations grew in intensity. But with it, so did her divorce from feeling, and instead she grew an increased attachment to ideas of revenge.

'You did this to me, John Black,' she'd whisper to the dark, the walls and into a dirty mattress.

On the island, she left the car unlocked. It'd be a sorry, bloody fool that tried anything with Snake Eyes asleep in there. A ticking time bomb of pain for anyone who dared peer through those windows. He'd gladly pluck their eyes and eat them for breakfast without a second thought.

She walked towards the priory remains.

Tall stone archways spanned crumbling old walls; 1400 years old. Now a ruin. The 'Holy' island was named such after Christianity had been introduced to northern England via the island itself. Now, a decaying gateway to God. She emanated contempt; her visit would destroy what was left. Accelerating God's retreat. She bore an army and strength that came with no limits to how far she'd go.

She'd said goodbye to what little remained of her own faith, long, long ago. It had washed away and ran down her legs as the first guard zipped up and spat on her before leaving the cell.

She sat on a rock, stirred and savoured the ruminations that had brought her there:

All I was, was a fucking DJ, John. You got us all locked up. Because of that stupid bitch you tried to save, that took a gammy pill. Fuck me, why? And why didn't you… Just, fuck me?

John had brought the Manchester club down, a house of cards, barely held up with insolvent cash flow from drug dealing and credit card mirroring. Cards were taken from bags in the cloakrooms. By the time they were used, and the punters found out, they didn't put two and two together. The police never did. Not until John abandoned his allegiance, testified against them all for that, the drugs, beatings, connections to the other gangs and much more.

So, you thought you'd get us all behind bars then take over his mantle did you, John? You pushed him over the edge of that building like he was a nobody. He was mine. I was next in line. It was all mine. I was meant to be next, to rule over—it's not yours, John, and I'm here to take it back. But, not before I've cut you and those around you. They'll all feel the restraints as I did, boxed in, as I pierce them. Uninvited, just like I was.

She stood, closed her eyes and took in the sea air.

Nina had looked up to her gangland boss as a father figure. It was an unrequited affair. She didn't know that, and fantasised over her eventually taking his role from him. Each day and night as she'd spun the black circles for them to rave around to, from the DJ booth, she'd imagined her next role: Queen Bitch.

She'd started collecting tattoos of famous gang sign offs. A new tag each weekend. At home she drank cheap vodka and put out cigarettes on them, on her own skin, as it seethed, she'd be grinning as her flesh bubbled away—permanently scarred for her unreachable desires. She was going to out match them all, she'd decided. No man would match her. Then, she would roll down her sleeves. Smile. And adopt the masquerade that was her life's compliance in the current order of things—until it was her time, and the main man handed over his throne to her.

Until you fucked us all over, John. I had a plan, and you fucked it.

Nina sat back down on a rock near the priory and thought through the detail of how she'd go about her revenge. John would be there for his mother's funeral and Nina felt the need to make a statement. They had time to lead up to that end piece. First, a little game with all those he thought he knew and anyone else who got in the way.

She saw the old man's approach. He walked like he had gout on one side, an ingrown toe on the other, and rickets in both. His clothes were so old and unwashed they practically camouflaged him into the greys, beige and dirt of the landscape around him. Only the sea gave him a slight silhouette, and today's waters were more grey than blue.

All she saw were those greys.

He got close, was about to speak, despite being out of breath. She didn't have time for small talk. Her residues of patience had been used up by the seven hour drive up the country. She had nothing left. It wasn't going to be his day.

What's this old cunt want?

Birds called in the background as the waves broke over rocks.

In a flash she stood up and her right hand whipped past his head in a grand theatrical gesture.

He smiled, confused. Then his throat opened up where she'd sliced the curved razor through his trachea. A moment later he sat, as if to prey. Another, and he fell back looking at the sky as angry looking cirrus clouds rushed past covering the sun's attempt to shine for him that day.

She watched a while as the black blood pooled under his neck.

A moment after this, his eyes glazed over and he was gone, to meet his wife. His face morphing from confused shock to empty lifelessness. Then she walked away, each step as calm and normal as the next. Nothing unusual had happened in her world, even as what was left of the sick, already previously dying old man's blood had finally soaked into the sand beneath him.

She opened the door and jumped in. Snake Eyes was already awake and sat to attention, woken by the smell of blood in the air that came with a fresh kill.

4

THE SUN INN

A PIG'S HEAD sat on the bar's counter top with its dead eyes staring blankly at the sweaty, overweight barman who was to finish carving it up. The barman was currently busy doing nothing, as usual, with his stretched and stained once-white T-shirt struggling to cover a deep, hairy belly button that no one wanted to see. Including the dead swine.

The Jukebox played Talking Heads' *Psycho Killer* as Naresh and Pete sat in the background looking up furtively to where John leant on the bar, between the pig's head and a retired copper who had an old police radio hissing away in front of him.

Pete and Naresh both whispered, just like they were back at school again. And as if John had just knocked the school bully out flat on his arse. A one-punch wonder, even back then. As adults, the wonder of his brutal powers weren't diminished. In retrospect they realised John always went for the weak spot, hit it hard, once. You have to have a savage heart and disregard for the recipient to play rough like that. It's all it took, and still takes. You can be a kung fu master but if someone punches you in the balls full welt, you crumble over and cry like hell. It's the brutality of the streets, wars and a desire to win, or survive, at all costs, and John always had it. They had shied away from it.

He did the same take down to 'Captain Heinz', the bully in their Primary School, at age five or six. Again, only once—it's all it took. A smack to an exposed windpipe and Heinz spent the rest of the afternoon avoiding his past victims, and the rest of the week croaking like he was a forty-a-day middle aged man. He was just a *four-a-day* at the time—with fags nicked from his mother's stash. His drunken mother gave Heinz another beating when he got home that day. Beaten again, for being beaten. There was no escape anymore or therapy in dishing it out, his angst, onto his classmates. John had shattered that. And nearly his larynx in the process. To this day the mention of John's name made him do a little involuntary throat clear. Any phlegm on the floor after was joined with a muttered curse, 'Johnny Black, the twat'.

The sudden influx of police and John visiting was the first interesting event Pete and Naresh had to talk about in ages. Well, since Pete's piano string got ripped by Toya, out the back of the pub. He'd come back in that night, crashing through the doors, looking sheepish. Twenty minutes previous, he'd expected to be gloating like that cat that had got the cream—he thought he'd stride back in like he'd conquered Everest, naked. She'd been the one who walked in first, giggling and wiping blood and what was left of him from her mouth. And then he'd followed, looking a bit pale and with a growing red Rorschach blotch to his crotch.

'Whiskey makes you frisky,' they used to say. Well... for Toya it made her chow down like a rabid wolf and left his dick end in tatters.

It was no coincidence, to them, the police action and John's return to the village. Their hushed talk and glances drew lines connecting the two. Like the pale horseman had ridden into town just before it was burned to the ground.

John was aware of the effect he had on places. He loved Bristol and Manchester. They coursed through his veins like they were the waterways, byways and back alleys of both places, but after he'd left, and if you read his books, you'd have thought he worked for the anti-tourism board for both cities. And everywhere else he wrote about. He held respect for his homelands too, but as soon as his feet left the train, the ground beneath him vibrated with mutual sorrows and inevitable conflicts to come.

Pete and Naresh continued their hushed chat, murmuring and clucking away like a couple of old hens. Soon, the rest of the punters, as few as they were, and scattered around the pub, joined in as they began to notice his presence and got brave enough to reach out from the dark corners:

'Black's back. Who would have thought?'

'Was he not shot dead or in prison?... Who does he think he is, the nerve?'

'They all come back, in the end.'

'Always... in the end.'

'Even that dumb fuck.'

'Umbilical's been cut now for good. Maybe this is it. A last return?'

'Mad-Jack Hall will be turning in his grave.'

'Shut it you crazy old bastard.'

Sirens blared, as more lights flashed past the old dirty casement windows, and the ground shook as if a Roman infantry was marching past. John looked at the reflections glancing off the window ledges, from the bar, and as they flickered and shone back over to Naresh and Pete.

They both looked scared.

He could tell they weren't getting used to it all, or him being back—to the idea: the shock of the day and John were one, somehow. John felt it too. He carried the responsibility with him everywhere he went. Maybe he should have stayed invisible, in Witness Protection. But it wasn't for him—the demons and monsters were way worse closed off; in the solitary confines of his head, alone. Out here, on the open battlefield he could face them head on.

He couldn't shake his past. They all felt it. He was tainted by the kills. He knew what that amount of police attention meant: more death and murder.

'What's with the pig?' John asked a sweaty back.

Alfred, or just Al, the barman, was slow to respond. Nothing would ever happen fast in his world, except scratching his arse, and he did that first before responding to John. He got his chubby finger into the hairy crack, wiggled it down into the crease and brought it back up to his nose for a lingering, self-satisfying sniff. He'd been known to cup a load of his own fart, before handing the darts or pool cues over for players. Each of his bodily outputs was paired with an action, cancelling out any degree of conscientious customer service and repelling any fragile tourists—exactly why it was all welcomed by the locals, adding to the endearing charm of the place that never changed.

The sweaty old dog on the floor knew even less etiquette. Only just making it outside to shit in the yard. Often getting caught short for a piss and spraying up the corridor walls to the gents.

John looked at the pig's head and waited for the answer, and some drinks to be poured.

'Pig? What, P.C. Ferguson? Old daft Fergie?' the barman said over his shoulder. 'He's always sat there propping up the bar, useless old fuck. Don't mind him, harmless now. Always was. Couldn't catch a cold that one. About as much use as tits on a hen. He's stuck here now... been there on that stool longer than Billy Idol on the Jukebox.'

'Get fucked,' said the shape from the end of the bar. The old boy slowly looked up to inspect John. The retired copper had struggled to let go, now with nothing else to hold onto but his pint. He was using the old police issue radio in front of him to follow the events like he still, or ever, mattered. He too was joining the dots from John to the unfolding mayhem. But had kept quiet so far. There were no coincidences around those parts. Either when a stranger was in town. Or worse someone from there, who'd left to bury their secrets, and now returned to unearth them. It was always the same.

They always return. Then wish they hadn't.

'Not him,' John said. 'The fucking hog's head bleeding all over the counter.'

'Oh the guffy's heed. Handsome wee fella isn't he. Fancy a kiss?' and he grabbed and held up the dripping pig's head to face John. The barman puckered his lips and smacked them together.

John didn't react at first. Then moved his head back.

'Not your type eh? Ne'r mind... He's gonna be scratchings, son. Right tasty, too. Fat and crunchy. Gimme an hour or two with it in the oven out back and you'll be pickin' hairs out ya teeth with the rest of us.'

'Not me,' Fergie said from the bar's end.

John looked around. The mangy, old, fat bulldog sat in its bed, farting through the smoke in the air. The place felt dead, despite the sporadic scatter of punters: John, a few lone faces hiding in corners, the lads he came in with, a retired copper, and three under-agers in the back room secretly drinking and playing pool.

They were like a mirror image of John, Pete and Naresh when they were that age... twenty plus odd years ago. Knocking balls about. Keeping their heads down to avoid a clip around the ear from any coppers in there, and mouthing off about the music on the jukebox. Pete, John and Naresh all played guitar back then, dreamed of it being their ticket out of the malaise; bedroom rock stars. By assassinating the jukebox offerings, as each track started, it bigged up their imagined musical prowess—the imagined band in their heads that never toured, lived on another evening, drinking hard, and never playing a note.

'You got the law in the front and illegal drinkers out the back. Just like old times,' John said to Al's sweaty arched back as he slowly pulled the eyes from the pig's head.

Pop. Pop.

'Don't want them eyes exploding in the oven again. Made a right fucking mess last time,' Al moaned with a final twist and yank of the cords to release them from the sockets, nipping them with his dirty nails to sever their hold. He dropped the pig's eyes to the counter.

Thud. Splat.

He launched both eyes and cords casually over his back and started the Guinness pours. One at a time, the eyes staring ovals arched with trailing tendrils dripping blood, then landed with a dull thud on the dank stained carpet by the dog. The hound had been eyeing the pig's head longingly, and knew they were always going to be coming its way. The dog lazily stretched its jaws, opened up and then slowly popped each eye like they were the finest of truffle balls.

Pop. Pop.

They left a mix of drool, vitreous and blood oozing from the dog's smug jowls before it returned to the efforts of an endless nap.

The lazy fat beast was in heaven. If Al the barman came back after he died, more than anything—he wanted to be that dog.

'Them young drinkers out the back, playing pool, will get barred. Just like you did back in the day, John. Retired P.C. Fergie-fuckwit here can even do it. Might even give him a smidgen of pride back if he likes.'

'Get fucked, fuckers,' Fergie grunted, twisting a knob on the radio from the local police to the ambulance channel with a crackle and a hiss of official codes and number-signs.

'And you'll let them back in at closing time... If you don't have a lock in. And then it'll all start over again tomorrow. The circle of fuckin' life, just like old times,' John said, smiling.

The drinks' sediment tried hard to settle.

''Spect so. Gotta eat. Their money, nicked from their mother's purses is as good as any. Besides, it's training them up for the real world. Don't you think?' he said, putting the pints from the drip trays down in front of John.

'Or sedating them from having any chance in it; having a life,' John said to himself. He picked up the three pints of Guinness that were still clouded over; vortexes of silken black swirls, and carried them over to Pete and Naresh.

'We'd ask you what you've been up to...' Naresh started when John sat down.

Pete finished the sentence: '...but we've read all about it.'

'In the papers, or my books?'

'The papers, then the books,' Naresh said, speaking for himself. Pete hardly read past The Sun or News of the World. Even then it was the background blurb that went with the tits he saw on Page 3.

'Probably the best order. No truth in any of them though.'

'Just the papers for me. Don't have time for reading fiction,' Pete joked.

'The papers *you* read are more fiction than most,' Naresh said.

'Your pulp-hardboiled trash is all this guy here talks about, and says it's all true too,' Pete went on, gesturing to Naresh with a Newcy Brown beer mat. Then started to nervously rip at its corners to create a pile of soggy, beer-soaked confetti on the table.

'At any point... writing those... did you ever think to protect yourself? Just make it up rather than make it real?' Naresh asked. Worried. It was true, he had studied John's books and he knew what tended to happen by the end.

Naresh was scared he'd end up a castaway disposable asset in one of John's next novels. He looked around the room, anxiously imagining the scene. Him, a red sweater trainee member of crew, beamed down to the alien planet with Captain Kirk, only to get eaten, slurped up by a hungry plant with blades for teeth, and a mouth like a giant pulsing shaved cat's arse. He wouldn't even make it to the next episode. The one with the fluffy cuddly tits bouncing around the Enterprise as they smothered everyone into a happy daze.

Fuck. He wanted to be in that fluffy tit episode more than ever.

The Jukebox flicked, tripped and started up *Walking on Broken Glass* by Annie Lenox.

'You still with us, Naresh?' Pete asked.

Naresh was still there, but gone.

'Don't worry, John. He gets like this. In a trance. Always has somewhere better to be than in the moment; off into his imagination again—I guess you know all about that yourself too?'

'Have you ever noticed...?' Naresh said, only just back in the room. 'How some people create art and it gives them a breakdown. Minds can't seem to handle it. The free thinking and altered states actually breaks them apart, like glass...'

Annie Lenox backed up his words.

'And then others, maybe like you, John, if they don't create, that's what tips them over the edge, and they... never come back either.'

'I know which sort I am,' Pete said. 'There's all the creation I'll ever need here in this glass of black.'

'It's nearly empty, Pete,' Naresh said.

'I'm always part full, Naresh. Even at closing time.'

John looked back at them, but said nothing.

A lot of the time he never even saw a glass and it wasn't part full or empty. He said nothing to them of the need to write this out. How his therapist showed him how to draw out that inner angst. 'Fishing out the fool,' she called it, by writing broken words rather than ruminating on them.

He said nothing of the terrors that came and went. Walking through him like he was a dilapidated corridor in a rundown mental hospital, channelling shadows of lost minds. Nothing... of the ghosts he saw and that never left, always there, gathering an army of hate.

Nothing.

It wouldn't do them any good to know.

He could see in Naresh's eyes he'd already read and knew too much from his books.

Naresh had a coping mechanism. Whenever things got too heavy he'd disappear into a Trekkie daydream and it seemed it was happening more than ever before.

His focus had left again, the drink was starting to work too and Naresh's gaze went out and past the back walls, off into some far, far away planet, with Amazonian women chasing him. He was firmly somewhere else, more cosy, less dirty-real. Just dirty.

'Very profound, fuck-stick,' Pete said, waking Naresh back up. 'Now let's get battered.'

The first round of Guinness had lasted all of seventeen minutes. The first of the catchup drinks were always the same, to lubricate the uncertainties. To see if they could all still get along, regardless of how their lives had moved on—or not, for Pete and Naresh. By the second and third pints it would be like they'd gone back to how it was. Regressing like it was old times and John was still just a man. The scars hadn't been cut and the women hadn't cut them.

'What's with all the police and flashing lights,' John asked the barman when he went to refill. He asked like he was just one of them; disconnected from outside, and like he'd only just noticed. Innocent. Ignorant. Idly curious, like them.

'Girl out walking her dog found a body,' P.C. Ferguson butted in, sitting up straight at the end of the bar. He addressed the room with some misplaced sense of authority, 'Nowt special, no drama, always been bodies turning up there in those dunes. No big deal, just some flashing lights is all. Piss into the wind. You know how that feels, John. People forget sometimes, is all, we all do.'

'Forget what, Fergs?' the barman said, opening up the taps again.

'That it's the old graveyard over there on Cross Hill. River changed its route ages ago in a storm, biblical it was...'

The room started to tune out, they'd heard it all before. The old stories. Fergie was full of them.

'Well before all our times it was, when the village was full of pirates and smugglers. Our Wild West era. The river changed course, cut the graveyard and graves off from the village. Then, over time, the sands shifted, they move. It's what it does, it shifts, doesn't it? A spilt hourglass, throwing history back out at us.'

The dog farted. Long and hard, with a wet finale, looked up. It lifted its head slightly and like its owner, took a self-satisfied sniff, then laid back down to sleep.

'Remember those old WWII shells you used to find over there as a boy, John?' Fergie went on. 'Just like them. Churn, churn, churn, and the beach spits another cadaver out. Spit. Drop. Out they roll. No big deal,' and he gestured with his hands; a body rolling from an imagined re-opened grave.

It fucking was a big deal though. The body the girl and her dog had found was fresh.

It was typical, alcohol-bolstered, small village, inverted snobbery shit that followed from Fergie: 'Nothing special happened here just because you showed up, John.'

John looked to the pints willing them to settle quicker, so he could get back to his table.

Fergie kept on the offensive: 'Why'd you go coming back anyway? Spent some time in the big smoke and firing blanks at Paddies, and you think you're something now, do you? I've silenced a 'rag head' or two my time, son—what of it? You're not welcome here. You're not welcome at that funeral either.' His act was commonplace, played up worse to anyone who dared leave and then paid a return visit—John was no different. All of them hated those who returned to differing degrees. Some just did it more secretly than others, under their breath, around a corner, or, like Pete and Naresh, quietly, under breath, whilst their pal was at the bar... The old-timers with less time left to get out, and escape the town, hated the 'returners' most of all. As those other people, with high adventures and movement, highlighted their own restricted motions in life to date.

'Think you're better than us do you?' Fergie went on.

John had long since switched off and looked at his drinks like they were the door to an engaged toilet cubicle when he was bursting to go.

The barman shook his head and put a finger up to his mouth to tell Fergie to keep quiet, to stop mouthing off, to simmer back down from the soapbox he'd drunkenly clambered onto.

'There's no sodding drama just coz you show your face, son.'

They weren't related. The term 'son' was a mode of control elders used over anyone younger. Like they had authority to say it, to do and order around who they liked: with a 'son' dropped in. From their point of view, they'd earned the right through age alone. Wisdom was assumed; not gleaned through experience or knowledge.

'People die whether you're here, or not, son. Don't be thinking you're special.'

There was no subtext, John wasn't welcome as far as P.C. Ferguson was concerned. And as he was tuned into the police radio, John assumed *they* all felt the same as well: the real police. He walked back over to the table with Pete and Naresh waiting, with heads down like neglected Whippets. Embarrassed on his behalf.

There was drama unfolding outside on the beach. It was a big deal. The body's blood was still wet.

Regardless of Fergie's mouthing off, fuck all had happened in decades—let alone a fresh dead body, other than through age or boredom. Fergie was in denial and gutted to be out of it; the action. He wanted back in and winced with each touch of the radio dial, almost in pain, knowing that was as close as he was ever going to get.

Twist, hiss. Another station.

A weary old drunk that had previously been invisible grunted and cleared his throat at the opposite end of the bar to Fergie. 'We know all about you, son,' he said to the room. Everyone knew it was directed at John again. 'You're that writer guy that was an informant against the Manc gangs, ended up killing the mob boss, now you've got protection from them all. Both sides... what the fucking hell is that all about?'

Pete, John and Naresh looked at the table top.

Whilst Fergie... looked nervous—like he'd missed some key information. Like he realised he had been poking a sleeping monster in John, and now regretted it.

The barman scratched his right ball through his sweatpants, then glanced at Fergie with a 'told you so' face. Then, mouthed: 'Now, shut the fuck up.'

'Whatever. One for the road in another place?' John said, still looking at the beer mats, and downed his pint. Then he looked up. As he went to stand and they looked up, he saw fear in both their eyes again.

John'd really changed since they last sat down for any length of time together, they weren't getting used to him after all. He realised, it must have been years ago, when he was still in the army and had come back on leave, that they'd last tried to spend any time together. It hadn't worked then. It didn't now.

He'd just changed, more. They hadn't, still.

PETE SAID OUTSIDE: 'Well, we're still barred from The Anchor, The Red Lion and The Schooner, and you are from all them and everywhere else...' the joke continued.

'The Schooner it is then,' John said. 'Like they give a shit, the amount we drink.'

The door creaked open and they entered another sorry old ancient seaside boozer. You could feel lonely fishermen, sailors and farmers' memories soaked through the wooden beams and sticky carpet. Smell them too. A Joy Division song played: *Transmission*. And for a moment John was snapped back to Manchester, his love, wanting to protect her but knowing the best way to do that was to get, and stay, as far away as possible.

'Going to look any old flames up, John?' Pete said, when they sat again.

They existed and spoke in superficialities, unaware of the full weight he carried. Although Naresh had an idea, but was scared to approach the matter further.

Pete started asking about if any memories remained of past almost-loves, lovers and haters. If John had held onto any of the many failed exploits and affairs of his past. Or, had they 'come and gone'. So it went on, for Pete's invented banter's sake—a distraction from the seriousness of life John had brought down on them.

John hoped he was on a path to forget these half-truths forever. John thought about his only love, left behind. And how these distorted pasts Pete alluded to lingered and hid around every corner—waiting to jump out, whilst the one woman that mattered, the one he cared about more than life itself, was untouchable and miles away.

He closed his eyes and could smell her deep red hair. Taste those strict pouting rose bud lips, wet to touch.

'I've met someone,' he said, and they both jumped at the seriousness.

Silence.

'Meet this!' a woman barked, and slapped him hard, on her way past to the toilets, battering him from romanticising any further. And startling the other two to jump again.

Pete and Naresh started to laugh, as John shook his head and rubbed the hand print reddening across his face.

'Someone's already beat me to it have they? Poor, sorry bitch,' the woman said, rubbing her hands together in satisfaction, then strutted away, wobbling as her worn heels rolled in the carpet and she got out a packet of blue Regal King Size cigarettes.

None of them recognised her for sure. Chances was it was a random drunken lass flirting a little too hard. Or, maybe it was one of John's invented semi-exploits by Pete, hitting hard from a past he'd forgotten or had never happened.

John could taste the iron in his blood mixing with salt carried in the sea air from the opened front door.

On the wind through the doorway came a whispered message, 'One down, more to come.' John knew it was death on the wind.

5

BAMBURGH

HEINZ WAS TOUCHING the wrong side of thirty to be living the way he did, that's what they all said and thought, reminding him of it over and over. He was in denial, drank through it, same as the rest.

As he sat on the sea harbour wall looking out to the Farne Islands, that's what he thought too. That he'd been treading those waters too long; he needed to move on. Nothing exciting ever happened here, in Seahouses. The county of Northumberland's borderland glory days were behind it. It was a living museum and giant nature reserve, that's all.

It was for the birds: fucking puffins, gulls and cormorants, he thought.

He knew there had to be life out there somewhere. He'd seen it on TV. His own life, it seemed to him, was consigned to that of a mangy dog living next door to a butcher's shop, too scared to leave home. Too much of a failure to even scavenge the scraps that were on his own doorstep.

He stood up and the bottle of Newcastle Brown Ale he'd been drinking from fell in the water with a plonk and a couple of bubbles. A seal bobbed in the water in front of him, mocking him with its playfulness. Further out, dolphins broke the surface as, overhead, the birds too flew free. Swooping, gliding and catching currents of opportunity, eager to see where they would take them.

Another dose of self-medication in The Olde Ship, he conceded.

'Tomorrow will be another day, and that's all,' he mumbled then coughed, cleared his throat and cursed, then spat a dollop of self-pity into the water. It floated there, the scum. The lining from his polluted airways joined with the sea. Even his own sorry contribution was more adventurous than the body that produced it.

First, before going to The Olde Ship, he had to get back to his bedsit and put on his uniform. A volunteer policeman, he hoped for action without ever fully committing enough to go full-time into the force. He was a Hobby Bobby. Another cause for the digs and jibes that would put him deeper into a depression or push him out of town altogether.

In the bedsit, no sooner had he buttoned up the silver buttons on his jacket than his radio buzzed to life.

Well, fuck-a-walrus, he thought, if he wasn't needed for something after all?

'Heinz,' it crackled. Even *they* called him that. His so-called respecting authority he volunteered his precious free time to every day. Such was his low standing in the community. And such was his own self-worth, that he didn't ever challenge it.

The name Heinz was a nickname from primary school, and because he hadn't evolved, moved on, or moved away, it had permanently stuck well into adulthood.

As a child, his single parent mother had struggled. Most do. This was a different level. She dosed herself up more than the others, to sedate her predicament, to placate her emotions from the fury over a one-night stand made flesh: him. She would watch TV on a couch between the hangovers and extended efforts to create them. Bottles and ashtrays with spilled ash lay in amongst toys he'd stolen or found on the streets. Litter and broken items were strewn everywhere about the tired council flat. At five years old his improvised school uniform looked laughable, almost fancy dress, and by 7, 8 and 9 years of age, he'd created a caricature; a superhero for himself to weather the never-ending storm. To exist in fantasy rather than suffer the reality. A wall of denial. Other parents would cast hand-me-downs his way in carrier bags, out of sympathy, when they picked up their sons and daughters from the school. He took what he could carry.

No one ever came to meet him. He walked himself there and back each day, alone. Once she did try. She'd woke early one morning or had drunk through from the previous day and not slept at all. He was so happy, walking along the street with her, just like normal children.

'Alright, Pet?' a voice asked, walking behind them. Another mother, pleased to see her out and about—being a mother.

She couldn't handle it. Feeling the shame and paranoia as the alcohol faded and her brain chemistry struggled to right itself. She walked through dog shit and screamed, turned and marched back to the flat.

'It's okay, Heinz,' the other mother said. 'You can walk a little of the way with us if you like? Just let us walk the last bit on our own. We don't want our little Jack here getting picked on by anyone thinking you two's friends or something,' she smiled, but was serious. They all worried for him. But were also sealing his fate before he'd had a chance to be anything other than he was already. Condemned to lone thoughts and conceded to be outside from a normal life.

All he ever ate was beans, cold, straight from a tin with a plastic fork, or whatever discarded chip shop rubbish he'd found on the way home. The cutlery in their flat had long since evolved an ecosystem of its own, and was unusable.

Children and adults could smell him if they were downwind of him, and from up to half the town away. His noxious arse quakes shook the school assembly too and kept the other kids running from him in the playground. Naturally, he evolved into a lesser rate school bully. Despised by himself, he let the hatred overflow onto others.

The irony being, this name stuck: Heinz. And all *she* could ever afford was the cheapest watered down home brands. When she was able to make it to the shops, it was for drink, and the shopkeeper would throw tins of beans in the basket—knowing they had to eat something if she was to live long enough to return to the shop and buy more. By the time she was fully incapacitated, the assumption was it was all the boy would eat, so what existed of the town's charitable nature deposited weekly tins as rations on their doorstep. As misjudged as this charity was, an occasional home brand bottle of vodka would be there too.

A school bully anti-super hero persona stuck. The only one to fit: Captain Heinz. It was a lonely role. Arms out of the sleeves of his hoodie. Hood over the head, and running around like it was a cape—hitting out at the screeching little girls and boys, if he could get close enough.

He loved the sound of their fear. It comforted him to know others could suffer too. Their screeches, moans and yelps became like bird song to him. Each lunchtime, it started with the first initial nip, kick or punch. A push down the hill was even better because as they were righting themselves at the bottom he could attack again. Whoever was first in line would erupt in tears, the screams started and then they ran. All of them. Before long he had tens of them scuttling between the trees, trying to hide in the concrete tubes of the playground or dashing behind the bike sheds. He always caught them before the bell rang to go back in. The teachers never stopped him. They were usually at the other side of the main building, smoking fags, talking down the simple life graced to them. At bell time, he would walk in last, alone, grinning like the cat who got the cream. Proud to have purpose.

There wasn't any solidarity and companionship to be found in that role, and by adulthood his superhero powers had fully weakened. This wasn't helped by when, in the last few weeks, one of the boys, Johnny Black, punched him so hard in the throat he couldn't scream his battle cries anymore, and just croaked instead. In the very last week, they'd started to call him Froggy instead, and his powers were fully depleted. Having left school, his name about town reverted back to the more humiliating: Heinz.

By adulthood, at least he'd progressed on to *that* brand; his namesake, and he now warmed them to eat alone with dry white toast in his bedsit. Always white bread. Never brown. At weekends he treated himself with a large squirt of ketchup. Added sauce to what was already an overflowing plate.

'Heinz, you fucking there or what?' the police radio buzzed aggressively. 'Pick up, you prick. Good job you're not a real copper. Fuck's sake, man, answer the call.'

'Yes Sarge,' he quivered.

'Finally. Fuck me, lad, you're about as much use as a chocolate teapot. As usual.'

'Sorry.'

'There's something we need you to check out.'

'Okay, sir.'

'Some tourists… Japs, I think. Sound yellow on the phone anyway. They've come across something in the graveyard by you, at Bamburgh. Grace Darling's grave. Blood everywhere they said. It'll just be animals, kids or something or someone dicking around as usual. Get there and call it in.'

'Badgers, foxes or stoats, I imagine, sir.'

'Who gives a fuck—just simmer them down before Tripadvisor assassinates us, and call it in, will you?'

He looked at the radio like it was his drunk mother; with love and hate. This was all he was now—this was his only purpose in life.

'They're not making any sense, these Jap tourists. As if they ever do. Dunno why they don't get back to photographing distilleries in Scotland… They're all gibbering wrecks. Mumbling fucking messes they are.'

'Yes, sir.'

'Thought they were tougher than that. Samurai? My arsehole. CLICK.' And the voice on the radio was gone.

Finally, some action. Purpose for the little man.

HE VISITED MORE than his own mother's grave. It meant more. Like it was a beacon to all mothers, women everywhere. Then and now. Whenever he approached those eight pillars of that Victorian gothic shrine in Bamburgh graveyard it felt like it channelled all those women's lives and suffering back at him. He had visited it a few times through the years. The strong, stable, reliable female figure from history was something he'd craved. The teachers in school had tried to teach them all about Grace Darling in school and some of it had stuck. The rest he distorted and made up in his head.

This feeling he had as he approached was worse than in his past visits that conjured up childhood memories of his mother.

A torrent of relentless pain co-joined the stone memorial as coastal winds attacked his self-pitying face. Already, he felt he'd seen enough of the darker side of life. With his upbringing. Or lack of it. Watching *her* slowly die on that couch. It was two months before he told anyone. When the stench was the talk of the village. When her eyes pitted fully and she'd bloated and deflated out the noxious gas of her own for the hundredth time. 'Hissssss,' it went, and he stood from the spot he'd been sitting, crossed legged, like a meditating monk to watch her die, depart and then decompose. It was a long, hard goodbye and he still, even now, hadn't done with it.

She'd pleaded for him to bring her food, she'd lost the will and ability to move and feed herself. Only after she died, did he ritualistically start to wait on her, bringing the same over and over again... When the police had finally gone in they'd found the countless plates and bowls of cold baked beans. Those empty tins of home brand beans spilling out of the bins and all over the counter top.

Mrs. Heinz had drunk herself to a different place, not better.

Now, on duty, he held the helmet tight to his head with the chin straps like they were reins on an unruly stallion. Bamburgh castle loomed in the background; further crowning judgement from the ages over him. The tall castle structure peered down from the hard rock tor it was built on. A reckoning over his past, its shadows cast an eerie purple mask over the village graveyard, and the beach and dunes beneath it. The waning light picked up silhouettes of sharp grass on the peaks of the dunes. And overhead the birds saw the scene—another passing.

Grace Darling's ornate grave loomed in front of him, imposing and intricate. She was the daughter of a local lighthouseman. In 1838, she'd joined her father in rescuing nine people from the wreck of a ship that had run aground off that part of the Northumberland coast. Savage, rocky and ferocious waters were matched by a brutal storm and she had fought it all and won. She died, aged only 26, in 1842, from tuberculosis. An unfair end to such a show of strength. Her overly detailed and imposing grave was a lasting tribute. Her body having been disrespected and taken by ill health.

Now, she had been disrespected further. He could see this as he passed the cowering tourists in bright coloured waterproofs on a wooden bench, and edged nearer to the shrine.

The statue of her body had been drenched in blood. Pieces of flesh were hanging from the pillars as the full desecration to her glory became clear to him, and with it, all women suffered the insult.

As he stared at the scene, he heard the voice of his drunken mother yelling in his ears, which ached with the pain of it: 'Get me the bottle boy. Now! You're just like your father... Useless. A walking, talking cock... You'll see, when I'm gone. There's nothing for you out there. Knock a girl up and move on. All you're good for, it's nothing. Bring me my bottle. NOW!'

Closer, only a few steps away, he could see the face of the statue was covered in flesh too. A recent kill. Another person's face had been stretched over it like a crude mask. Words were scrawled to the base of the bloodied statue:

He did this to them. All of them.
The Anti-Christ, he may be. There's always something darker to fear.
You'll all join us to suffer, before him.
Then it's the end.
Rest in Hell.

He looked at the skin mask stretched over the statue's face. It seemed to channel his mother, come to life and talk: 'Why didn't you feed me boy? When I needed you. I kept you alive on my withered tits for years, boy, and you wouldn't even feed me... once.'

He closed his eyes and opened again—she was gone, for good.

'Sarge...' he said into a police radio over the wind, 'There's something bad gone on here. Real bad. I'll send photos. Get a crew here pronto.' He spoke with a new confidence. He'd be gone from this place. Her hold on him was weakening.

Then... he was sick.

He was getting used to it, one second at a time, and that's what really made his stomach churn: the getting used to it. The gore in front.

He crouched as the acid burned his throat, and he looked up through tears of disbelief at the makeshift skin-mask draped over the sacred stone face, and shook his head. The images and thoughts would never go. They were indelible. Burned into his mind. The precious stone form, now bloodied, was to be seen forever, like the image of his mother on the couch. This new vision was overpowering those that used to haunt him, his mother was leaving him with each second he forced himself to stare at what was now in front.

Only the Devil could do this.

A small village perspective, he hadn't seen just how cruel and dark life could get. Until now. He shivered, but wasn't cold.

Behind him the three tourists that had called it in shook too, rustling in their plastic coats. Expensive cameras at their feet. They sat on the bench holding each other, squeezing hands as if to pray through what they'd seen. To squeeze out the images. What they had been shown was a glimpse of the honest savagery that belonged to those lands, the type that didn't appear obvious in the guidebooks. The kind the Vikings knew. The Romans, Pagans and the Celts too. Primal imagery transcending usual forms of communication. Getting straight to the heart of the matter, one bloodied message at a time. Visceral, primal acts.

Overhead, clouds overlapped, bellowed and overflowed with dark greys and reddening washes as if painted by a master.

In a flash of black, a bird swooped down and grabbed a strip of flesh from the monument and was gone.

You got some excitement now, Heinz, he thought. Careful what you wish for in the future.

The tourists were being sick as he stood with his back to them, he looked out past the graveyard at the sea as it crashed in unison with a sky that continued folding and rolling in Constable and Monet ripples of deep reds, blues, pewter and red-orange breaks.

Now he noticed the dolphins, and overhead, puffins. Then... he remembered the seal from the harbour. Its playfulness.

His eyes had been opened.

'Goodbye, mother,' he said, then was sick for the last time.

6

THE DIRTY BOTTLES

JOHN CHECKED INTO the White Swan Hotel. A three-hundred-year-old coaching inn with wooden wall panels and fittings from Titanic's sister ship, RMS Olympic. The irony wasn't lost on him. The hotel was decorated and fitted out with the fixtures from the *one* that didn't sink. Whilst all around it, the town was in decline; a cultural wasteland. An economic dead end waiting for the planners—it was a historic market town lost to the ages. Now a mass of museum pieces that should have been shut up behind the old town walls ages ago. To protect it from the outside world that was sure to shatter it as the property developers watched on with pound signs in front of their eyes.

The front desk had a brown A6 sized envelope waiting for him. The hard edged capital letters spelling his name looked like his mother's regimented shouting handwriting, but they couldn't be.

They all have a way of reaching us from the past and over the distance. The cord is never really cut.

The envelope was pocketed without another thought.

Only the concierge knew how long John had stood fixed to the spot, staring. To John it was only a flashing moment. To the concierge it was a long impatient minute before he took himself off to the disabled WCs to cheer himself up with an overdue wank.

John expected to be found staying in the hotel. The most expensive hotel in town wasn't ever going to be a convincing hiding place. He didn't mean to make a statement. He just wanted every chance to sleep whilst there. He'd also been turned down for a job there when he was a boy.

'Too ugly and ginger to be bar staff,' they'd said.

So he'd stay, run up a big ugly bill, empty the minibar, and fuck 'em if they thought he'd settle up at the end.

In his room, the high ceiling, four-poster bed and moulded fittings were a far departure from what he was used to in the recent grots of Manchester and Salford's bedsits, flats and doss houses. Before getting back to Alnwick, Rain City had stayed true to its namesake and he was yet to find a place that didn't leak through. He didn't think to stay with any old acquaintances or family whilst in his hometown. He didn't trust his own presence around them, or their reaction to it. If they saw a scar they'd belittle it like it was a smear on their own flesh. If they saw him sleepwalk or hear what he yelled out at night, they'd be equally as unsympathetic, before the trauma set in. And, as usual that would happen after he'd gone and it had fully sunk in.

He closed his eyes as images of Cherry's injuries echoed about his brain, traumatising him with each glimpse and flash. Her pain. Bruised and cut love. He wanted distance and felt sure if his demons came for him, it would be at night. He looked across at the mini bar, sure of making the right decision—he really didn't want any more witnesses to those night-terrors that would sweep through him. He'd hurt enough.

He sailed his ship alone. And it would sink one day that way, alone...

The holdall he'd dropped on the bed's end looked half empty. With a few bare essentials. He looked at the ceiling, the mouldings, the history of the place. He closed his eyes slowly again, as sleep moved to touch him, and went to drag him into one of those memories. To relive the unliveable. He snapped to. This wasn't the time.

He took out the A6 envelope and ripped it open. It was a folded, faded, lined sheet with pencil scrawled on it. A child's writing:

John, Aged 7
Alnwick South, Primary School

Today, I saw a white dog shit on the way to school. It's always there. It started greeny brown, slimy too, slowly turned white and now has hairs too. Maybe it's growing into a new dog. Maybe it's a dog's egg? I always wanted a puppy.

Yesterday, I went out on my red plastic tractor, and pretended it was a motorbike, and I was in that American TV show, CHiPs... I love that. When I'm watching it, I'm there. Not here.

Last weekend, some boys hit me. They wanted me to break into the building opposite. It's not been finished, they're still building it. I think the boys wanted me to hurt myself. Wanted to push me off the scaffolding and into the cement when I was up there. Then, say it was an accident. I wonder if someone told them to do it? Because they wanted rid...

I ran and knocked on the door to get back inside my home, I was crying. They stole the tractor whilst I was gone. Mum wasn't there. I think she was in bed. An angry sweaty man, with hairs all over, banged the door open, wouldn't let me inside. Where it was away from the boys. He shouted at me. Smelled of grown-up drinks. I told him about the boys. He hit all these nails, giant ones through a bit of wood, told me to belt them with it, then he slammed the door shut and went back to mum, inside.

The boys weren't there anymore. I don't know what I'd have done if they were. Maybe if I had done anything with the nails through the wood, I'd have had to go away too. Just as if I'd fallen from the scaffold. Maybe someone just wants me to go away?

I work hard at school. That's how I'll escape one day. I'll go away if they want me to.

The teachers give me Ds and Fs. They smell of grown-up drink, and the smoke smell too. I know it's better than that—my work. They act like they want to keep me here. They don't want me to be more than them. And, I don't want to be anything like them.

Tomorrow's the weekend. It'll be sunny. It's always sunny at the weekend. Even when it isn't. People smile more then, or sometimes. I'll walk in the dunes, collect war bullets from the sand. I'll use Nanna's tea tray as a sledge. Going over where the bullets lay. Dead Vikings too. Those bullets, the ones that didn't kill anyone. I'll play on that main dune—the really big one. My favourite. It's like the sun. Everything looks to it. The spiky grass on the top of it tickles my legs. There's big concrete blocks at the bottom there too, on the beach. Grandad says they were to stop German tanks. Like the bullets. They didn't do what they were meant to do. I haven't seen a real tank. They haven't either. The bullets didn't hit a German soldier and the blocks didn't stop a tank from attacking Grandad's golf club... Like grandad said, they were practising. This place is full of things that don't do what they could have. Then... after the sand sledging, I'll sit on Cross Hill. I like it there. I like the birds. They seem to know who's coming and going. I've seen them, the birds, when there's a dead seal. They care as if it's one of their own—the crows most of all.

On Monday, I think the white dog shit will still be there.

Nothing changes, it'll just be a bit hairier.

No one tries but me.

One day—I'll be gone forever.

John looked at the writing. Words from the past. The smudges on the edge of the paper by a child's still innocent dirty hands. He tried to rediscover the memories of writing it, and looked at his hands now; pitted, scarred and scratched.

Not so innocent now.

Too much had happened since he'd made his 'escape'. So, no fond childhood memories came back to him. Having re-read the inner workings of his childhood head, he wasn't totally sure they were ever that 'fond' after all. Maybe whoever had left the note was making that same point—that he was better off away from the place, and he shouldn't have returned, regardless of the reason.

He screwed up the letter and threw it in the waste bin, with a subtle care for who had left it for him, or tracked him down to the hotel, and sat slowly upright. A family member trying to show they cared or an old teacher showing how he'd done it, finally escaped. Without fully knowing what he'd escaped to, and how he'd suffered for it.

Or, maybe it was M. Pamplemousse. She loved a mind game, M. Pamplemousse did. Fucked with him constantly. She was a master puppeteer, and would be impatient for her next book draft from him, and knew how to stoke the fires in him: a pull at a family memory here, a tug at a doomed love affair over there—yes, he'd decided. Let it rest, and say it was her, and not someone who still cared. If they ever did.

He left the room and pulled a hair, licked his fingers and stuck it over the door frame from the corridor side and put the 'do not disturb' sign on the handle. Life made him that way; paranoid. To be cautious. Things could be sweet. Rosy as fuck. He'd still be looking over his shoulders, like a wolf. Wars, gangs and life had shown him—he couldn't ever be too careful. He saw victims everywhere. Loyalty had shown him pain. And what it was to be cautious of himself most of all.

Outside, the streets seemed ghostly. A window through time. Wet cobbles bulged with tree roots and under the weight of carriages and carts that had turned into cars and trucks. Victorian street lamps flickered as the moon highlighted droplets mid-air, and on the translucent leaves of the trees.

A decrepit old Ford Cortina drove slowly past as an even older man hobbled over the cobbles, clutching a bottle of Laphroaig Whiskey.

Rush hour, John thought.

Further down the street a man attacked a dirty old silver Ford Mondeo. The drunk was frustrated at locking himself out and being unable to drink drive himself home all of the one mile away.

'I'll give you fifty quid for the car.' John could see the man had dropped his keys behind himself whilst fumbling to get them out his pocket. It would be a public service depriving the drink-riddled maniac from his car.

'This piece of shite… Fifty quid?… Have the fucker.' And he gave it a last kick, losing his balance and stumbling backwards as if the car had pushed back. He took a close look, making sure he'd dented the wing for good measure then stood upright, expectantly.

'Gimmie my fookin' pennies, son.'

John put some notes in the man's hand which automatically clenched to take them. A few steps away the man stopped, seemed to reconsider, then forgot in a moment and went to walk away again. Oblivious to anything other than the call of another drink and grateful at not having to raid his wife's purse again that night. He thought he'd knocked her round enough recently. His shoulders hurt from the effort of swinging and his palms burned from making contact.

John bent over, pretending to do his laces, whilst palming the keys he'd been standing on. The man stumbled further off for another drink with his prize of easy notes.

Later, the man spent most of the night in a cell for beating up his own ex-car again. He'd returned to vent and punch out frustrations hours later, after unofficially selling it to John Black. He came back drunker, less capable of standing, let alone driving and without the keys. The police didn't care less. They called to tell his wife she had the night off, and the kids didn't have to hide in their rooms until late the next morning.

Turns out she was walking her dog, Marlie, on the beach and the kids were with the neighbours. She'd end up speaking to the police again later the same evening anyway.

THE DIRTY BOTTLES, or 'Thi Dorty Bottles' as the locals called it, had a curse. It'd been a pub for over two centuries. The building itself was built in the 1600s. If the town was haunted, this place was overridden with the afterlife; horrors of the past. Old drunken pub brawls, murder and suffering had seeped through each dent of the door frames and every hanging splinter from the furniture.

It used to be called Ye Olde Cross Inn but, due to the curse, it had changed its name. Unofficially at first, but then the new name stuck and the sign went up to confirm it. The actual glass bottles remained untouched in one of the front windows and a sign was affixed at the window, which read: 'Dirty Bottles', so most local Alnwick folk used the name.

Legend had it that, centuries ago, an innkeeper dropped dead interfering with the bottles in the window. The widow sign declared that anyone who tried again would go the same way. As a result, the dusty old bottles were sealed between two windows for eternity—and *the curse* was set as legend in the mindset of an already overshadowed community. The imposing castle in the town, built in the 1090s, had set that feeling in stone for centuries already, with the ghosts from its dungeons overflowing and free to roam alongside the living.

John got a drink and sat down at the small round table, alongside the bottles in the window. In the past, he'd always sat close to them. Now, after so much, they seemed even more connected to him. The background music jarred comically against the setting as some euro-pop crap attacked his ears and made him want to hit something hard.

A male stripper did his best for a girl in the corner of the room, he got leered at and slapped on the arse, and then on the face. Then he was gone before he could get his pants back on.

The music switched: Led Zeppelin's *When The Levee Breaks* built up as the rain outside started on cue, and crashed against the lead-lined windows with a 'ratta-tat-tat'.

Out came John's notebook and pen. Both like second and third limbs. The dark ink, like blood on the pages, was his deepening connection to a moving past, and present, that never stayed still long enough for him to be sure of the truth in either. He couldn't fully remember the first therapist that had originally made him aware of them, the tools to exercise his mind. He wished he could thank them. He couldn't speak to them, and wrote that down as well:

Thank you.

He was meant to be back home for the funeral. But a story was there; more death than expected. He'd changed and *almost* wrote as much as he drank these days. Almost. So, he scribbled manically. Let it flow. And drank that one drink, for now.

'Ring. Ring,' his phone lit up. Onscreen:

M. Pamplemousse

'Yes?' he lifted it tentatively to his ear.

A horsey, deep and sensual voice breathed down the line from the opposite end of the country. 'I can feel it, when you go at it, John... It's almost a sexual thing. My pulse goes up, my nipples get hard. You can't hide your vices, Johnny-boy. We're connected now... I'm your agent. You fucking walk past a quill and I get wet.'

He spat out most of his mouthful of Guinness... the rest came out of his nose. The whole pub noticed. Her energy was colossal and with tendrils that easily crossed the miles and airwaves.

'You are, aren't you? At it, John? Don't tease with me now. Enough foreplay—cut to the money shot. Give it me hard, Black.'

'Lucky timing... I *might* have just opened up.'

'I knew it. You dirty bastard. Now, put down the pint you just spurted out and get right to it. Get another book draft down. We need the money. Do it for us.'

'Alright. Maybe. Why did you really call?' His hand holding the pen hovered over the page below.

'I thought you were quitting the drink anyhow, cutting down or something?'

'How is she? Cherry?' He changed the subject. He might have quit or cut down on *it*, but *it* hadn't quit chasing him.

'Cherry... She's okay. As expected.'

'Really. Have you seen her? How... is... she?'

'Seen her once, or twice, is all.'

He breathed, listened hard, willing her to be safe, healed, and at peace with them being apart.

'She's sad, John. Hurting. Strong though. You know that. That's why you're into her. Otherwise, I'd have you all to myself, wouldn't I?'

What was left of the Guinness left his nostrils and hit the page.

'Honey, don't worry. She'll mend. I guess we'll *both* just have to wait for you to bury your past and come back to us, again.'

'Yes.'

'Same old story, John.'

He could see her winking down the line and licking her top lip. The retired stripper, turned literary agent, was quite something. She could tighten a man's sack from hundreds of miles away. She was a master of her abilities. She could also cut balls off from similar distances and wasn't to be fucked with.

'Get off my bar you hairy-arsed-biker-prick!' she shouted to one of her punters on the other end of the line. 'Down, NOW! And put that away, or you'll fucking lose it for good this time.'

'Still pulling pints then? How about you get to selling more books?'

'How's about you write one people want to read,' Again another flirty wink was inferred across the airwaves.

With a smack of full, dark red lips, and a 'click' she was gone. Back to her bar, The Hatchett, to wrestle a half-cut biker off the countertop, and out of one of the doors. His trousers would still be around his ankles as he lay in the gutter wondering what had happened.

The ancient doors to The Dirty Bottles rarely opened and only a handful of shadows ambled around its front and back nooks, snugs and lounges. John left his notebook and pint, and went to the gents where a unique historical aroma, haunted by ghosts all of its own, awaited him.

His flow created a familiar noise as it splashed against the back of the urinal and the drain conjured up a foul, demonic collection of smells awoken by the new addition.

Layers of scratches, pen and pencil were on the wall in front of him as he aimed straight ahead. The wall looked like it might have been once a mustard yellow. Although years of fags, dirty hands, wiped snot and smegma may have been its defining everlasting shade. Farrow and Ball paints could name a product line after it: Shit House Ghosts.

Back in Black, he read in an 80s nail's scrawl... A nod to ACDC and the passing of their singer, Bon Scott. John looked down, shook off, nodded in some kind of respect, an understanding, then walked back out. He didn't wash his hands. No one ever did. He'd been nearly killed more times than he could remember. Personal hygiene wasn't a priority in there.

And even if he did wash, the previous two hundred years' worth of hands to touch the door handles to get out sure as hell hadn't.

Back at the table, three of the pages from his notebook had been ripped out. One had been rolled tight, made to look like a snake or a worm with a fat head. Another, was made into a small origami box. The third sheet had pencilled numbers on it: coordinates.

He stopped.

No one moved, or looked over in the room. All busy in their corners.

Hands at his sides, he was ready to form any shape, fist, block or reach required. He slowly turned 360 degrees, scanning the shadows, the shapes hunched on the bar, distant tables and the barman. He looked for movement, a tell. Someone would want to know he'd got the cryptic messages or whatever in hell they were.

Nothing. All just drinkers, drinking. A lone, tired server, serving.

He picked up what was left of his pint and poured it into the nearest plant pot then sat to look at the numbers. The barman looked up, only now seeing what had happened as John discarded his drink to the cheese plant. He poured another and brought it over.

'Bad pint, John?' He looked apologetic. He hadn't cleaned the pipes that week. It flowed so regularly whether he did or didn't he saw no point in it. An Aussie couple once had the shits after a pint of McEwans each. He didn't read too much into it. Didn't want them hanging around anyway, and no one else touched the shite.

'Should have taken it with me... Someone has been here, touched my stuff. You see anyone over here by my table?' John looked up. His facial expression had returned to war.

'Paranoid a little since the army are you, John? Not sure anyone gives a shit where you've been or whether you're back.' He played it down. His heart had skipped a beat and changed rhythm when he heard John was back, same as the rest.

'Maybe,' John stared, serious.

His notebook was sacred. He'd had his writing used as a set piece before, against him. He should have known better than to leave it on the table. Maybe his subconscious wanted to fast forward the game... to get on with the show.

He should have known better than to publish them, his thoughts. Exposing his mind to the eyes and ears of others. It all becomes an ever-changing Mobius strip exposing your mind to the enemy. Your thoughts change, secrets too. And no one knows what's actually true anymore as you write the new ones out again.

The barman's expression changed, like a penny had dropped from up high and hit him in the centre of the skull. 'Mind you... have you just come back from the bogs now?'

'Yes.'

'Then yes, a minute or two ago. Shit, John. I thought it *was* you. All in black, sorry. You spooks look all the same. Our usuals are a little dustier.' He gestured to the bottles in the window. 'Take it,' he said, and put a new pint on the table and turned to walk away.

'Aren't you gonna ask me why I'm back? After so much time?' he asked the barman's back.

'They all come back. For death usually. A family member gone, or they want to be near their own one last time before they go themselves. Funny that, isn't it? They *all* do... come back... return, in the end. How *have* you been, John? Close to the end?' he said, still walking away.

'Still breathing. Must be another's death brought me back.'

'Was sorry to hear the news, John.'

'We all go... in the end. Death and taxes,' John said, focussing in on the folded paper snake and origami box on the table, which he slowly realised was meant to be a coffin. It was obvious now. Was it meant to be his mother's, his own, or someone else's?

A snake and a box.

Was it a riddle or a signing off? A hello?

'Death, *drink* and taxes,' the barman said, putting both hands back on the bar. It was a busy day if he had to think and speak at once. The interaction had drained him. Slowly his right hand reached under the counter and he poured himself a large one from a bottle there.

John looked up the coordinates that were left on the third sheet, in his phone. All landmarks, National Trust sites and tourist hot spots. The county was full of them, if you actually had the interest to go looking:

Cragside
Bamburgh
Vindolanda, Hadrian's Wall
Kielder Water
Alnwick Castle

He took photos of everything, a close up of the coordinates, and sent them with a message:

FAO Prudhoe Street Station Commander:
I think this is the start. Check them out. I doubt they're in any order.
I guess I'll see you there.

He knew whoever laid the bait must have been and gone. No one's that mad... Telling you where a crime's going to be committed in advance. Whatever they wanted found at the locations wouldn't be good. And the police would likely just pull him in, in connection, in cahoots—the only one with any real evidence. They liked to bash a stranger in town, a tourist or even better. And a local returned thinking they're better than the place—that was the real prize.

'YOU AND HE were marras, weren't you? Friends?' the barman asked Marshall. 'He was just in here, sure as life, stood right where you are; John-fucking-Black. Soldier-boy come home. Thought he was shot ages ago, and there the moody fuck was, right where you're standing. Ordered a Guinness as black as his shirt... As black as his heart, name and jacket too.' Again, the barman was exhausted. Thinking. Talking. It was too much on minimum wage and even less brain cells.

'Sounds 'bout right,' Marshall muttered. Without the confidence to look the barman in the eyes. He never held eye contact, Marshall. A blind man's stare could rattle what little confidence he had left in him. If there ever was anything.

'Were you... close?'

'Played pool a few times, that's all. Not sure someone like that really gets close to anyone. Do they? Otherwise, how could they do it?'

'Do what?' The bar tap spluttered as he spoke. 'Time to change another barrel. Great.'

'Kill people and all that...'

The town was closed off, and Marshall Nichols was closed off from the town. He ventured out of his bedsit once every blue moon to raid the local charity shops for Asian horror DVDs, the more obscure, the better. And occasionally for a pint or six to self-medicate his mood. Which meandered from a nihilistic: can't be arsed rage, through a zen like comatose nothingness, to on occasion, depressed and drinking through it to the other side of melancholy madness.

This was such an occasion. Although the mention of John Black added a new toxic drop to the mix.

'You were friends though, I am right?' the barman insisted, putting the pint down.

A figure at the end of the bar adjusted the edge of his dark hoodie that was up over his head. He tilted his head slightly as if it helped to listen closer to the men nearby. In the bar mirror, his snake eyes glistened and he ate up the words. Delighting in the opportunity of a new prize.

'Guess we were close-ish... Suppose so,' Marshall said the words without conviction. He didn't care for John, but liked the suggestion of normality by someone. With those insincere words, overheard by a stranger, he unknowingly sealed his fate.

Snake Eyes grinned and only he saw it. The next person to see this empty smile would be dying in agony. No chance of saviour. A destiny sealed an hour earlier, whilst he pretended to be normal, with the barman... by lying about a friendship with John Black.

MARSHALL WAS FOUND tied to an old stone cross in the town's market square.

The police approached the mangled stark effigy very slowly, creeping quietly like the dead body was asleep and they didn't want to wake it.

Steam rose up and around the shape of the man like smoke from a dying fire.

They could smell Marshall's soiled clothes as they entered the square. The moon lit up his stillness from a distance like he was a permanent fixture. Another defaced statue. A wooden post had been forced down both sleeves pushing his arms out as if in a makeshift crucifixion. The post was pushed so hard his elbows and wrists had no skin left, and his left hand was bent back on itself the wrong way, splintering bones and gristle out at the wrist joint, as empty tubes, veins, bulged and popped with nothing left to expel.

These surface injuries were post-mortem.

His body had been treated like a rag doll. A decoration for effect. The minutes before his death, he'd been a different type of doll for the killer's entertainment in a black magic game.

Blood had run from his body and was now congealing on the ten stone steps beneath the stone cross he was tied to.

They opened his coat, slowly. It was stuck with more congealing blood. On the other side of the market square, a butcher's shop window proudly displayed a pile of black puddings, from drained pigs, with the reflection of Marshall's body in the glass as the officers teased his coat to open further.

They looked—stared—eyes widening as they took in the full gore.

Rusty six-inch nails had been forced into his torso. And in the end, his eyes which now left black trails down his pale gaunt face which was sagging to one side to form an accidental, open, twisted grimace of a grin. A retired joker that never smiled while he'd lived. His empty mouth was wide open—an empty, laughing scream to match the nailed hollow eyes.

Birds sat on the roof tops surrounding the square.

'Someone's used him like a Voodoo doll,' an officer said.

'Clearly to cause maximum pain. Before he went into shock. It's like his killer knew where to pierce... skirting past vital organs... and which once to pierce to extend the suffering,' another said, scribbling in, and shaking, a notebook.

'Who is it?' the first officer said, then threw up. They weren't used to this kind of work.

'Marshall... I haven't seen him in ages. Was like a fucking vampire, only surfaced once every...' one said, then they all stopped.

They looked up at the *full moon*.

No one saw or heard a thing around the square but an occasional flap of wings. Marshall's tongue had been torn out, and one of his ears was found in a nearby waste bin.

The police had been called because a couple had stepped outside The George for a quickie in the alleyway. When they hurried back in, the man had complained that the smell outside was so bad that it *almost* put him off his 'vinegar stroke'. Almost. Not quite. When the barmaid went out to check, she was sick too, then she called the police to deal with it.

'What's going on here, Sarge'?' a young PC asked.

'*He's* brought all hell down us, that's what... Put out a call. Get John Black to the station,' the Sarge said.

They all looked at the thickening blood pooling on the steps.

'And call Queen Bitch. She can squeeze him,' he continued. 'This shit's way over my pay grade.'

'Yes, Sarge,' one said, and turned and went on the police radio.

The Sarge finished: 'Now, let's get this poor sad fucker photographed, bagged and outta here—have they cleaned up the piss and sick from outside The George yet? I need fucking drink.'

7

CHEVIOT

THE OLD MAN wheezed as he leaned forward to stoke the fire in the stone farmhouse that had been his home, and to those in the countless family generations before him. He was the only one of his family to do it alone, almost. He had his dog. The weight of his belly momentarily stopped his full stretch to the hearth. Eventually, with a strain, his mass spilt out at the sides increasing his reach enough to provoke the flames to life with the iron poker. The fire re-sparked alight. Enough to endure then placate under another round of contemplation and mindful sedation by the flames.

He did this a few times in as many hours as the logs shifted, crumbled and sparked again for another shift as coals re-glowed underneath.

'That's enough exercise for the day, pet,' he said to the grey sausage dog curled about his feet. He looked to the window and saw a break in the weather. An opportunity to do his duty and stay dry and also to collect more wood for the fire.

The dog's yap evolved to a bark then a twitch turned to a jump as its excitement grew expectantly.

'Right,' he said. 'Alright, pet.'

His voice soothed her. His monotone mutterings were at the centre of all the love in the little dog's world. The heart of her universe.

'I know, I'll check they're all locked up… You can take your shit. And we can get back to the fire with some new logs. I'll find the biscuit tin too. If you're good.'

So went the two's cycle of life. Happiness, when he allowed himself to accept it, and the little dog's elation in the simplicity and rewards in his companionship.

The biscuit tin always came out. The dog could do no wrong in the man's eyes. Unconditionally his.

The little dog barked again. Excited by the small things and routine again that made up life with the old man. Every day was the same; in and out of season. He'd walk past the tired old caravans. Check a stray sheep hadn't made a home in one, or under any, then he'd stop at the stone wall with the little dog. Sometimes he took a leak up against the stile and laughed at all the hikers that would use it that day to go over the drystone wall.

They'd look up at the Cheviots, the sweeping hills; a heather covered range straddling the Anglo-Scottish border in Northumberland. He'd never been up Cheviot itself, and the little dog wouldn't go without him. Not even chasing a rabbit or hare. Furthest she'd ever got was the far side of the campsite after a stoat, and she soon backed off when it was cornered and bared its teeth. Cheviot, the highest point in the Northumberland National Park, on his doorstep, and he was lazy. He'd spent a lifetime, happily looking up at, but never down from it. Besides he was scared of snakes and there were a ton of adders up there. He hated their beady little lifeless eyes.

Snake eyes were the worst.

Tourists stayed in his caravan park using it as a base to explore the area, walk up the hills and look at the stars — admiring the clearest night skies for miles. On a good night you could feel like you were seeing God's entire playground as you shrank into insignificance under it all. The fortunate visitors brought their own accommodation; tents and vans and didn't risk the facilities. His laziness knew no bounds.

'WHAT DO YOU think? Would make a good base, no?' Snake Eyes said from the passenger seat of the Range Rover. They both looked out at the caravan park at the base of the sweeping green and brown hills, with patches of heather dotting purples and deep blues, all spread out in front of their car. For a brief moment they were touched by it. Something greater and more important than their own impulses. Then, because unacknowledged by either of them, it passed and they returned to a bloody river of thoughts that polluted everywhere they travelled.

'Yes,' Nina said, 'let's go and have *word* with the old fat man.'

'A *word*, yes.'

The subtext and insinuations were well known by each of them now. A car journey the length of the country and they knew what each other meant, instantly. The only thing that wasn't clear yet was how far to go each time. Although they had a base level violence, that was only ever the starting point.

They eyed the old man hobbling between the caravans with his dog. Him: the injured gazelle. Them: bored, hungry hyenas looking for a slow drawn out kill to pass the time.

HE SAW THEM eyeing him over the fields from their 4x4. It was out of season and he was closed for business, and with it all the fake pleasantries he had to usually put on in order to face a visitor. He only just about had patience for people, barely, when it was the height of summer months. He loved his dog. That was it in his life. In the height of activity on the campsite, when the place was all booked out, he'd manage an enthused grunt at best. If the tourists were lucky he'd kick his dog's shit off the main paths for them. He saw no point in offering up any more to the strangers. Still, they came, returning year after sodding year. Although he often wished they wouldn't. But he didn't know another way to get by. Dog food wasn't free and he struggled to think past the field end on most days. It took him three strong coffees to function and move half as much as the average man. The first problem was the effort and initiative to make those brews in the first place.

He saw the steam rise from their engine as they slowly started the car and began their creeping approach.

'Here we fucking go,' he said to the tired grey sausage dog. She started to shake, looking nervous. Overhead a kestrel circled and even higher the clouds were filling, waiting to break again with a heavy downpour. They parted slightly to let ethereal beams of light scorch through, lighting up heavenly patches of the hills as if spotlights for unseen dancers, and for a moment they had his attention.

'Pots of gold, pet? What do you think?'

If he'd had the will, he'd have taken a spade to dig for the gold under those spots. He kept telling the dog as much every time it happened. He never did anything... The heavens kept up their gestures. He took the joys life offered to him, as long as they didn't involve an ounce of imagination or physical effort — simplicity, happiness and poetry laden with inaction.

The skies were in flux, again. Something unheavenly was about to break and spill over the ancient land, the hills and campsite with it. The area had seen border wars, blood shed in gallons. Savagery and brutality.

Today: evil would soak through it all.

'WHAT'S IT WITH you and boxes?' Snake Eyes said to Nina and then stoked the fire with the poker. The farmhouse was small and they weren't sure they did want to stay after all. The fire was toasty but there was a dampness and musty smell that would never shift.

'Oh, this?' she said, looking at the wooden crate at her feet which had streaks of red and brown handprints over it. She feigned a look of innocence that lit both of them up, inside.

Muffled sounds and whimpers came from the box.

In the corner of the kitchen the dog looked on, wide eyed — gripped by terror. Something bad had taken over what was left of her simple little life. Way worse than she could have imagined. She shook, longing for it to leave; to have her master back, and return to the fireside with him.

'I was kept cooped up too long is all. People thinking they could take what they wanted from me,' Nina whispered and took the red hot poker from Snake Eyes' hands, that had been heating up in the fire. 'I was trapped, boxed up, and pierced — deep. Again...again...' she dangled the poker expectantly, and in a last, 'and... again!' she forced the glowing red hot poker down through a crack in the box, which immediately released a guttural howl.

Blood, piss and shit ran slowly from the box.

Then came the beautiful silence. They sat and enjoyed the quiet stillness; fully appreciating a mutual release by her action. Maybe this was how a relationship started, he thought; in the world of monsters. Maybe... just maybe... One day, they might touch each other. Sparks and electricity would pass between them. Would that mean they would no longer need to do this to other people? He didn't stay there longer than those few thoughts.

NONE OF THESE thoughts crossed her mind. She felt an ounce of pressure release from the memories she carried. Snake Eyes might have found a connection, a glimmer of humanity, or a glimpse at potential normality... There was such a long way to go for her to get to that point, she thought nothing of it.

'More fuel for the fire?' Snake Eyes said, bring the room back into darkness. He looked at the dog that was shivering uncontrollably up against the kitchen units.

'Why not... Tastes like chicken. Or, so I've heard.'

Snake Eyes stood and took the poker from Nina and walked into the kitchen. Expressionless.

Outside the heavens opened; a downpour of tears over heather. It was out of season for the trailer park, but evil had come to stay anyway.

8

CRAGSIDE

JOHN SAT IN the tired grey Ford Mondeo. He was sticking to the seats as the engine tried to rattle to something resembling life. Like an old man's lungs before a marathon, it wheezed with the futility of effort. After some time, smoke coughed out the back and the engine ran. Clicking, chugging and splattering away.

For how long it'd go or how far he'd get, he wasn't confident.

He looked at the coordinates for Cragside on the scrap of paper as the radio played *There's No Other Way* by Blur. The car's heaters finally were up enough to release some warmth and with it came a stale, burnt out reek that circulated back into and around the car. It was like being trapped inside a drunk's arse.

His mind eventually went back to the radio and responded to the song's lyrics as if the chorus was a question.

'There's no other way…' it went.

He nodded involuntarily along to the track.

OUTSIDE, THE PREVIOUS owner of the car had been tapping on the driver's side with his tattooed knuckles. He'd chosen the 'hate' emblazoned ones intentionally. He was angry, and a little scared. John's face carried an unknown risk for him to provoke. But he was dumb enough to do it anyway.

He saw familiarity in John, and knew a little of him from his past and in the murmurs about the small town. Drunken gossip of the rogue soldier turned gangland boss bounced about in the enclosed rumour mill. Maybe they went to school together also, and he'd forgotten. Fuck it, he thought, he just wanted his shitty car back. The fun of drink driving just wasn't the same without wheels. And his wife's unsaid disapproval, which opened him up to deliver his 'love' fisted disciplining on her, was growing boring. He much preferred his favourite excuse to go at her, other than the kids... the one that was, 'he just wanted to.' Like he had the God given right and she couldn't do anything about it. Trapped. Just like he was with her.

John's frame was slowly overshadowing any confidence the man had. His appearance was that of a hostile stranger who didn't care less what he was looking at. The semi-sobered up drunken angry man was just another stain on the window, and he felt like using the mains head to clean it.

The man had seen degrees of this before in the tourists. The disdain, from those well-travelled that had gone off track en-route to Edinburgh and landed in Alnwick town by accident. They didn't tend to hang around. Took in the castle, some sights, usually for half an hour, then fucked off before they got put in the stocks, or burned in a straw man or something else medieval. That condescending glower never left them, the entire time they were there. The man saw the same look in John's black eyes.

Tap-tap, he continued on the window.

Inside, John turned away then back again. Like a statue, no outward emotion.

The man stopped... mid tap. His finger hovered, wavered, then retracted to form a shaking fist.

John's reaction, or lack of it, as if the car's prior driver was invisible, was enough to rattle him to the core. So, like a shamed football hooligan under the shadow of a police horse, he turned, dragging his fist and knuckles away, over the cobbles for a bottle of Newcastle Brown in the nearest pub.

He didn't have the balls. Fuck this shit, the man thought, as he left.

With each step his fingers slowly re-extended from their retreated position. By the end of the drink, he'd be a cock-sure prick again, ready to beat and be beaten mindlessly. Boasting to bar stools how some idiot had stolen his car, and how he was gonna kneecap them. He wouldn't dare say who it was though. The man that had stolen his car. The ghost that had come to visit.

JOHN PUT THE car in gear; his foot getting the last word in as it answered the call to action.

The man would have heard it from the pub, as John revved the sorry engine, then floored it, and tore through the old stone streets.

The car wasn't used to going past the town walls and chugged up an endlessly steep hill that made the old Ford grunt and fart black clouds of despair. Having made the repeated new efforts it would kill or cure it to clear out the valves, exhaust and tubes of its making.

The car sighed in relief as it crested the top of the hill onto an old Roman road, and was opened up to cut through moorlands, with pheasants and grouse flying up and over the road from both sides, skirting suicide with each glance of the windscreen or wheels.

John rolled a smoke, half-looking at the road. Old bad habits were re-emerging. As he flicked the black Zippo open one handed and lit up, he wondered more and more if he was going to have to return to his worst habit of all — and kill again.

By the time his slow meditative exhale came, and the Golden Virginia fumes left, carried on his breath, he knew it for sure. It wasn't *if*. It was *how soon* and *how many*.

CRAGSIDE IS A vast Victorian Countryside mansion, built amongst an eclectic mix of giant trees. The Baron that had built it as his home had collected the mass of trees from around the world. Tall and wide now, they frame the roads and house itself in a blanket of branches and leaves.

Its Tudor Revival architecture is as mixed as its surrounding shrubs and trees. It's hundreds of years old and never has looked the same, one angle, season and period in time to the next.

Always in flux and open to interpretation. Like a complex ageing wine. A built-up jigsaw of architectural tested imagination rather than a set timepiece formula.

John parked up and walked out into the forest path that led up to the house. Today, it looked like a tall Tudor-esque bastardisation of a castle. Black wooden beams and slats crossed high walls under a section of castellations and thatches. Perfectly inharmonious yet perfectly balanced in its jarring juxtapositions. The wind through the trees formed some kind of personal, familiar feeling that felt welcoming, though it was the same for everyone—nothing unique or personal about it. They sang their own song for themselves—regardless of the audiences that came and went.

The giant, metal-studded, wooden door loomed up in front of him beyond the pebbled drive.

'Are you a member?' a jobs-worth, tweed-wearing gent said around the slightly opened crack of the doorway. He clearly had no intention of opening it any further. The metal studs that dressed the door's surface looked more like weapons than decoration. The door was a giant defensive shield.

'Someone suggested I be here.'

'You've an invite? A private appointment?'

John's patience was thin. The place was generally open to the public. Occasionally the caretakers would play guard if they thought a visitor wasn't worthy, or was a threat to the estate and its artworks inside. The door's brutal studs looked increasingly tempting to push into the cranky old bastard behind the door.

Then the rage faded. He wasn't that person. Not anymore.

Was he ever?

'I'm a member, he can be my guest,' a female voice came from behind on the gravel.

He jumped slightly and turned.

It was like looking into a circus mirror. A female image stood there, an alternate reality version of himself reflected back at him. Different hairstyle, bobbed deepest dark brown. All dressed in black. And baring a stare halfway between loneliness and independent strength. She looked back and through him.

'It's alright I won't expect anything in return. I just want you in... And, out of my way, so I can get in too,' she had a Northumbrian accent, but her demeanour could have passed for some art-house French chic. If she had taken out a cigarette in a holder and spat in his face before slapping him aside, he wouldn't have been surprised.

Her high black boot heels clacked up and stood alongside him on the top stone slab step.

The door creaked open and she was greeted by the old man on the other side as if she owned the place. The old man's country-gent tweed outfit—complete with plus fours—annoyed John, but he reframed the judgement before the needless aggression built up too far.

We all have our uniforms.

'Viki, sorry miss. Didn't see you behind him. Please... Please... Come in.'

'Thanks,' she said, brushed John to one side and marched into the entrance hallway.

'How're the dogs?' he said and took her coat.

'Sleeping off a shoot. Wet. Tired. Bloody jaws and muddy paws. How they're meant to be. I work them hard. Just how they like it,' and she looked John up and down.

'Get much?' the old man said.

'A brace. Enough for tea. One to spare. One for you if you like?'

'Thanks miss. Will go well with the neeps 'n tatties I've got waiting.'

John looked to the slabs of the stone floor and shook his head as if disapproving a stuffy royal, knowing he was to suffer for it, to be beheaded, if they clocked him.

They both did. Looked at him. Shocked.

Their pleasant-mock-regal-banter was for show, to the unknown visitor, to set a scene — to put up a class divide. They meant for him to be impressed, obviously, and it didn't wash. Exactly the opposite had happened.

'Inverted snob prick. Just let him in. He's definitely just *public*,' she barked, then walked proud and hard down the corridor, as if she was related to the characters in the intimidating giant framed paintings of dignitaries lining the high walls. The gilded framed faces look down from both sides. History's jury. John still wasn't impressed.

'Well, if she says you're a guest of a member, and can come in,' his face winced as he stood to one side and waved John further in reluctantly. Neither of them had any real authority to turn him away, and he was firmly past the threshold now.

The place was open to the public, but historians, National Trust members and staff treated it like some kind of personal heirloom—a private clubhouse. He assumed the woman was an art historian, librarian, studier of books too—she carried that kind of air of pretentious superiority that comes with being buried in a subject so long, you think you are it. It was like she had travelled, seen and been places without moving. An unproven wisdom and confidence easily broken.

John moved down the corridor and between the rooms.

He didn't know what he was looking for but felt sure it would find its way to him, one way or another, and would speak out. He walked room to room, all filled with over-ornate pomp and regal splendour that made him uneasy, hanging under high carved and embossed ceilings, painted and shining in brash splendour, even brasher, given the time they were created.

What he searched for nagged at him more than the ill-gotten gains of past high society. He was being played, again. Clues and signs would be here. The coordinates had pointed the way.

Viki appeared in a doorway. Looking. Judging.

He had already grown used to it.

John ignored the background prejudice and looked up at an oil painting of a flame haired girl on a beach. She was maybe twenty years old in the composition, at most. The girl held a golf club and wore a black knee length pleated skirt, a white shirt and red tie. Each of the paint strokes were drenched in symbolism. He looked into it, transfixed. Even then, women of stature were forced into male imagery and stereotypes, styled up in order to succeed rather than flourishing as they were. Like the female authors of the day masquerading as men in order to be read and taken seriously.

'Do you think she gave a shit about golf?' Viki said from the doorway.

'Expect it was to show her ranking. Her place in society. The painting. The pose. The activity. That... she was capable of being as good as a man—and all that shit. And, that the reason it's hung here in the smokers' lounge, for a load of old cranky gits to letch at, is pointed too...'

'What about it?'

'Maybe it was just to titillate the old fuckers as they knocked back a scotch.'

She didn't respond. Instead, there was an air of respect. He'd obviously paid the painting, and her, some thought—enough to try and wind Viki up as he danced around truths.

'And what about me, do you think I'm a woman pretending to be a man, to get by in society?' she asked, and brought out an antique shotgun she'd been concealing behind the door frame, and pointed it at him. Cocking the hammers slowly one at a time for effect.

Click... Click.

He didn't flinch. He'd had a gun pointed at him before and knew when someone meant to pull the trigger. She didn't and the rusty old piece of shit she held would probably smoke out and fall apart, or blow up in her face first.

'Ex-services?'

'S.A.S.'

'Of course.'

'Want a tour?' she asked.

'This one's got my attention, this painting. Don't know why.'

'Maybe it's the red hair? Or, maybe you're drawn to the strong ones?'

'Possibly,' he said, and thought of Cherry.

'It's a painting of *his* daughter, Lord Armstrong's: Vera. Liked golf is all. Not everything is shrouded in cynical manipulations here. You don't have to go through life like that, sabotaging the joy out of everything... you know?'

'There's always more to see in these old paintings,' he said, as his eyes focussed in on something.

'I prefer the Japanese prints. Less colonial or old establishment feeling. The baron, Lord Armstrong, wasn't all that you despise. He was more of an inventor.'

'Tanks and bombs,' he stated as his eyes closed in, 'I know.'

'Hydraulic power as well,' she said, trying to defend a legacy.

'This girl?'

'Yes?'

'If she's all that... Happy? His daughter...'

'What?'

'Why is she crying?' he said and turned, like a lawyer making a case, looking at Viki to gauge her response.

'WHAT?' SHE WAS shocked, and put the gun down, clinking it against a glass table top, and walked quickly over to have a closer look at the painting.

'There,' he pointed slowly at a small red tear that was coming from her right eye.

'That's not meant to be there.'

'Didn't think so.'

'No. No. This just isn't right. What have you done? Why?' This time she was visibly moved, hurt. Like he'd cut her. Uncontrollable. She loved the art in the old place like they were all living breathing things. 'Fraser! Quick. Fetch the ladders. NOW!' she yelled into a Walkie Talkie. 'If you've done this I'll have you banned from all National Trust sites!' Even she cowered at how ludicrous it sounded, out loud. She quickly turned from pink to red, embarrassed. Still, she'd said it. She was flustered by the disruption this stranger had brought with him.

She wanted everything back to normal. But also wanted him to stay.

'I guess I'll take the rough with the smooth. Enjoyed it whilst I was allowed in. Suppose you won't be offering me a discount on membership,' John said, looking back up at the defaced oil painting.

'Sorry. Of course it wasn't you. Or, I hope not. You've just got here. And how would you have reached—you're not an ape. Not that sort, anyhow.' She softened and let her feelings show in a fleeting glance. She could see he was as concerned she was, and it went deeper than the vandalised image before them both. She felt the cogs of his mind whirring away like he was a detective and privy to a much bigger picture than the defaced one in front of them.

Fraser appeared in the doorway. 'Yes miss... step ladders coming up,' and he scampered off like one of her spaniels to retrieve a downed grouse with lead shot in its lungs.

Whilst they waited, they looked up at the painting, unmoving, still. Eventually she looked back to study him.

Who was this stranger that had brought excitement where there never was?

Silence.

The girl in the painting looked sad enough. Trapped in her established role. A painted societal slave oiled onto canvas, lasting the ages, shining out for all to see her predicament. There was no need for the addition of the teardrop. So dark. So red. A bleeding Mary statue. It just wasn't necessary, all conscience bearing spectators would carry one in sympathy for her anyhow.

Fraser pulled up the step ladders, scratching the parquet floor as he went. He'd spend a week polishing it out. Now, they focussed, fixed on the painting. Viki gestured for Fraser to put a foot on the bottom step as she started to climb up towards it. Her heart beating faster with each rung of the ladders.

She was still in control.

Viki stopped at the top and looked into the little girl's eyes. They connected. She welled up then swallowed it down. She wasn't sure whether it was the girl's recent defacement or something deeper down that drew the emotion out of her, like pulling out a bee sting.

Both artists knew the effect they'd have: the one of the original painting, and the one that added the red teardrop.

The person to daub the bloody tear took time and formed the perfect hanging droplet. It looked real to her.

Carefully, arms spread, she gripped and lifted the painting. Teetering slightly then brought it slowly down, her hands trembling on the gold gilded frame. All the while her and Fraser stared at the crimson teardrop marking the girl's cheek.

When she reached the bottom step, she sat the picture in a chair then took a tissue from her pocket, folded it into a triangle and wet the point with her lips.

The old man panicked, 'Just a tiny drop, ma'am. Fresh too. I can clean it off this afternoon,' he stammered, gripping her wrist, preventing her touching the painting with the tissue. He touched the corner of the frame like it was the shoulder of an elderly relative.

'How did it get there?' she asked. 'The bloody tear drop.'

'Maybe a random act of god. A drip from the ceiling. Condensation or a leak. Copper tainted water to her face,' the old man said as they both remained transfixed by the girl's spoiled image. In their world, whether it was an act of God or man, it was sacrilege.

Did the recent addition of teardrop reveal the true nature of the girls pose?

'Maybe *that's* why she's crying,' John said.

'What?' Viki said and looked at him, realising he wasn't fixed on the painting anymore and he was staring wide eyed at the spot on the wall it used to cover.

On the wall, previously hidden by the painting, there was more blood. Words, lyrical blades of text, stabbed and scratched into the plasterwork, shouting out at them to see. Written and sliced into the wall with a blade that must have been dipped ceremoniously in more blood.

'Someone knew we would see this,' she said.

They all looked up at the patch on the wall:

> *These ancient lands, buildings and people carry ghosts.*
> *Some you've known.*
> *Some you've lost.*
> *Some returned.*

Don't worry. All precious memories and corpses you'll get to meet
again sure enough.
Yes, sure as hell, John Black, it's coming for you.
Like a comet, curse and a disease we all ignored.. until it was too late.

—

By the time you read this. There'll be more ghosts added to the crowd.
And they can't wait to see you again, John.
You discarded them in life, but you'll meet again in death.
You can't run from your destiny.
But it will be fun. The chasing...

—

THE HUNT

What the hell?' Fraser said, and held his hand to his chin.

'Who are you?' Viki said to the wall and the mystery man who stood next to her.

'I'm John.' John said. 'John Black.'

There was silence. For a while.

'I've heard of you... Died a few times I thought. Definitely thought you were dead and gone the last time.'

John said: 'No one ever goes away from here. They always come back in the end.'

9

THE SCHOONER

KIT RAYMOND HAD worked the little coastal village pubs all her adult life. When she'd had the looks, she bounced around them to the highest bidder. The bids never came in high enough to bounce her out all together and into a happy life.

Now less striking, she faded into the crowd. The Schooner's bar taps had stuck to her in those cruel later years where she'd felt the onset of obscurity as insignificance approaching.

Like the tired old carpet, she had been there long enough for the punters and savage rude tourists to have trodden her down so hard, she lay stained and threadbare, not going anywhere else in a hurry. Dark wood panelled walls were made darker by generations of farmers' smoke, stale farts and potent breath, and the Jukebox was stuck on a series of '80s hit parade repeats: Rod Stewart, Billy Idol, Elton John and Toto. When The Smiths came on she used to hide and cry under the counter.

She was now immune to ambition. Any of it.

That afternoon she was half asleep when the skinny man with the snake eyes came in. She was passing time thinking of the few lost love opportunities she'd had that could have been her big ticket out of the place. Once seen as a village rose, her straight black hair and Spanish olive skin was now the wrong side of a certain age. A number she'd attached too much importance to.

Here, if you weren't married off before nineteen or twenty, you were shelved for good. And she had well and truly hit and passed the village's unsaid marrying 'sell by date'. She swallowed hard when she noticed the new punter approaching, and turned to pretend to do something behind the bar, so she could secretly check her appearance. Touch it up a little here and there: straightening her top, assessing how much cleavage to show, and to check if she had a bit of a Frazzle or a chip left in her teeth.

Who knows what the future might hold in a new stranger entering the pub? It still might come, that ticket to happiness. A kiss that means something. A hold that lasts after they climb off.

She didn't think anything of the man's straight up, without introductions, incessant asking of questions at first. She welcomed it. Loneliness had settled deep. Anything beyond the usual sexist flirting, drinks orders, barks and bites for change, all felt a welcome change—for a while.

It soon started to feel like an interrogation.

This man was different. How she imagined a serial killer behaved when there was no need to hide their motives any more. No pretence. When there was just the killer and victim, alone.

Her blood chilled as if she'd stepped into a freezer. 'Why do I go thinking stuff like that?' she thought. 'It's why I'm still alone.' Always a drain, never the radiator. Her mum had told her all about 'radiators' and 'drains' and since then she quickly pigeon-holed people on first impressions. She'd always thought that people were unaware of which they were. But she was aware of her own 'radiating' or 'draining' rises and falls and could change, at will—a super hero barmaid.

I've still got a lift in these two, she thought, cupping herself with one hand and attempting to flick herself back to 'radiator' mode

He looked about as confused as a snake could.

She shook her head, smiled and looked back at the stranger. She looked around. The room was empty. But for her, him and those staring... snake eyes. This was going to be hard for her to shake. The guy was creeping her out.

This time she tried a wink, but it came out all wrong. What the hell was she doing? He wasn't all that. In fact, was he anything? Was she that desperate?

Nothing. His tight lips just got tighter, and those dead eyes, deader.

Did he ever blink?

'John Black?' he asked like a detuned radio. Words forced passed tight lips.

'I haven't heard that name in a long, long time,' her eyes went off to another place. A rosier place and time, filled with fun fucks and no ties. If only she'd expected or asked more back then.

The man with the snake eyes stared hard into her.

A glint of moisture rested on her lips that quivered at the mention of John's name.

The man looked like he'd scored something he desired. Carried in her words—not her.

'Do you want a pint? Or, do you just want to ask your silly little questions?' she adjusted her top. Pulled it down to show a fraction more cleavage. *In for a penny, in for a pounding,* she and the girls used to say before a night out. Before they'd all settled down and left her behind. With their lives filled with kid's craps, potties, pushchairs, and... a once-a-month fumble if they were lucky. Whilst she stayed fused to the fucking pumps.

Snake Eyes seemed robotic, an automaton. As though her chest was invisible to him. He must be gay, she thought. Then, the jig came to life, creaking into action:

'Pint. And a shot to go in it. Both black.'

Her face screwed up, confused. It was an involuntary reflex as she tried to think of what dark pint would go with what dark shot.

'I'll leave that with you whilst I go for a slash,' his skinny lips said. And the stranger went off to the gents to prepare his own dose of something special for the crazy, inconsequential barmaid.

TWO CUSTOMERS IN half an hour, this day of the week, she thought. As the door opened again. It must be her lucky day... Then, she realised the uniform.

'Shite,' she muttered under her breath.

Roy Blackwell hadn't drunk on duty so far that week and wasn't about to start. He still had remnants of a bastard behind the eyes from the last dirty pint he'd had in The Schooner, and hadn't forgotten who served it to him.

'Cleaned them fucking pipes yet, Kit?'

'I could say the same, Roy. Trudy says you gave her the clap last time you guys were out back against the bins.'

'Now then. Remember I'm an officer?'

'Yes, sir… eww, so strict. I'm just jealous,' and she winked. It was a forced act. But she was good at it. If she kept it up with every sad bastard that came in maybe she'd strike lucky, and get fingered before closing time.

Already, she was forgetting the stranger in the toilets out back.

She wasn't really jealous of anyone that had been with Roy. Despite her words. He was a wanker, kept barring teenagers and the next generation of drinkers. He'd killed Saturday night in The Schooner last month and was on track to do it again this one.

'Seen any strangers in town, Kit?'

CHINA BOB LOOKED at his 'snake eyes' in the dirty pub mirror. His empty stare was well practiced. He'd ran out of martial arts trainers to be taught by, then dispose of. Ultimately, he had no soul to shine through and reflect, although the mirror still tried. He cut a vial of powder on the counter top. Mixing the dose just right to knock her out, but not too much, he wanted her still to feel everything when the time came.

A sound came through the cheap paper-thin door to the side. Chattering. And with it he smelt the filth. Bacon. His senses were as finely tuned as his lack of empathy and emotion. He could smell a pig, one of the police, through a wall of lead. And this was a hollow core door hanging off its hinges.

Sniff. Sniff.

He hated small talk. Didn't see, or hear, the point. The small talk between 'the law' and that dimwit, failed cock tease of a barmaid, even though it wasn't directed at him, boiled his blood. He nearly ripped the handle from the door in eagerness to get out there and silence them both. Then the training kicked back in. Mindfulness for serial killing, psycho sick-fucks Part 1: take a deep breath, hold it. Smell it, taste it. Hold. Hold. Just hold it. And now... breathe out.

His eyes darkened over.

He folded up the carefully prepared dose in a cellophane wrap. Put it in his back pocket then went 'full ninja'. Like a shadow. A reaper. A cat with razor sharp teeth creeping up to a couple of wounded birds.

Last orders at the bar.

'FUNNY YOU SHOULD ask, pet... matter of fact, yes, Roy,' she said to him. 'One fella is just out the back. Real funny one too,' she giggled. 'A weirdo. Haven't seen him around. He's taking a...' her ramble was cut short.

The expression on Roy's face misted over. Like he'd been switched off. She'd bored a few in her time but this was different.

His eyes went from overly inspecting her and the place, analysing and jittering about like he always did—P.C. Jobsworth that he was—to being fixed straight ahead, and passing right through her. It was like watching a TV and it being switched off mid-show. The screen reflections and the mind's eye echoing what you were seeing when it was on beforehand only those few moments ago. She had a delayed reaction to his sudden lifelessness...

'Roy?' she looked nervous. 'Roy, you okay?'

His mouth dropped open and a small drop of blood pooled, then fell from the corner of his lips. His mouth fell fully open and there was more blood. He slumped to his knees as his jaw bounced, snapping shut off the edge of the bar.

Crack.

His body collapsed fully into a curled heap on the carpet. Like entrails recoiling into a bloody sloppy pile. Behind the space where he was, a spectre now stood: Snake Eyes. Holding a dripping blade as if it was part of him; a finger or an arm. His eyes, face and everything were expressionless. Like he was a mannequin and someone had put the blade in his hands.

His face was more lifeless than Roy's had become on the floor.

Beyond the snake's skin, and mask, she knew he was smiling inside and had relished taking another life. His lack of outward emotion made her sure of it. And she grew sure that she was next.

Her lips quivered, and she started to whimper.

He's done this before, many times, she thought. She was so scared now; she didn't feel the piss start to run down her leg.

He was Death.

'Now then, now then,' he whispered without moving an inch. 'No need to worry. Now where's my pint of black. And a shot of black I asked for? You are, are you not a fucking barmaid?' he stood in the pool of blood growing at his feet— the darkest, blackest blood.

She stood, caught by the moment, in shock... Transfixed to her spot on the floor like she was concreted into it. She should run hard. Escape. Life had prevented her thinking she could ever do that. She should have run long ago, away from that place. She'd been killed years ago, only now she realised it for sure.

He saw her hopelessness and hated her for it. He felt the frenzy brewing.

Mindfulness for serial killing for psycho sick-fucks, Part 2: Breathe, relax. It's just another bit of meat. Old flesh to toy with. Nothing special. We'll be done here soon enough and can move onto some newer flesh. Take your time, savour the aperitif. The main course will come soon enough.

'Tut, tut, tut,' he said, and shook his finger slowly, gesturing like a parent at a child in an insincere disapproval, usually to be followed by a tickle or laugh.

There would be no tickle.

The snake's eyes blackened over and the man sprang to life. Leaping like a cobra and grabbing Kit about the neck, pushing her behind the counter.

The Smiths came on the Jukebox: *Girlfriend in a Coma.*

He wrapped himself about her and started to go to work. She didn't stand a fighting chance. Not least of all because she had no will to.

10

PRUDHOE STREET

POLICE REGULATORY standards specify:

Interrogation rooms should be adjacent to the processing area. An enclosed space that is 8 x 10 feet is preferable (about 2.5m x 3m). All within a secure part of the facility. Transporting suspects into or through any other parts of the police station creates unnecessary security risks. These risks are not to be taken.

John sat quietly on the cheap plastic chair in the centre 6 x 8 foot room in Prudhoe Street Station. A building with all the charm from the outside of a Victorian mental asylum. And on the inside, it vibrated with the unhinged mania of what could have been the inpatients.

He was motionless, with a heartbeat calmed to a monk-like standard; Bruce Lee would have had respect. The windowless room was to its own standard. Everything about that town, the people and streets, were of their own design, evolution or specification. The rest had been scarred by history, the police station was no different. They didn't give two flying fucks if you couldn't breathe in the interrogation suite. It all added to the atmosphere and desire to cough up, and so to get out quicker.

The intentional confines of these spaces were undoubtedly to create a claustrophobic panic prior to, and during, any questioning, and in those well-placed waits of lone introspection created before, during and after a harsh grilling.

When Simon, one of many local booze-hounds, knocked his wife around having been in The George all day, the officers would man-handle him into a cell. Give him a once over, then boot him out the next morning. That's because they knew his wife, you see. Some of the PCs had been with her, the others wanted to, or just felt a tiny degree of sympathy for her. However, when Antonio half-killed his wife during a double espresso fuelled barny about the pizza dough his fag ash had dropped into, and whether or not he should just serve it up anyway, the police didn't even turn up. Despite the second-generation Italian immigrants having some of the broadest Geordie sounding accents in town. To the local police, they were and always would be outsiders. By the end of the night her blood had been added to the tomato sauce with his cigarette ash and no one was any the wiser. They super glued her eyebrow together and by the following weekend she'd clobbered him back with a frying pan for suggesting she'd looked at the waitress 'funnily'. She'd been intimate with Vicky for some time, it only bothered him when he wasn't getting any.

If the officers were sober at that station, and didn't lay a hand on you, you were in a different place.

A camera moved in one corner of the room above John's head. The humming and hissing from the device sounded more like it was a cornered alley cat. It all added to the Big Brother atmosphere. He ignored it as the lens adjusted, taking aim and zooming in on his face. Analysing. But who was on the other side, down the lines and behind the mirror? Like telescopic sights before the assassin's squeeze, it seemed to pause its close up.

In front of him, in the corner of the room was a lone white door. To the right of that was the mid-height one-way mirror across the rest of the wall's width. Enough for a small army and their wives to hide behind.

'WHAT DO YOU make of him?' said the plainclothes officer on the other side of the mirror.

A woman in a black suit standing next to him thought, as though wondering if the officer was worth, or capable of grasping her response, the situation or how much he and the station was going to have to change if it wasn't to be flattened next year.

'He's been back here a handful of times,' she started.

The officer listened hard. A sycophant. He rarely got close to the top brass or any special agents. He wanted to make an impression—he knew this small interaction was as close to an interview to move on or up he'd get.

'A few times again, since going into the army. Maybe a weekend or two's leave.' She leaned towards the glass to inspect John and steamed it with her breath. 'But, during the SAS years, he didn't return at all. Then by the clubland bouncer days, never.'

'So, he grew more and more out of love with the place?'

'Not sure he wasn't born into something else anyway,' she admitted.

'Loves lost and torn apart,' the officer muttered.

'You been drinking again?' she snapped. 'I know you want out, Rich, but you don't stand a chance. Not even if you grow a pair of tits and start respecting women. No one here does. Why do you think they call me in every time there's real work needs doing?'

He instantly realised why she'd earned her nicknames: Iron Bitch, Frosty Knickers, Razor Snatch... he remembered them and grinned.

'Snap to,' she barked. She hated not having brought more of her own crew and so having to interact with the local town muppets. Times were tight though. With the constant bomb scares and operation Tayberry, trying to track down and clear up establishment indiscretions with under-agers. Everyone was busy and tied up. So, she'd ended up there, in deepest darkest Northumberland, trying to find fault with a man at the orders of high command. On paper John had grown too powerful on both sides of the criminal fence—in their opinion.

John had never accepted the call to arms for either the police or the criminal underworld. But, it was always assumed he wore both crowns. The caps fitted.

'Somehow…' her words grated with frustration at having to interact with the man beside her. 'He's managed to become both a police secret agent of sorts and a gangland mafioso.'

'And some bullshit crime writer... documenting his actions.' He hesitated to speak, but the words fell nervously out of his clumsy mouth.

'Yes. And now... he's home for a funeral... his own mother's. Who knows if they're actually related? It's hard to believe he's connected to anything here anymore.'

'He's not from round here. Not any more,' the officer attempted to mirror her.

'I don't give a shit what it says on the birth certificate. And, I don't buy any of his bull shit back story either. It's as made up as his dime-store-pulp-shit-novels. Other than the funeral, I get that. She is fucking dead. But he's nothing up here.'

The officer squinted. She seemed to be on a passionate roll. A soapbox rant. Her professional guard had dropped.

'I don't care if he's some big black star in Manchester and Bristol... He needs to pick a true vocation. He'll be judged on what happens here—we owe him sweet F-A. Sure as hell. This guy's past, his history...' she focussed in on the glass again, '...is as dark as fuck, and he's brought it down on all of this sorry town. I can feel it. He takes it with him, place to place.'

'So, *we* think he's connected to the deaths?'

'You catch on quick, son. Been a copper long? Fuck me. You know he is… And, you know what he's become since he left here. Of course, he's connected—it's just how much. Is he driving, being driven or did he pack the boot?'

He looked confused. She didn't care. She'd been saying the words to get her own mind straight, and he wasn't much of a sounding board. She needed to go in and talk to John.

'The Manchester teams say he's onside, Bristol too. Like some black ops undercover super-agent or some shite,' he said; last chance to win her over.

'Bollocks to all of it,' she said. 'He's a failed author is all. With some gonzo-gangster-method writing issues. Running short of material, he'd just fucking crafting and carving it out of another dank place. Not here though. Not here and now. No.'

Again, he looked confused. She still didn't care—she was ready to face this two-faced demon.

'This will all end up in a book, really?' he quibbled, then shifted to minor excitement. 'We might be in it. You think it will—be in a book?' He grinned.

She stared him down with a look that could stop a pit bull. 'Mark my words: it will. And those dead girls will never get to read it having filled the pages for him.'

'How long can we really keep him, ma'am?'

'If he is all they say he is. And I doubt it. It's how long he lets us. Before all fucking hell breaks loose.'

'I'm not sure... if I want to go in,' he said. His chance at promotion was over, and he knew it. He was scared of her and of John. He wanted to go back to his desk to process the parking tickets he was wiping for the cash in his pocket. 'You've got the bigger picture here. I'm just sorry he came in on my watch. I really don't want to go in.'

'You're not,' she pushed him aside like a branch in the wind and opened the door. He was as feeble as the rest, and she had a fire in her stomach that John had put there.

JOHN LOVED STRONG women. His mother was one, God soon to rest her soul, or the devil be waiting. Cherry was one, hard as stone. In recent months, she'd made him what he was— or at least helped him survive it, head high. Her love had made him detach from the criminal world he'd previously toppled and picked up the mantle of. She'd got him to drink less, and to write more. She was his everything. Now, with her safely distanced for love's sake, he was sure of never seeing her again. And old instincts begged to take over his actions once more. Ancient demons were reaching out from their graves to mix voices with fresh victims about to be buried alive..

So he welcomed another berating attack and exchange from a steel lady. He'd missed it. His emotions simmered, wilting below his subconscious. It would take a strong hand to drag him back into the fight.

Maybe this was the one.

He looked straight ahead.

Before she opened up and went at him. Her bobbed straight black hair hardly moved—like it was painted to her head. Although outwardly unmoving, she emanated contempt. How couldn't she? Women had died. Men too, which she cared about almost as much. Almost. John just didn't know how many victims there were yet. Or did he?

Her eyes focussed, tightened. Like she was trying to figure out if she liked a painting, or at least respected the artist who had created it. 'They haven't seen you back here in a long, long time, John... were you even planning a return?'

'We all do, eventually,' he said to her, then looked to the table.

'Quite a colourful background now... haven't you?'

He touched a scar on his hand. When he kicked Manchester's Mr Big from the rooftop, he'd grabbed the belt that the criminal had around Cherry's neck. He'd kicked into him, pulled on the belt that cut into her neck, and transferred his weight to pull her up. He'd been shot, grazed too, and he only realised after she was back up on the rooftop, that his hand had been in a shard of broken glass left from Mr Big's shoes. It was this that left the lasting scar. And it was this that he toyed with and thought of Cherry, as the cold face of the interrogator opposite looked to hate him. With man-hating eyes that didn't realise he was only alive—to love, write and be—because of women.

'Most lads from your old school are driving tractors. Or trucks up and down the A1 and A69. Carlisle to Newcastle. The rest are in The Dirty Bottles testing the local healthcare's capacity.'

'Guess so.'

'You couldn't have just settled for the easy life, could you?' She inspected his file on the table. 'You could have just become a barfly like the rest?'

'I've done my fair share of that. Drinking.'

'I can tell.'

'I'm dryish now, but for special occasions.'

'Funerals?'

'Yes.'

'Going to be a few of those coming up.'

'Expect so.'

'Enough small talk,' words of hardened grit left a face that had changed again, another face, another war mask. She went for him hard. A fierce monster showed its teeth opposite, she wasn't there for idle chat, 'You're a killer, John.'

'I've killed, yes.'

'I'm not talking about overseas. For your country. Or even that gang boss you kicked off the roof of those flats. What I mean…'

'Real people?' he interrupted.

'YES.'

'No such thing, officer… sorry, I didn't get your name?'

'Forget my name.' And she didn't give it. 'Here's a few you might recognise. See if anything jolts a tell-tale twitch. And I'm the fucking master of tells, John. Voight-Kampff test has nothing on me.'

'Okay.'

'Let's start: Cherry.' She barked the name closest to his heart like it was an insult.

He looked up straight away. Glared.

'That was easy now, wasn't it? I have a benchmark…'

The air froze. No punches pulled. It was clear the woman opposite meant blood. No respect for John's service, duty and achievements in and out of court.

Maybe he should have stayed in Witness Protection, he thought. Protection from people like her.

'Now, let's really get started.'

He winced a little. His trained interrogation demeanour was already broken. He breathed in, then slowly out to recalibrate. His heart was still a mess by the time she got going again.

'Kit Raymond?'

He said nothing.

'Rachel Norcross?'

Nothing.

'Claira O' Neilson?'

He stared. Nothing.

'Simone Rockson?'

His right cheek twitched.

'Ah. There we go. Getting it yet?'

And he was... It was slowly sinking in as a picture emerged. They were all exes. Of sorts. Flings, one night stands that had overrun. Some weren't even that. Just ideas, names he barely recognised. They weren't tangible love. Not real. They weren't Cherry.

'It's a small town, Alnwick. The village where I did most of my formative drinking. Everyone knows someone, who knows someone.'

'Well. Looks like all these women, you knew, are now missing or dead.' She threw a picture on the table.

He looked down, then back up. He barely recognised the girl's face from the photo. Both his memory and the sea, her attacker, and the birds had all taken a brutal toll. Shrunken torn lips bared to yellowing teeth. And bloodshot eyes looked to nothing.

'It doesn't add up, that your train was literally arriving, pulling up to the station, as we uncovered one. But you must admit your connection, past exploits and colourful history is a little too dark to ignore. Given your status in Manchester now, particularly.'

'If it is... like my past and recent events... the police will need me. To draw out and deal with whoever's really at the heart of it.'

'You're at the fucking heart of it!' She slammed the table.

He didn't move. Only his irises tightened as the force of her strike echoed about the room.

She kept her hand there an uncomfortable amount of time. Like a chess game with broken bones, it was his move.

'That'll smart later, your hand,' he whispered. 'As you cup a double-something, stare at the flames of a fire. On your own. Thinking why you did or didn't let me go.'

'There's no way out for us, is that it? We might as well just let you go?'

'Either way, no one wins. People die. This doesn't have a happy ending. They never do. It's life... My life. Read the file.'

'Great. Black by name, Black by fucking nature. Weren't you under Witness Protection, John? Lying low, anonymous? Why leave it?'

John ignored the question. He knew she'd read the file; would know he'd left it for a case driven by Cherry. He slowly stood and she didn't stop him. Sorry, I didn't get your name?'

Again, she didn't give it.

He walked just as slowly towards the door, opened it and left with a quiet authority of being above the station and everyone in it. No one looked up as he walked past. They knew who and what he was, and how it was going to go. He was untouchable, for now. And he was right, one way or another, with or without him, people were going to die. He was better let loose into the melee to take the blows so they didn't have to.

They weren't used to this level of evil in their small town. The same evil that had chased John homewards. It happened wherever he went. It's why Cherry was where she was and he was there. This town he'd left behind all those years ago now shook beneath their feet with vibrations of evil. He was less welcome than any that had returned before; he had brought death with him.

11

CROSS HILL CHAPEL

KIT WOKE TO blackness, restriction all around her. She was bound hard, hurt, hungry and so very cold. Her flesh likely frozen, frost bitten and blackening. She'd shiver hard but couldn't move an inch. She was confused between the bordering patches of overlapping pain and numbness that now mapped her entire body.

There was too much sensation, all bad, it wasn't clear where the burning, freezing, cuts or dug out holes to her flesh started and finished anymore. Or when they'd started doing it to her. Her temples pounded from the chemical assault that had put her there, in the box, and she was braced by the most primal of fears. A wounded, battered and neglected animal. Trapped in something and gasping for the air that was tainted by her own fluids and soiled clothes. Worst of all, beyond the pain, her remaining senses felt someone, and something else's excretions had been imposed and violated throughout her.

Although her head, arms and body were fixed into the confines of the dirty shell of the box, she felt a drop of temperature and air across her backside and vagina. All open to the elements and the demon of her predicament: a tormentor who held the hammer that had nailed the lid closed.

She heard the wind. Birds. Sea. Footsteps. The box was still above ground and the ordeal wasn't over. She wanted more than ever to die.

Her heart tried with what strength it had left. She willed it to stop in an instant.

'Please,' she whimpered. Put an end to this agony, she thought. She tried again, to will it to stop, her to give up, to switch her senses and being to 'off'.

Footsteps.

'Goodnight sweetheart,' a voice whispered alongside her makeshift coffin.

Her heart exploded with panic as irregular beats forced waves of pain to her chest and made her temples throb. A life as restricted as the box flashed before her. Miles never travelled. Places not seen, lives lost, and those never embraced. And one embrace in particular rang through.

The box fell with a thud and she felt the temperature drop further. With it came the presence of a hole about the wooden shell. Then sand and soil falling on top of the makeshift lid.

By the time the sounds of the sand piled up on top, and was muted by the following layers, she'd conceded her fate, without resistance. Welcoming the passing. Her life wasn't much to regret. Her only real regret was that she hadn't lived enough to have any. No regrets. Her body and bones making up an empty vessel that would break down, and be cast out to sea in the tides and then broken down on the shore.

Then, as the last muffled heap landed on top, one image came back to her. A dull flash, before she was switched off from the outside world. Memories of a weekend emerged: long ago now, with *him*. Then *he'd* left. He always did. And that was it. All she had was parting thoughts for the world, before she resigned her lungs to what was soon to be struggling final breaths. That single regret; a shining black penny in an empty barrel; that it was only ever the *one* weekend they'd spent together. Neither of them had worked at it. *He* had gone back to fight unknown enemies overseas. And she was left with her own battles, buried deep inside—faces no one had ever seen but her.

By the time *he* was back from service. His internal wars had long since eclipsed, over spilled and muted the memories they'd shared, and feelings, if any, he might have had for her. And by then she had already become that nothing-woman. Dead before death. The burial, barely alive, in a splintered wood crate, was the encore to an act no one had cared to buy the ticket for.

Curtain down.

'John,' she whispered into the darkness, through bloodied cracked lips. 'Why didn't you save me back then?'

Above the reams and layers of sand, a crow mourned her burial. It stood on one leg then slowly lowered the other. Black beady eyes that had witnessed her pain, torture and suffering. Now respected her conclusion. Then it flew. Taking off, circling overhead before landing on the ancient cross on top of the hill to caw loudly; a salute. Sixty seconds to cry. Then it froze, like a statue, and waited for her passing to be complete.

She closed her eyes.

'...John, why haven't you... saved me... *now*?'

12

BLACK EYES

IT WAS 1985 and an unusually hot Summer in the North East of England.

'What ever happened? What lit that bitter fuse in you?' Margot asked looking out the kitchen window as her hands idled away, not really washing the dishes in the plastic bowl.

She'd watched as the flame-haired young boy marched up and down her sunny garden all day. He was oblivious to the colourful blooms around him that she'd tended so well. He was bathed in the glorious rays of sunlight, but only carried shadows, and a look of forlorn pain and abandonment more suited to a lonely old man walking a graveyard path, rather than a young boy staring out on life's colourful journey.

She'd minded the boy every weekend since he'd been born: the year of the dragon. Her single parent-working-mum-daughter was always busy. Had to be somewhere else. Had to be somewhere away from him. On the rare occasions she was in the same room as him, she had her back to the boy. There was always something more important to be doing. Or, maybe she'd seen the shadows in him too, and didn't want to anymore?

Margot's mind glanced over her own past in her head, then moved her eyes back to the Northumbrian coast scenery that formed the backdrop to the house she'd shared with her husband of fifty years. They'd built it. The aspect of each window view was designed—it was her therapy. And with the sun came the sweetest of pills. Her and her husband had been around the world. Initially having considered living anywhere, *but* there, on the Northumberland coast. Austria came a close second, but in the end, they chose to rest back where they'd been born, in Northumbria. Right under their noses since birth. The scenery, coast, sweeping hills, castles and history were like the greatest hits of everywhere they'd been and loved in their lives.

If only her daughter could see and realise it.

If only their grandson, that walked the garden like a wounded animal could stop, and see the sights, and smell those roses.

In the end, they realised, the soil and sands bore the blood and most treasured memories. And all those that had come before them. The hills where her parents farmed, the train track where her husband's father was an engineer on the Flying Scotsman. It went much further back too. Family tartans tying them back through the ages. They were always meant to be together, and be there together.

They knew the darkness lived within the family. Sometimes it skipped a generation. It was in the black eyes. Her own mother had them, the fury, and now so did the boy. It would take a lot to keep him on track. They didn't have a Bible to fall back on. It meant nothing to them. New world religions were imposed. They were insulted by the defaced cup and ring marks where the Romans had struck crosses through the ancient sun symbols, even now, so many years previously.

Only the land, animals and sea held true meaning to them. With it came nature's laws and the inherent respect for life that came with it—Pagans through and through.

As she looked out at the boy, she wasn't sure any of this would be enough. The sun didn't touch him and the flowers were invisible to him. She would cry, but hadn't given up the challenge, not yet. The boy was loved. Black eyes and all.

She looked out at the scenery again. The birds flying over Cross Hill. A visual feast and song. She always imagined she could hear the sea as she could see it in the estuary. She could feel the push and pull of the tides in her core. The cycles of the sun and moon ebbing the waters together out and then returning again: life's certainties.

'What are you doing now, John?' she said, as her mind was dragged back from the therapy of the ever-changing backdrop.

She watched the boy as he dropped a biscuit tin down, and marched back up the garden again to the raised patio in front of the French windows.

The boy knew she was watching. It didn't matter.

He had things, a mix of unsettled feelings, and a cloud ready to burst inside that he needed to get out. These things he wanted to tell her. Things that he should be telling his mother too. But she was never there. She was busy. Always somewhere else.

He was on a mission to destroy these notions that gnawed at him on the inside. His head, once clear and open to the blue skies and birdsong, was now a hardened skull with adult thoughts forced in to rattle and bounce around way ahead of time. A childhood stolen.

The scenes to delete these images was going to be quite something to see—it was going to be a firing squad.

THE BOY, only 9 years old, looked down at his Action Man on the sun-bleached concrete steps. It lay naked with its 'eagle eyes' pushed whimsically off to one side, unaware of what lay ahead. Next to him lay Luke Skywalker and Optimus Prime. All his favourites, lined up ceremoniously. Then, he looked back down the length of the garden, like a hunter stalking deer, glancing over a pristine lawn he'd been cutting for 50p a go every weekend for Nanna and Grandad. He surveyed the range, like it was the Savanna and there was big game hiding in there, wading through its grasses; waiting for him to spot, sight and fire down on them.

Beyond the fence at the bottom of the garden was a farmer's field with cows lazily chewing, slavering, shitting and splattering in the sun. Crusty pats littered the ground and clagged to their behinds in clumps of giant dangling turd. Beyond the cow field, was a village cricket club, then, a river that was filled with trout. The waters pushed hard to try and form an oxbow at that point, before running under a small road bridge, and eventually passing the fishing village where the trout were less and flat fish became plenty. Then, it hit the estuary and was dissolved and mixed into the ice-cold North Sea. Colourful Coble boats lay in the mud and sand flats. Testament to the once thriving fishing community, now long since retired from significance.

On the horizon was a lighthouse, and before that on the other side of the water to the village, Cross Hill dominated the view. With birds of black and white; swooping and soaring. Crows and gulls. Angels and demons. Dancing together. They mourned and signalled the dead and dying, sure as a compass points to North.

The boy's jaded childhood had projected enemies and tormentors so they were now firmly fixed; embodied in the plastic shells of the toys laid out before him. He wouldn't regret their passing. Not today. Optimus Prime, Luke Skywalker and Action Man had an appointment with a .22 hollow point delivered by a BSA Mercury air rifle and the clock was ticking.

MR TURNER HEARD noises. *Footsteps.*

He had a long day ahead of him and wouldn't stand for any disobedience. Zero tolerance was Mr Turner's policy and it wavered for no one; woman, child or man. No boy in the school dorm got up in the night on his watch. Never. The sounds coming from overhead were an insult to his authority.

The respect he instilled through fear must be waning and need a reminder. Balance would be restored and flesh marked.

There would be no excuses. If the young lads needed a piss, they could just hold it, sweat it out, shaking in silent tears or piss their beds. Just like he'd had to when he was back in his own boarding school. The runts would learn life the hard way. You can't always, if ever, have it your way. There's a line to be toed. And he had cast the rope out himself. You cross it. You suffer. Toughen up. And be quiet about it. They could tell their parents all about it when they were allowed home in four weeks, if they took them back—unwanted runts; the lot of them. See what their parents said about it. 'No harm in a little beating here and there to knock some sense in.' That's what they'd say. He'd been given a free rein to dish it out as far as he was concerned. And the few parents that did voice concerns were ignored.

This was Mr Turner's watch. It was Mr Turner's domain. His rules.

If the little shits dared try to tiptoe to the toilet in the night, they got ten of his best. If they wet the bed, they got ten as well—just as hard—there was no escaping.

He had his 'box of tricks'. The boys feared this box more than a letter home to their guardians, mums and dads. Every time the box was opened a part of their childhood was ripped apart, savaged and left red raw and bleeding as his back arched and he laid into them with a cane, shoe or strap. On Sundays it would be a hand. Closer. Skin to skin contact. He loved it when his hands burned and they cried. They always cried in the end. Always. He didn't stop until they did.

Overhead: *Thump... Thud.*

'Boy, you're going to wish your mam had kept your worthless arse at home,' Mr Turner said, looking to the ceiling, sitting bolt upright and swinging his legs out of the bed. Its springs creaked and moaned a mini orchestra, as if tuning up frantically for his most personal savage opus.

He slipped his feet from the cold floorboards into wool lined tartan slippers.

'She knew you needed this. Didn't she? When she sent you here, to me,' he said, imagining the boy tiptoeing about upstairs. He stood and walked over to his wardrobe and reached for the black box from the top. 'And, I know you need *this* most of all,' he opened the box and grinned as he carefully selected his tool. His hands shook and his pyjama bottoms bulged with excitement as he gripped the leather handle. He tucked his erection into the elastic of the pyjamas in an attempt to conceal it. As usual he'd finish himself off later, after he'd administered his punishment and they were back in bed.

THE BOY CHASED his mother but never got any closer. The beach's sand always swallowed him up; a foot, leg and arm at a time. He couldn't get up close to her. Never feel her touch. He tried and tried but was stuck fast in quicksand, getting deeper and deeper.

His grandmother appeared alongside, smiling sweetly.

'Come on. We'll catch her together. Look she's just there. Look, not far.'

The boy looked, squirming to be free of the smothering sands that were quickly hardening like concrete about his legs and waist.

His mother didn't look back. She walked briskly away, busy. She had somewhere to be. Her child was there, right behind her, and longed for contact but was invisible to her. His grandmother pulled at his arm again and again. Happy to try, smiling at life.

His shoulders ached. In the distance, his mother kept going as her image slowly faded through fine sand particles and fret carried on the sea air. Dissolving her away from him.

The quicksand meant to take her son... She had somewhere to be. She was busy.

A final yank at his arms by his grandmother and his shoulders felt like they would pop from their sockets altogether. He was out. His grandmother brushed him down then pushed him on. Forward. Ever optimistic that her blood lines would figure it out, be bonded, find love.

'Go on, catch her up. You'll be fine. She loves you. We all do. Run. Run.'

He ran towards her. She kept walking the opposite direction.

His knees buckled and he fell, he rolled, tasted the salty seaweed, grit in his teeth and pushed up and on. The rain started and battered his face. The force of the wind pushed against him, but still he kept trying. To reach her, hold her. Connect.

She kept walking. Dress flapping in the wind. To be somewhere else.

Eventually he was an arm's length away from her. Nearly able to touch her, and her dress as it flowed as if in stop motion. She didn't falter on her course. Didn't notice the boy struggling so close behind.

Nearly there.

Finger tips glanced at the damp cold material; her dress hem a mere centimetre away.

Snap.

The boy felt a shock. Like a brick, a stone. Something like a wall hitting at him from behind.

The sea rose up as the dawn light shone through, silhouetting the crashing horses peaking on mighty dark navy waves. Birds cawed overhead. Crows and seagulls danced a familiar waltz of celebration in the pockets of air.

Snap.

Such pain in his back, thighs and rump. Burning.

'Save me, mum. Save me...'

She had somewhere to be, kept walking. The distance between them grew again.

The skies, clouds of greys, reds and burnt siennas parted, revealing a dark room with faces that looked back from its shadows. Pale and scared faces. Young boys.

'FIVE... *Whack.*

'SIX...

Whack.

'Sir, sir... Mr Turner, I think he's still asleep. Been sleepwalking, sir, is all. Please stop Mr Turner. Please... stop. Sir, you're really hurting him.'

'You're next, Darren... SEVEN!'

Crack.

The boy, Darren, looked to the floor, whimpered. His friend Jason put a hand on his shoulder. All eight of them shook in the dim light of the master's torch. It rolled menacingly on the floor with the sheer force of each of the leather strap's impacts on the bent over boy's bare arse.

'EIGHT...'

Smack.

The boy that was being hit slowly opened his eyes.

'NINE.'

Craaaaack!

Emotionless.

Mr Turner swung his arm back for an almighty lasting imprint to the boy's flesh and memories.

One day the boy would write about it.

All of the master's own demons were conjured up before him. The previous strikes had been a warm up... This was the one to put them to bed. All of them. To sleep forever. All those times he was hit, he was getting his own back. Now was his time to purge the barrel of unspeakables from himself.

His arm tensed, muscles a coiled spring, then swung forward, like lightning.

Slap.

And stopped...

His arm couldn't move. Like it had hit a slab of stone; a tank on a beach hitting a concrete block. His wrist burned as much as his shoulder throbbed. Jolted, jarred and impacted. Like he'd been in a mini car crash.

He was trapped in a vice.

In shock, he bent and stretched as much as he could and scrambled with his spare hand, fumbling on the floor like a mad drunk for the torch.

One of the boys nudged it with their foot and it rolled towards him.

He grabbed it, rattling the batteries inside and shone it back at his right hand that was trapped in the vice-like grip. He moved the rays from his hand and pointed up at the boy's face before him then back down at this iron hand that held him. Twisting. Mechanical and fixed.

The boy was possessed. Mr Turner winced in pain and disbelief, squinting in the dim light. Shaking his head, trapped in his own nightmare.

He looked at the boy that held his hand. The victim had turned tormentor. Black eyes now looked back at him; soulless black circles looking through him. Deconstructing him.

The eight boys still looked scared, but not of Mr Turner as much as the other new force in the room.

The boy used his free hand to take the leather strap from the wilting master. He felt the burning pain that the man had inflicted on him and his eyes tightened. He contemplated the strap. Its contact across the man's face. Tearing at the man's eyes and crushing them in front of him. He thought of kicking the sad little man's body 'til it went limp. Getting the others to join him to dance on the twitching body. He contemplated it all, let the master see it churning away behind his eyes, that he could and would do it. Then he stopped. He felt no pain any more, only pity.

'Goodnight,' the boy said and released his hold.

He walked past the others, dropping the strap by the foot of his bed on his way. It creaked as he lay down and he pulled the thin sheets up and over his body.

He looked up at the small postcard above his bed: a Northumbrian castle overlooking a sweeping sandy beach and the sun casting serene colours over the shore, sea and turrets.

He closed his eyes; to go back to the beach. To try to catch up with his mother. This time, he hoped she'd wait for him.

She kept walking away, always did. Next time, he'd catch up with her. She'd be unable to run. She'd be dead and he'd be at her funeral.

JOHN LOOKED AT the Action Man that he'd previously propped up against the biscuit tin at the end of his grandmother's lawn.

'How you feeling now, Mr Turner?' he whispered and prodded the Action Man's shattered leg. John had spent the previous hours creating hollow points to each of the air rifle pellets using a drill bit from his grandad's tool box he'd found in the garage.

The toy's leg joint had exploded from the pellet's impact. And the shoulder, foot, hands, the head too, split, exposing the workings of the dolls moving 'eagle eyes' — not looking so whimsical now.

The boy nudged Mr Turner to one side, and he flopped from his perch; deader than dead.

He marched back up the garden.

He paused and looked to the kitchen window. She looked puzzled at him from the other side. He wanted to tell her what had happened. Why he was so jaded. All about that school they sent him to. She seemed to falter as he looked back her and her gaze grew, looking through him and over to Cross Hill behind him in the distance. He knew the birds above it would be starting to move again in a frenzied celebration.. It was their time. Their dance:

Of the dead. The dying.

'So, Mr Peters, you're next... any last words?' the boy said, cocking the air rifle and inserting another pellet as he looked down at the toys.

Luke Skywalker looked up from his concrete slab, blank-faced, vacant, resigned. He couldn't change his fate. Not now. This was always the way it was going to go. Bad things happen to teachers who use a size thirteen Dunlop to batter a young boy's legs in a classroom in front of everyone.

'Not for you, Ms Graham,' the boy said, shifting his gaze to a spread-eagle Optimus Prime, basking innocently in the sun. 'You don't get off so lightly,' John took out a Webley Tempest air pistol that had been tucked in the back of his belt, and shot Ms Graham in the face. The plastic exploded and the memories rested.

IT WAS A dark and rainy day of 1995, in Belfast City, Ireland:

John looked down the barrel of his SA80, deep in the undergrowth that he had burrowed out for cover. The boy in his sights couldn't have been more than fourteen, maybe sixteen, at most—a child. When John was that age, he was still firing pellets at his toys, playing soldier. Exacting virtual revenge over any memories of teachers laying a hand on him.

This boy that was now in his sights and waving an AK-47 about, ducking and diving, nervously kicking up dirt, and dancing with death. He should have been kicking a ball with his friends instead.

Despite the distance John could see the lad was shaking.

He wasn't cut out for this shit. John or his target.

They were political pawns, tools. Trigger pullers for cowards failing to make more important decisions with discussions. Meanwhile borders cared little about which side the bodies fell and history would celebrate the inefficient policymakers not the unnecessary dead.

John longed to be in nature. And not just the hedgerow that dug into his stomach where he lay. Leaves and thorns dug and stabbed into him to remind him of nature's inevitable truths before the bullets flew without solid reason.

John was invisible to the lad and his pals. An unknown and unwilling executioner waiting for the signal. The one he didn't want to hear. Wished it wouldn't.

Then it came.

'Take the paddy prick down. And his pals, John,' the radio shouted in his ear.

It was the moment to make him.

He breathed in, held it. His finger started to squeeze. Stopped. A dummy run. He flicked the safety. Looked at the boy, his freckles, the red hair.

It could be him.

He saw his grandmother's garden again... He didn't at the time, but now he could smell those beautiful red roses, not just the shadows they cast. The sunlight's warm touch to his skin. The fallen toys: symbols of pain.

He wanted to be back on that beach by Cross Hill and his grandmother's house. Digging up old war bullets, chasing seagulls and sledging down the sand dunes on a tea tray. Not, firing bullets at children for a politics with words so weak they had to be emphasised with violence.

'Take the fucking lad out. NOW!' the radio insisted. 'NOW! We know you've got a clear line, why haven't you taken the fucking shot already, John?'

He clicked his radio to acknowledge hearing, but not wanting or being able to speak.

His body went through the unsavoury motions again. In preparation for taking the shot. He looked hard at the boy's face and connected. The boy felt it and looked in John's direction and the reflection from John's sights. He gestured and his pals started to fire at the bush John was in. The shots skirted around John's prone shape as it blended into the hedgerow and grass. Then one nipped his left shoulder. The next buried into his right shoulder — held in place painfully by the edge of his flak jacket.

He lay flat. Re-focussed on the boys all knelt firing at him and his squad who were behind and alongside him. John tightened in on the boy's face, cross hairs between the eyes as his red hair blew in the wind bouncing off the church image.

Those eyes. Black, like his.

Flames erupted about the boys as a fire bomb they tried to light dropped and lit itself from one of their fumbled Zippos.

Out of the flames marched a Viking. Striding. A history of war in each step.

He walked straight at John. He carried a connected past, heritage and links to everyone on that tiny battle ground by the small church, filled with boys and men in that messy war. They were all each other; blood-connected.

The others didn't see or feel, but John did and the Viking's aura touched, burning more than the growing flames around them all. He rubbed his eyes, sure of the apparition and wanting the others desperately to see it too.

A sign. To wake up.

He followed an invisible line up from the boy's face to the bell tower. Then his SA80's sights followed too. He aimed and squeezed.

The bell rang out: 'Clang.'

A mighty toll from the heavens to reckon over men that pitted themselves against mere boys, in a drawn-out conflict that was long overdue a resolution. Things had gotten way past ugly for all of them.

The bell rang out again in a final distress call and fell, silencing the gunfire below.

The boys surrendered and a rain of boots over their heads was their olive branch from the other side. Children stamped within an inch of their lives as John was dragged, numb, from the bush. Unflinching, like a toppled statue.

He came to, when the others continued their barrage on the boys. As if stoned then sobered, he jumped up, swayed, swung a fist, and was blocked. A forearm was broken and then he was knocked down by the butt of a gun. He felt no pain. For the rest of his life, fragments from the boy's bullet that had pierced his shoulder would be with him.

He looked over from the ground where he was dumped, no longer valued. Before passing out, he saw six-foot high Action Men dolls, they moved like man sized wooden jigs, beating the children on the floor. A macabre dance in view of a silenced church where John had brought the last ring of its bells.

The toys wreaked their revenge.

The young lads were locked up and John was shamed, court martialled and dismissed.

He searched hard to find another way. New loyalties. There were none at home or in the army. He meant to make a change. Then the drink took hold, masking PTSD screams and yells from the soldier-boys. Gangland Manchester eventually welcomed him in, silencing the screams with her own noise. Music.

A soundtrack to die for.

13

SNAKE EYES

IT WAS 1995 and raining. It always did. It's why they called it Rain City:

A *different* boy, soon to be a man, sat at his desk in a cold room in a shared house in Longsight, Manchester. Outside, birds sang as if Spring brought a bountiful feast, and for the time being, the cats in the neighbourhood didn't exist. He didn't hear them. The song. Beauty. Not in the notes or the spaces left between them. Nature meant nothing. Only pain's chorus meant anything to him, after the dull melange of life's initial verse.

He existed in another place. In these notions that fell between life's joyous notes.

Downstairs *his friends* partied on from the night before. That's what they called him: *a friend*. He didn't hear them either or accept any of their gestures towards this imposed friendship.

A light bulb flickered overhead. Nothing.

A dog barked next door. Silence.

All he heard was the zip on a small leather case as he tentatively started to open it up. All he felt was numbness. He was a cannonball somehow floating on the waves of life and he knew he was due to fall, sink and rest on a bed of nails. And it was going to come someday soon, maybe he'd be lucky and it would be today. It was going to be quite something—a dragon's awakening.

His adopted mother hadn't said a word as she'd helped him pack his bags to leave for the city. She'd ironed sheer hell out of everything, as she compensated for the weight she knew he carried inside. She saw it in him, what she hoped was anxiousness, but knew really was something much darker and harder to placate. It was like he had a crack-filled balloon in his belly that was about to pop. She knew what that was like. She hadn't had it easy. She'd done her best. It was just that this level they'd carved out was lower than most people's worst.

The boy spent a lot of time with his door locked in that shared house. When he occasionally ventured out, the others were drawn to his black heart. It oozed shadows and left invisible bloody footprints as he skulked around that tired old Victorian house. They all thought he was cool, that it was an act. For a while.

The mirror of their projected desires, of wanting him to be like their idols, soon broke

Then they realised...

He embodied an image the others normally saw onscreen or in music mags. But, he was the genuine article. They assumed there was some degree of simmering anxiety behind it too. They were wrong. Unlike those they'd read and seen on screen, in bands and in those mags. He was... for real.

The zip went all the way back on the small unassuming black case that carried infinite possibilities to him. They were his real friends—his own instruments and tools. He imagined flying insects buzzing at his head. Carriers of distraction trying to pull him back into life. So, he swatted them away from him and the black case.

Rusty shiny blades looked up at him like longing lovers for a first or last kiss. The sweetest touch. A gentle, teasing stroke to climax.

He was in control of all of this. He was a god.

He pulled back a shirt sleeve and saw each one of the fresh scars. Pushing. Making them seep his own very personal fluids of pleasure.

He turned up the radio that he wasn't listening to. All white noise to drown out a world that wasn't his.

He used to cut himself, to test if he was still there. To see if he could feel past the numbness. A reality. Then he cut himself to have this control. There, with them, he had complete orchestration over his pleasure, pain and when it started and stopped…

Then it had evolved. These exercises became more mature, and an intimate study in the languages of pain. Boy to man. Pleasure to pain.

He sat back. Tears of joy came as he was sensing the caress in the slightest touch of the blade into his nerve endings. Blood flowed. Trickled. Mapping tributaries of layered sensation over the cuts; past and present.

'Yo, we're having a brew… you want one?' a voice came from the other side of the locked door…

His eyes narrowed, tightened by the interruption. They became animalistic slits, like a reptile's.

Like a snake's.

He wiped the blood away. Put on a plaster, another of his closest friends, and rolled his sleeve down to conceal the twisted kisses from steel angels, as he called them.

'Yo Bobby, you in there?' They'd taken to calling him Bobby for some time now without any idea of his real name.

Silence. Then a zip. Radio turned down.

'You knocking one out in there, Bobby? Filthy—you'll go blind.'

'I'll just be a sec…'

'Dirty bastard.'

'Be down in 5.'

He'd learned to act with his body when he saw the need to get what he wanted. But his eyes only knew one performance: Snake Eyes.

THE REST OF the household thought Byron Walters was a public schoolboy prick as soon as he turned up on their doorstep. There he stood; way too fucking proud in his fake-tan skin. Posed catalogue-regal style, like the shitty neighbourhood didn't matter around them, and the shared house was his new castle. His black designer holdall bag that hung from his hand was worth more than the rent they would all pay each quarter.

In the kitchen, the peeling walls bellowed with Byron's shit and the others were glad Bobby was locked in his room. They could tell Byron's brash banter would send Bobby spinning off and goodness knows where his head would land. They'd have to ease them both in together. At least Byron wouldn't be mouthing off as he took a sip of something, surely. So, they plied him with coffees. But, soon regretted it when the bull-shit-spreader was turned up to eleven by the injection of caffeine.

One of them went up to grasp the nettle. To get Bobby from his room. Better he met the new housemate whilst they were all there together. For the newcomer's protection.

Byron kept laying it on, trying to sell himself. It was like he was a market trader with an open suitcase of knock-off aftershaves. He kept misjudging his audience—no one was buying.

Bobby started to come down the stairs.

The others looked at each other as they heard the footsteps overhead.

Byron didn't notice. He was too busy with stories of girls in each port... How he couldn't beat them off with a shitty stick—how he was the fucking *man*. And, how all these girls... barely pubescent, were his disposable trophies. To fuck, finger and forget.

'They fucking love it,' Byron said. 'It's all any woman wants, to be boxed up and fucked—no arguments. Then left. Disposed of.' He laughed, alone.

Bobby, Snake Eyes, could hear the words from the kitchen. It didn't matter who they came from. He'd never forget them:

'All any woman wants: to be boxed up, fucked. And disposed of.'

The fabric of the house and kitchen changed with each of Bobby's steps, getting closer down the corridor. He slipped easily into the room behind Byron and leant in the corner out of sight. One of the others nodded, stretched over behind Byron and switched the kettle on.

Click.

Bobby rolled and lit up.

Another *click* as his matte black Zippo snapped shut.

Byron sniffed the air, looked around and jumped at the new member in the room. Bobby was all in black, like his lighter, looking like a priest.

'What the fuck? You a fucking goth or something?' Byron laughed. 'Thought this was Manchester… all indie kids, baggy trousers and Reni hats n' shit. What the fuck are you meant to be? Joy Division is over. Didn't you hear, there's a New Order to things now.'

Bobby was like thin ice with a bed of broken glass underneath at the best of times. You could joke about him wanking through a locked door, but that was about it. The others felt the tension before his response to Byron.

Bobby breathed in, meditatively, contemplating the bigger picture.

He knew how to act. To get what he wanted. Only his eyes didn't follow suit. Only ever: Snake Eyes.

Then he breathed out.

He gripped his forearm. Teasing the fresh slices enough to feel he could leave the room, at any moment without moving. The stranger's words bounced straight off of him.

'I'm going for a piss,' Bobby said to the floor, rollie hanging from his lip.

He left his smoke hanging in the vacuum where his body had stood.

'That's quite an act. Fucking dark arts reaper or something. Watch steam doesn't come out when you take that slash,' Byron said to Bobby's back.

Bobby walked up the corridor to the stairs.

'Ain't no act,' a voice said by the sink.

'Bollocks,' Byron barked. 'Kid's been listening to too much of The Smiths already, that's all. We'll get some Boddingtons in him, pills, poppers… Get him out into the heart of the big bad city. That's just some small-town country repressed fuck up waiting to get laid and come out the other side a real man. 'Like me,' he inferred. They all heard it.

'Really? Not so sure about that,' another voice said.

'Bull shit... He can have one of my birds. Got two turning up tomorrow. It's a nightmare of a juggling act anyhow... ships passing in the night and all that.'

Byron's coffee had kicked in and the others had wished they'd given him tea instead. He was off on one, again. The gobshite was churning it out double-time. Hyper. Like a dog busting for a piss, hopping on the spot between two lamp posts.

Bobby's footsteps started again overhead. He was coming back down.

'Wait... I've an idea. It's a belter—check this out!' Byron announced to the room. 'Everyone, hide. NOW! I'll get behind the door, I've got just the thing for the fucking 'Crow' up there,' he giggled.

No one joined in the laughter.

The others looked around, beyond worry. Not confident enough to rein in his dominating ego that filled the room more and more with each drop of assumed wit and wisdom he expelled. They were a little curious to see what was in store, despite knowing it wouldn't end well. They knew it was a car crash coming and they were fixed to the back seat anyway.

Byron turned up the radio in the kitchen. Radiohead was playing *Creep*.

'Perfect,' he grinned and knelt down, unzipped his black holdall and quickly took something out, putting something black under his trackie top before they could see it. Then he stepped behind the door and pulled it in front of himself so he was hidden.

The others all found a spot, and hid as well.

Tick tock. The time bomb moved in only one direction.

From the top of the stairs Bobby had a Joy Division song in his head. By the second to last step of the stairs, Nine Inch Nails' *March of the Pigs* was playing and he floated with it to the bottom.

His feet padded down the dark hallway. A thrown beer can had blown the bulb two nights ago and they hadn't replaced it. They never would. The kitchen door was open, but he couldn't hear voices. This was normal over those that whispered in his head and whatever soundtrack he played there too.

He stood in the doorway to the kitchen.

Where had they gone?

The cellar was full of shit, nothing to see down there but a broken toilet. And there was nothing much outside either…

Manchester's Longsight district wasn't a place to go sightseeing. Unless you liked boarded up windows, smashed out bus shelters and a hidden ferociously hungry population; only emerging in darkness to rob, break and piss on the streets.

They must be hiding.

Maybe they've been burgled? And the rest are in the cellar tied up.

The area was rough. Only a few nights ago a taxi driver had been mugged and killed. Some lads had jumped into his car, put a gun to his head and a noose around his neck. Told him to drive or be shot. Said they'd let him know if he could stop before the rope tied back to a lamppost snapped his neck and his head came off. That's if he was going fast enough for a clean break. He'd given them everything and showed them pictures of his wife and kids. Pleaded with them. It didn't make any difference, they were bored. It was something to do.

Bobby had understood this world. Only too well.

The taxi driver's head was found by school kids the next morning on the road, and the car crashed into a Heras metal fence a hundred yards up ahead. The motor still ran as a piss and shit-soaked leg was locked in position by rigor mortis—the accelerator pressed relentlessly to the floor.

You can't outrun death.

Bobby had heard it on the local news, and replayed the scenes to himself over and over again as he masturbated, in sync with the imagined events as they unfolded. As the last fluid that his body had to produce dribbled from his clenched knuckles he still kept going. Red, raw and bleeding. Firing nothing from his body but an unrelenting focus.

The man was forming.

Bobby grinned by the doorway as the others hid from him. He touched his forearm again. His nervous excitement went past boiling point wrapped in a well-practiced, zen-like shroud.

The cocoon was splitting. A head slowly emerged.

It was like the calm ebbs and flows moments before going over a waterfall in a small boat. Knowing… The boat always goes over.

He went fully into the room.

He looked out of the kitchen window to the sun, feeling nothing other than a thirst for conflict. For them to be tied up in the basement and their captors to show face, only to be demolished in a torrent of his controlled rage.

The door behind him snapped open crashing against the counter. He felt a gun barrel pressed hard against his temple.

Yes. Yes. Yes. I want this more than anything. A body was following the head, pushing out from the cocoon.

'Haha,' a voice said, spitting over Bobby's face. 'You're gonna get it now… Say your last fucking words, CUNT!'

Bobby breathed out, his *snake eyes* looking down as he embraced the moment, then he slowly closed his eyes one at a time, as if going in for a kiss. 'If you're gonna do it, do it,' he whispered, intimately.

Bryon started to shake.

He saw the Devil.

The others stepped out of the shadows, from behind corners and the worktop.

'Like we said,' a voice said. 'He's for real.'

'Fuck,' Byron muttered… Gasping, his breath taken.

'Just pull the trigger, will you? So I don't have to.' This time Bobby's words even more so a lover's whisper.

Byron jumped away, scalded, as his feigned aggression morphed into extreme fear. He saw Bobby welcomed a bullet. But all the while was somehow bulletproof.

A shrivelled cocoon dropped to the floor, a dragon with snake eyes now stood where a man once was.

Byron slowly put the piece on the worktop, delicately, like a priest holding out a communion wafer. He'd been christened and embraced by a loss of control. Now, he felt true darkness. Byron's image-persona was destroyed. 'Pint?' Byron's lips quivered, conceding his comfortable life was now over. He was defeated and needed to be re-built.

'Yes,' Bobby said. 'And you're fucking buying.'

Byron put a hand on Bobby's shoulder as they put on their coats to leave. He told him he'd wished he hadn't pulled the stupid prank. He was sorry. It was just a toy, it fired blanks.

Bobby wasn't listening.

They walked towards the nearest pub, and saw the rope dangling from a lamppost up ahead. It trailed up the centre of the road to a burnt-out Vauxhall Astra that still smoked.

Bobby smiled, as a sensation tingled in his trousers.

Sitting in a beer garden, by the fifth pint, Bobby told Byron not to worry. He didn't need to tell him the rest... That he welcomed a live round. To stop him from what he was going to go on to do next. Because after that point, there'd be no going back.

They sat in that beer garden in the pouring rain, getting soaked through, drinking down pints quicker than the heavens could re-fill the glasses. Small victories.

'Some fucking Bruce Lee calm fighting shit you got going on, Bobby. I don't get it.' Byron drank the beer down. 'The Zen-like meditation. I had a gun to your head and you fucking loved it, man. Didn't flinch. You must do some Kung Fu-Karate-type shit or something.'

Bobby closed his eyes and imagined all the training he'd done in secret and all that he had planned to complete the metamorphosis. Then, he opened them again, hiding the disappointment he was still only there with those flies still buzzing about, waiting to be knocked away. He composed himself.

An act.

'China Bob. That's what we'll call you. China-fucking-Bob... Or, oh...even better: Snake Eyes!'

'I'll take that,' Bobby said.

The beast was free of the cocoon; about to fly.

He closed his eyes again, to see how easily he could make these people all disappear, as the clouds took a rest and the sun strained for a chance as much it could in Manchester.

Snake Eyes looked into his glass. He saw just how much Byron had been shaken. He saw what was in himself. He saw blackness, then flushed with embarrassment that morphed to exhilaration. He was bashful of his new powers. It felt like receiving an unworthy compliment—a lover's gift. Then, it drained away, and the calm washed over again.

He rolled another cigarette and eyed a broken bottle with shards of razor-sharp glass by his feet.

It welcomed him. It spoke to him.

His new wings were stretching out. Droplets of rain resting on the veins of his skin.

The broken bottle's neck formed the perfect handle to hold. He nudged it with his feet. The glass shone. In it, he saw a crossroads, choices. Each, with a release. All of them red as night, dark as sinkholes, and humming like the finest ever long embrace.

He saw the Devil.

He was about to take off. Free.

AS HE WALKED down the street, he heard the traffic, could smell the fumes mixing with the fresh blood in the air, on his hands. He felt the pavement, each crack under foot. And he heard the screams from the beer garden behind him.

His senses were heightened where previously they heard and felt nothing.

The sirens wouldn't catch him.

He walked straight up to the first nightclub doorway he saw, started a fight with the doormen, and won. By the second and third club he had job offers from all three.

China Bob, with the snake eyes, had arrived to start his further training.

The dragon flew.

JOHN WAS TIRED that night working the door of The Church nightclub, like every night.

Every so often his boss would ask him to run an errand, to go collect, and he hoped it wouldn't be that night. He just needed to drink through it and collapse into the bedsit he called home.

'John, he wants you to go soften someone up out back. Some dealer's been selling some unlicensed powder, making people shit themselves. We can't afford the bog roll or to lose punters due to any more slackened arses. Go have a look. Sort it out will ya?' the fellow bouncer shouted in his ear in front of the queueing customers, not to be put off by what they'd heard. The club had a reputation. And they'd get one too. Just by being there.

John got back from softening up the dealer and saw the rest of the bouncers were all holding their heads, moaning. And that's when John initially heard of, and nearly first met China Bob.

Next, he became a name whispered on the wind of the underground, 'China Bob' a hired hand. For the *real ugly jobs*. And there was plenty needed doing in the city. He didn't even ask for money. Pain was his payment. He was honing a craft.

By the time they met face to face it was too late. John had taken down the infrastructure that supported China Bob's sordid outlets. Then he had to take down China Bob.

In prison the cocoon regrew around Bobby and a new monster grew and developed inside, waiting to emerge. When it did, Snake Eyes eventually left the prison gates, with any semblance of China Bob and Bobby locked up behind him forever.

14

HADRIAN'S WALL

CARSON TENDED THE ancient stones with a trowel, toothbrush and a magnifying glass. She obsessed over each tiny detail, finding history and aeons of adventure in each small crack, slight patch of moss and nondescript stain. Hadrian's Wall had stood nearly two thousand years and what was left of its forts, stones and paths had centuries of stories to tell her. She buried herself in that past. A welcome feeling; safer from her own.

She had her stretch on the wall to tend to with its own unique tales to discover and ruminate over. Hers to protect. Each year the visitors came and went, and she remained the constant feature growing old amongst the roman relics. She was both guardian and custodian to the centuries of stone elements left behind by the invaders.

Often the weather was too much and the tourists just got out of their cars, nodded as if completing a test, did a mental 'tick', and then they were gone. Done. Left to shit on another tourist border checkpoint. The Chinese were the worst. They got way too close for Carson's liking. Like they were studying an insect or prodding a dead corpse. They swarmed over all the historical pieces, the wall and its artefacts, dropping wrappers, cans and leaving undersized footprints in the peat. They moved the full length of the wall like locusts, from Carlisle over to Newcastle and back again. Coach loads of them passing each other on the A69. They photographed the shit out of everything. They stole its soul with each shutter and flash. She was sure they meant to recreate it back home. Piece by piece—'Made in China'. Didn't they have their own fucking wall? She thought.

She walked out of the Vindolanda fort area. Past a burn, a copse of trees then up the hill to that stretch of the Roman Wall that was all so familiar and mysterious to her. The one she felt closest to; her stretch. She loved the varied scenery in that couple of miles. It could go through all the seasons in one day for her. Some weather which she was sure only ever graced that patch of land and nowhere else.

She walked along the wall, whilst looking out on either side and imagining what it must have been like for all those legions of Romans back in its hay day. The more native Celts, just previous invaders, were designed for that harsh sweeping unforgiving landscape. Low to the ground, stout and bulky types with fiery hair you could use to cut granite. They must have been ferocious pagan beasts to the Romans. No wonder they built the wall—a defence. A blockade. To keep the wild 'animals' out. They'd made an empire of most of the world but got stuck at Caledonia; now Scotland and the Borders. There they built the Antonine wall. Then, they were pushed back and built Hadrian's Wall, in order to keep the Scots, Celts and Borderers out—those Pagan heathens keeping the entire Roman empire on its toes and up to their home-sickened necks in mud. They must have longed to retreat back to Rome and the rest of the empire. Something kept them there. The romantic sweeping lands and skies that spoke in stars and ethereal sunsets evolving to sunrises. How could they not make a go at it before finally heading back into Europe?

An adder snake slithered out from one of the stones a few steps ahead. Its beady lifeless eyes glancing at her, like a warning. Its tongue flicked the air. It didn't seem as scared as the others she'd seen, like it would gladly chase her and strike had it not somewhere else to be.

Further on, down the wall and over a series of foot-traffic smoothed stones, an old gnarled tree played host to a murder of crows who watching her approach along the top of the wall. As she passed them, they subtly flapped and repositioned their wings, staying fixed to their perch.

The wall started to crest a mini cliff down to a patch of water. She stood, breathed it all in. Felt the ages coalesce in her lungs as the crisp air opened and purified her lobes.

Again, it all came as nature and history's welcome distraction from a past she'd grown used to hiding from.

She'd be lonely if it wasn't for the air, birds and that wall. Protecting her patch was her everything now. It was her baby. A lasting monument that had existed way before her, and the stones would long outlast her. She couldn't imagine wanting any more from a lasting legacy to be nurtured and cared for—before she was gone to ruin, herself.

Looking back where she'd walked from, the top of a 4x4 now poked over the hedgerows and drystone wall by the visitor centre. Light bounced off its rooftop. A giant crow scarer to scatter the birds. They would soon resettle, made of harder grit around there.

The car wasn't there when she'd left, nothing and no one was.

'Fucking rich tourists, these ones,' she muttered. 'Ripping up the world in their shitty-city tanks.' She pulled her hood up over her head and yanked at the cord, concealing her long blonde hair. She wanted to escape and hide but knew she had to approach them. Keep them on the paths. Stop them stealing any mementos—for the wall's sake. If she didn't there'd be another random block of the farmers dry stone wall lumped into the back of the Range Rover and mounted over a fireplace in London. Or worse they'd bother to grab a real piece of the Roman wall. Once, she had to stop a couple of Aussies that had pocketed a spear head from the main exhibition hall. It was a plastic replica—they didn't know that. And she was distraught more by the disrespect and sentiment than their naivety of its real substance.

Her phone vibrated in her pocket.

'All go,' she thought. 'If it doesn't drizzle, it pours.' She looked to the sky which had yet to commit to which combination of the four seasons to reap at her and the surrounding landscape.

There was no name on the mobile screen. Just a photo of a pile of books with an empty bottle on its side. She'd picked the scene especially for *him*. The top book, *Untethered*, was dog eared and stained.

'Long time, John.'

'Carson, listen... I don't have time.'

'You never did.'

'I'm on my way, but you need to listen.'

'But I thought you always had to be somewhere else?—I wonder where you got that from? The urge to shun love?' She knew John well enough. She'd heard his dreams.

'Listen, please—for fuck's sake, Carson!'

'I'm finally in one of your books, am I? About fucking time,' she pushed the phone under the rim of her hood, to avoid the winds.

'STOP! LISTEN!'

The skies had suddenly picked a composition: a bellowing storm brewed with fierce changeable ambers and graphite greys.

'It's not good.'

'Is it ever, John.'

'This is different, Carson, please—the reception is shit.'

'Always knew you'd come calling one day. You rejected my advances. But today's the day is it?' She yelled against the wind's attempt to silence her, and John's attempt to get the dominant word in. She would make him hear this time. It's what she'd always tried. Despite never getting through, whenever their paths crossed, she never gave up on him totally.

'Carson. Listen,' he repeated, pleading.

'John, I only have ears for you now. You could have had the rest. You turned them down, remember...'

'I think there's someone, or some people, bad, headed your way.

'What?'

'You see anyone, anything, get your head down and let me know. I'm on my way. I'll be thirty minutes. Less if this farmer moves his sheep out the road quicker.'

'I suppose police won't help?'

'They're en route, behind me.' Where they tended to always be, chasing John's destruction... 'I think they all agree you're more of a force than they'll ever be.'

'I should have retired to China,' she said.

'You'd miss the weather.'

'It's got a bigger wall.'

She looked at the 4x4 in the distance. She wasn't scared. She'd been living with centurions and legions about her all her recent adult life, and had seen all sorts of savagery; past and present. Only last week the bones of a young girl were found in one of the Vindolanda pits, where a Roman drinking den once stood. It was a dark crime, hidden, a dirty secret. They always buried their dead away from camp. This was an ugly incident, on site.

There was more, she knew it. Felt it in the stones. Much more to come.

'Just call, please, Carson.'

'Maybe, I will. Maybe I won't...'

'Carson.' He knew she was as stubborn and strong willed as hell. But even worse, enjoyed him having to plead for anything. She was as strong as anyone he knew. Even Cherry.

'Nothing going on here,' she said, watching the two characters walk from the 4x4 in the distance. They were dressed all in black and as sinister as hell.

It was exactly as she imagined *he* would eventually write it.

Both like upright ravens jolting and snapping around. The Devil's messengers had paid a visit to her wall.

These were no tourists.

She knelt and pulled her hood down and let her long blonde hair free to blow around her head again, and for the mobile's mic to be exposed to the wind, to crackle in defiance at John's end of the line. Then she lay on the earth amongst the grass and stones.

She didn't take orders anymore. No more than he did. She'd left, done her service as well. And she had no intention of ever taking them from him.

'Carson!' he yelled.

She hung up.

Behind her, the branches of the tree mirrored her hair's dance: waving frantically; an electrified octopus as it manically wrangled and twirled about her head. The crows were fixed firmly to the branches. Watching. Waiting. Spectators of fate pausing before celebrating the weather's decision to cast her rolling black blankets over the land.

JOHN DROVE HARD down the country lanes as a squad car appeared behind. Lights glaring in his side and rear view mirrors. Hedgerows, trees and banks on either side of the road seemed to take on the now dark red hues of the sky that grew deeper with each mile. Then another car appeared, then another. Lights flashed and several sirens started to scream.

An emergency drew them, filling the lanes with noise and light.

A suicidal pheasant flew across the road, narrowly avoiding getting clipped. John nudged left to avoid a dozy rabbit as well. It wasn't so lucky with the squad cars that followed and its guts sprayed across the hedgerow leaving fluffy tufts behind on the potholed tarmac.

When the police cars sped up to, tailgated, then overtook him, he knew: it was too late.

They weren't for him.

Carson was surely gone.

CARSON LAY FLAT on the hillside. Thick grass just about covering her. From the distance she could have passed for a rock or patch of fading heather. The Roman Wall was behind her stretching the width of the country. It gave her resolve. Like she had something to fall back to. A position of resolution. It was too late to stand and fall back to it now without being seen. But if they approached, she'd pick her time and be over it and gone.

She took out a pair of mini binoculars and held them to her face.

The walking ravens moved slowly together, then separated. One went into the visitor centre, then out again. They seemed to be looking for someone or something. The other one ambled about the old fort. No respect. Jumping on and off the sacred heaps. They might as well have been jumping on her friends or slapping her mother in the face. God rest her soul.

These visitors were on a mission. This wasn't a casual, curious browse. They were looking for something. It was a hunt.

She clenched her jaw. Who were these people? What were they to John? It wouldn't be good for any of them. He'd made a mess of his life in and out of the army. All in the name of doing the right thing or whatever moralistic divining rod he chose to follow day to day. This would be the same. A shit storm. MI5 hadn't been any kinder to her than the SAS was to him. They were more alike than he ever cared to openly admit. Morally fixed, loyal and stubborn to do the right thing at the expense of their own skin and bones.

Why hadn't he just settled all those years ago, into an easy life?

For her.

She reached into her fleece and pulled out a small Celtic cross and rubbed it slowly. The sky froze and the ground hummed. She felt the moisture from the peat beneath her body soaking through and touching her skin. The same solid, acidic and mineral rich as touched the centurions and that the Celts and Pagans worshipped.

She felt it all.

She felt the ceremony.

And spoke: 'Ladgerda, be with me. Winds, soil and land, be with me too. Skies open and close for me. As I dispose of those, like dust, that are mere grit and specks of insignificance. I'll stand with pride before the gates of Valhalla.'

Overhead the clouds co-joined, overlapped and burst. The heavens heard her. Responded. Waiting for her last lines:

'Odin, I'm coming for you. But not before I bring fire and the iron bones of our dead down on our enemies... these enemies,' she looked down the binoculars at the walking ravens.

The tree that had mirrored the motion of her hair stopped, even though the harsh winds were stronger than ever around the wall itself, and showed no signs of easing.

She squinted down the lenses.

'Fire... and the iron bones of our dead,' she repeated.

The two human-sized black birds regrouped again.

They stood looking up at the wall. Their heads moving in unison, scanning, bobbing and nodding as their eyes panned left, and then right, and back again. Stopping occasionally to analyse an outcrop, feature or... a reflection—in glass.

She'd gotten sloppy, out of practice. Out of the service.

She froze. Then slowly she lowered and covered her binocular lenses.

She lay still. Her heart beat slowed and dissolved into the peaty soil beneath her. She put her face slowly down into the earth, moved it left and right then looked up. Her face was camouflaged, streaked in the land's soil marks of acidic darkness.

The strangers looked the other way, distracted.

A kestrel flew overhead. Carson rolled on her back and looked at the bird as it majestically circled, marking her spot, as if she was prey; a wounded rabbit or fieldmouse to be plucked from the grass... Its wings and body were silhouetted by light straining to filter through the dark billowing clouds from behind.

The day was done.

She rolled back onto her stomach. Looked. The walking ravens were gone and so was their car.

'YOU COULD HAVE just sent a postcard,' she said to John, who stood next to her on the stony track. The flashing lights made their shadows jolt, flicker and twitch on the stone walls alongside them. The moon fought the man-made lights for dominance. It was sure to win.

He said nothing, just looked at her. Grateful she was there still there, and able to make the words. The crusts of dried peaty soil, dirt and grass stuck to her face echoed his time in service. Fires in Ireland. Tanks in Bosnia.

'What did you see?' an officer said with a pen and pad.

'Just a couple of lost tourists. Creeps, creeping.'

'Sure?

'Yes. I think so. Why? What would I have seen?' Carson wanted to control it herself. These invaders. She wanted to go full 'Roman Legion' on them. Without police interference.

'More, like him maybe.' The officer prodded his pen in John's direction. 'A city gangland reprobate lost in our countryside.'

'One's enough for anyone,' she said. 'Besides, I thought he was a writer now—or has he lost that plot too?'

'Sooner we get the funeral done and him back to whatever fictional setting he carves up around himself next, the better for all of us,' the officer said.

She nodded. Looked at John. She wished she could get back to her home, to hide his books before they both got there. And she would get John back there, it had been a long time, she had to.

JOHN WALKED OFF, leaned against a squad car and lit a rolled cigarette. He felt rattled, as though his insides churned with emotional turmoil and confusion.

They were being hunted.

The police, him, Carson... no one was in control—only the killers. As they attacked parts of his world he hadn't thought to protect, and now it was too late—they were under fire. These pasts long forgotten. Erased by war. Overwritten by gangs. What was the normal life, if you can call it that, before all that? He just couldn't remember. Whatever was left, any semblance of innocence, it had been dragged into the mire with his army, gangs and written up psychoses in those books.

John smoked and listened to the policemen talking to Carson:

'We'll leave a squad car. No one's that stupid to come back. If it even was *them*.'

John wasn't so sure. He thought of talking to the police, convincing them to leave more men, but knew they wouldn't take orders from him, any more than he did from them.

He'd have to stay on himself, until morning. Watch Carson as she ignored the threat and sharpened her claws for John.

They stood in the lane and watched most of the police leave. They left one naive young lad behind. Both Carson and John shook their heads which did nothing for his confidence.

She told the officer where to drive, leaving John and her standing together.

'A drink?' she said, as the lad's police car tyres crushed age old stones, and his car lights beamed through dust and disappeared off into the distance.

'A drink,' John agreed. Knowing he would stay until morning. And hoped her image of him had faded, so that she had forgiven him. But not enough to want any more from him by being together.

'Don't worry. I still hate you,' she said, reading his mind.

They walked to John's car and she directed him, overly assertively, down the lanes, past the visitor centre. Then along the old Roman Road, now roughly tarmacked for good measure.

'This left,' she said, suddenly.

'Okay,' he slowed, then pulled in past a series of well used, rarely repaired farm buildings. Sheep and cows sounded off over barbed wire topped dry stone walls either side, in anticipation of being fed. The car bumped along the narrow road, passing the parked up police car, as they continued to the end.

'Here we are,' she said and pointed. She didn't need to. There was only one barn ahead—the last one on the road, and it had been converted.

'A picture postcard retreat.'

'Could have made a good writer's hideaway,' she said, jabbing at him.

She'd always imagined more from their interactions than he'd envisaged himself. It was why he liked her though. She'd always seen the metaphorical mountain tops on paths he'd hadn't ever thought to walk in their time spent together. He'd long since been distracted into his own solitary life's jungles and the warfare that waited.

She had too.

Even now, she was reflecting back on their past, or lack of it. As he carried tinnitus ringing from gunshots, a pain in his shoulder from a boy's AK47 in Ireland, and one in the other side from a Mancunian gang lord's bullet. All this and John's hands that wanted to clench constantly from some old Viking hereditary disease. Genes courtesy of his grandfather on his mother's side.

As her own wounds throbbed of broken bones, bullets and blades, she still looked and saw the romance in him. Mountaintops and glades, from their paths now split.

They went inside and closed the heavyset oak door. She made them drinks and they sat by the fire, which he lit.

'I read you'd met someone,' she said, in the seat facing him as the giant roaring fireplace lit the room.

'Our paths fused together,' he said, and straight away got his phone out, checked then put it away again.

'Sorry, you must be worried.'

'We separated. For her sake.'

'Why, if you care for her?'

'I love her,' he said to the flames.

She looked at him, madder than ever. Then it diffused.

She felt the anguish. It was part of her own fabric of emotions projected into the darkening room, soothed by flame. To care so much, but it was never meant to be.

'And here we two are, sure of a bond... choosing to be apart, for love.' She hated him again. She referred to them both, together. But knew it would pass that he interpreted it differently.

'You met someone?'

'Many years ago, John. You know that. It didn't work out.' She let the words hang in the air then changed the subject. 'You're under fire. Again. Is there any role out there you can go into without this?' She raised her arms as if pointing to demons all around them.

'For some reason, I seem to attract it.'

'What?'

'Death and violence.'

'I can see that… I'm curious, John, what comes first, the words or the death?' She looked over to the side wall. Dimly lit by the fire's light, a floating oak shelf held up a handful of books, two of them were John's.

He looked over at the wooden drawers, the only other furniture in the room. On the top was her MI5 ID card.

'Aren't you meant to go into hiding after what happened? And, retiring?'

'Who said I'd retired? Besides, you came back didn't you. And, anyway, haven't you heard? They *all* come back in the end.'

'And look at what good it does.' He opened his palms. Catching the demons. Then, like a cat, he stretched his tendons and heated his hands over the fire. She half expected him to start purring. As he moved, the sleeves of his black shirt went up to reveal scars on each forearm. Different encounters. Permanent reminders.

'So, are you finally retired, John?' She took a draw from the large Scotch whisky she'd almost forgotten she was holding.

'I've given up a lot of things,' he said, looking at his own glass by his feet, for now untouched. Not so long ago he'd have drained it and the rest of the bottle by that point.

They said nothing for the next twenty minutes as the flames reflected and washed over them. Her normally blue eyes flickered orange as his glowed red like a rabid hell dog's in a Hammer Horror film.

The night went on. The flames and fire did their work.

They drank more and both fell asleep where they sat. Closer than they'd ever been. He went off first and she smiled as he went to war in his dreams. Haunted by what he'd seen, done and had to do next.

In those moments, fused by the fire, she was content, oblivious to the full extents of his inner anguish. They were as close as she'd ever imagined, hoped and dreamed before.

Night raced from black to dawn and the roses' shadows by the window changed from moon to sun fed.

A cockerel's call rang out.

The sun's rays streamed across the wooden floor boards and lit up the tattered old chesterfield armchairs they were in. The fire still smouldered, embers glowing and hanging on as they waited for another day's fuel to pass the baton of life to.

She opened an eye. Looked at him. He was the same age as her but even whilst sleeping exuded several extra lifetimes pains in the rivers, scars and lines of his face.

He twitched.

In his sleep, he ripped the tongue from Hell's messenger who'd come to tell him something he didn't want to hear. His leg moved; kicking drops of life from Death. Then his arm moved too, in a mini punch; knocking out teeth that meant to bite him.

Still fast asleep.

'Chasing bunny rabbits, my sweet?' she said, still ignoring the darkness of his inner make-up. Always looking to the flower crested mountain top.

She walked to the kitchen to make a pot of strong coffee for them both.

When she came back, he was wide awake and putting another log on the fire.

'You've got to go... I know.'

'Yes.'

She put the mug of black, steaming liquid down, and a plate of toast.

'Eat, for fuck's sake. I know what you're like.'

'Have you still got a gun?' he asked, his mind elsewhere.

'I'm not giving you one, John.'

'For you I meant.'

'Don't worry about me...'

'I am worried.'

'Whatever shit-hawks have followed you up here, won't be any harder than what's come before them. These lands are used to barbarians, savages and rebels... It's what they call home. It's the tourists who should be worried. And these hobby-criminals you've drummed up,' she turned and took an old leather-bound Jacobean Bible down from the shelf.

He looked at her, about to plead to make her understand.

'A King James edition,' she said, slowly opening the Bible up. 'My relatives would have been hung drawn and quartered if Charles's army had found out they had this: The Heathen Edition. My ancestors, like yours, were all Border Reivers. Criminals for hire. It's what protected these borderlands, kept it what it was... And... what it *is*, John. Why'd you think the Roman's built the fucking wall right here all those years ago. To keep people like us contained. People like you... and me.' She reached inside the Bible's open pages, where there'd been a hollow cut out, and she took out a Glock 17 handgun.

'I'll be okay, John.'

He stood, drank the rest of his coffee down.

They held each other. As friends that had fought separate battles, and lovers that had never been.

She put the gun down on the kitchen counter on the way past the kettle and walked him to the door and locked it behind him.

No parting words.

She returned to the seat where he had been, downed his barely touched final drink from the night before and fell asleep to absorbing what remained of his presence from the tired leather seat around her. A lingered caress from the seat's memory. Casting away the spell of a hangover before it dared further ruin another new day, without him.

THE KNOCK ON the door woke her and she beamed, excited. He was back. She smiled uncontrollably. Stumbled, drunk again.

'Forgot your keys? Just like old times, John,' she stood up. The hair of the dog and rest not having quite worked the way she'd intended. She was giddy again as she wobbled through to the kitchen, blurry eyed and un-bolted the door.

She'd forgotten the threat. Only saw the roses. Looking to the mountaintop—where they could finally be together.

There was another side to their lives. The one she'd left behind. But it still followed him around.

She opened the door eager to see him.

There it stood:

A raven with snake's eyes.

She saw the hand holding a handle, before realising something was sticking in her, and before she felt the pain. She jumped back and kicked the door and relocked it shut. A reflex. The hand stayed still on the other side, holding the blade where her body had moved off of it, leaving the knife to drip. She screamed on the other side in angry defiance, then coughed and spat blood onto the back of the door. The blood in her throat quickly threatened to choke her, filling her up from inside.

Where was that uniform meant to be standing watch?

She hobbled, stumbled, fell...and crawled.

She struggled on her hands and knees back towards the living room. Over wooden boards that had lasted an eternity. And would now long out last her, long after her blood had dried up and only her bones remained. Behind her the raven attacked the door. It banged, kicked, with man-sized force. She was sure it would soon give in. The door was solid but the attacker was purposeful. This one wouldn't stop. Not this fierce man-bird. She could tell it would never stop.

She reached up, straining for the Bible she'd left on the drawers.

The door banged. Kicks growing in intensity. Now there was more than one attacking it as two pairs of feet and claws went at it from the other side. Both ravens she'd seen the day before had returned for her.

She fumbled, blurring eyes, fingers knocking the big book. It spun on the top of the drawers then fell to the floor with a thump into her blood.

The door burst open, splintering from its hinges. There they stood. All in black but for those piercing, hateful, beady, lifeless eyes. Especially the male one... Snake Eyes.

She watched the giant black clad beasts approach, wishing she'd drank more of the whisky. She grabbed at the big book of hope, pulling it nearer, as they walked slowly towards her undeterred. In all her strength she flipped it open.

Empty.

'This what you looking for?' a voice said from the doorway, then a woman's hand picked up the Glock by the kettle.

Carson collapsed flat, wheezing into the growing pool of black blood beneath her.

'MI5 eh?' the man one said holding up the ID card he'd found on the side.

'We're going to enjoy this, Carson,' the woman one said.

OUTSIDE, A SQUAD car sat with the driver's side open. A few feet away a radio lay, hissing: 'Come in... You there, Parker? What's going on? Respond. You better have just gone for a piss and got your hands busy, son. Come in. Now! This is the last time.'

Over the drystone wall the young officer, only a year or two in service, sat against a tree as if taking a rest. His trousers were around his ankles from going for a leak, as his dull lifeless eyes looked to the Roman wall in the distance, and his severed cock and balls now trailed from his mouth.

'Backup on route,' the radio finished.

15

RUMBLING KERN

JOHN SAT ON ragged rocks and looked out over the raging North Sea. An array of rock pools spread out beneath the imposing fossil lined cliffs behind him. The waters in front were where his ancestors had fished, sailed and travelled to plunder, invade and settle.

Tortured by events, past and present—he sought comfort in the forces as they coalesced. Seeking comfort in this inevitable union of elements coming and going.

Carson... was gone.

His hands shook as he opened the Moleskine he was holding like a wounded bird, and he began to write:

> *Babbling changes in dark pools and ripples.*
> *Touched by a recurring moon's pull.*
> *The skies light wars over land and seas.*
> *As she casts her bloody shades,*
> *torching each night, bleaching out every new day,*
> *through heavy clouds and wind.*
> *Tomorrow, brings a new dawn.*
> *Nevermind, the pains of yesterday will last... forevermore.*
> *Our burden under nature's changeable blanket.*
> *The sands will shift, the tides change.*
> *As the crows fly over Cross Hill.*

His hand holding the pen went to scrub out the last lines, unsure. Or, wanting to rewrite his mind and the deep-felt helplessness. He left the words, and his gaze re-joined the waters; a calming cycle of the waves.

Once, John had nearly died at sea. He was close to giving up on life, all hope was ripped into tatters. The scars meant nothing to him anymore. He'd swam out into the sea until his arms and legs burned as the last of his energy reserves were used up treading water. Eventually he sank to the sea bed. When he'd opened his eyes, *he* was there: the Viking. They both let out a primal scream that bent had time and nature around them in those waters. And with it, John had thought he'd let his weaker self die as he swam back to shore, reborn.

Illusion or delusion.

The hopelessness had returned. People were dying. His love was distanced, untouchable. The sea air he breathed and sands he walked had weakened its grasp on his vigour. But, not altogether.

He was unsure if he still felt his heritage reaching through time from the image of the Viking. At times it had reminded him where he came from—to stay on frequency, in tune with his making. Recently the ghosts had faded, leaving just a lingering imprint. He needed the image's strength to return, to being that keystone that held up a weary heart and sheltered his mind from ghosts.

He clenched his hands.

His tendons tightened in the cold.

The seas and wind touched him whether he recognised it or not. As sure as the sea would always break on the rocks and shore and the cliffs themselves would eventually crumble, piece by piece into the waters below.

The sea brought cycles, motion, an unstoppable force of attrition.

Now, as he sat on the rocks, he wondered: what was the point of living if it meant so much death? This wasn't how it was meant to be. When he refused to kill those boys in Ireland. Were one of their bullets meant to finish him? Is that where it should have finished, before he'd started this one-man crusade against the underworld. The one that now bit back at him more than ever.

The Viking had appeared when he had the young Irish lads in his sights. He had stormed from the flames that had eventually burned John. As if on side, the Viking deflected the trained bullets from a mortal shot at John and doused the flames. But by then, enough had touched him, burned and pierced his skin for him never to forget.

All the lives he meant to save by doing what was right...

That young girl he was too late for back in the club in Manchester. He'd tried to make amends, he'd stood up against those that sold the pills, the gangs darkening the streets.

He wrote:

All I ever tried to do right by has returned to haunt me.
Now, back home.
Will it ever release its hold?
Will I ever be free of death... to live and love.
Or, should I remove myself from the equation.
Dull the attacker's cause.
Go back to the sea.

He looked at the waves that drew him more than ever before.

A small fish, a blenny, swam then stopped in the rock pool by his feet. The birds didn't swoop down and pluck it out because he was there, and was leaning over the pool. A silent guard.

'Does evil exist because I am here? Or does evil just do what it was gonna do all along?' he asked the fish.

The fish blew bubbles, its tiny gawping mouth appeared to say, 'Drop dead, Soldier Boy.' And then it swam off... A far cry from the strength of the Viking.

He stood as the waves crashed against the rock cliff faces up alongside him.

He contemplated hard—to go into the sea.

It repeated its familiar call, more than ever. Would walking out into it and not coming back be worth more than not shooting the boy-soldiers in Ireland? Or pulling the girl from the club? Could he pull this evil that followed and killed a path all around him into the depths to rest? Or would cheating the demon of its prize anger it more? So there would be even more victims after he'd gone?

He couldn't fix it, the way he'd fixed himself. He knew that. He was just pulling at straws. The ones he had control over. The killers had killed with tenuous links to his past. And some complete innocent strangers. It's what they did.

These killers, they just wanted to kill. A grudge with John just gave credence in the act having purpose; more than it being impulse.

Who carried the heaviest grudge? Who pushed the blade?

There were two more co-ordinates left: Kielder Water and Alnwick Castle. The police would have them wrapped up. Alnwick castle certainly anyway, like it needed it. What protection did a medieval fortress need? As the Duke and Duchess were at home, it was closed to the public.

Kielder Water was another matter, eleven square kilometres of man-made reservoir, Surrounded by a thousand square meters of national park. Impossible to police from every approach.

He racked his brains to think of his connection to either. What clue, victim or trap might be waiting.

His phone rang:

'John... It's Carson,' Cherry said.

His throat dried. Why hadn't he called Cherry before now? How separated were they that all this had all happened and nothing? Only she would understand after what they'd been through, and he didn't think to call her. Was the distance they created, for her safety, worth more than a call for his own sanity?

And why had he left that young PC behind at Carson's.

'I know,' he said.

'Another mess. Isn't it?'

'It'll get worse before it gets better. It was always going to be the case. That's why you're there. And I'm here.'

'John.'

'Yes.'

'It's not your fault. We'll get away. From all this. I promise.'

'One day,' he said, standing up and looking out at the undulating horizon. 'Should have stayed in Witness Protection. Disappeared. Stayed invisible.'

'Then we wouldn't have met. And remember, it was me that pulled you out of it. You didn't have much choice at the time.'

'I could have gone back in.' He looked at the seas.

He knew what he really meant. He meant to leave everything behind and *go back into* the waters that were calling him. She obviously heard it too.

'I need you not to do that, John. That strength. The one we saw in each other. The one I love in you. Those black eyes. That Viking blood. Remember it. And most of all. More than my love, remember—people will do evil whether you're there to blame... Whether you try and stop it, or not.'

He looked out to sea holding the handset. Neither of them spoke until she eventually hung up. A text followed a moment later:

> *Forevermore belongs to us.*
> *I'm going to quit. You should too.*
> *C X*

He climbed a nearside cliff and reached one arm out as the other gripped the rock face. Stretching out to touch the splashing waves. Beneath him a cave mouth roared as it swallowed giant gushes of sea, then spat it back out in great rolling rips and splatters.

He climbed down slowly, eyes shutting, making his way by touch alone.

At the base, he hopped down, then walked into the cave in a timed space between battling tides as a wave covered the cave's mouth behind him. Sealing him in behind a temporary watery curtain.

He could see bones, shells and seaweed lying scattered about the floor and began tracing the cave's walls as his feet sank in the wet sand. His breathing echoed. And something vibrated, duller beneath that, a pulsing thud like a heartbeat a murmur through the layers of rock.

He used the light from his phone to shine ahead, exposing the pitted textures of stone, following it back where the walls got smoother and the ceiling lowered at the back of the cave.

His fingers traced the 'cup and ring' markings in front of him. Ancient old Prehistoric carvings. Concave lines and depressions, a few centimetres across, pecked into the rock surface and surrounded by concentric circles. John imagined the people that might have done it, all those years ago. Fighters, farmers, fishermen and explorers. Surrounded by death, love and hate. Life's ebbs and flows. Like the sea crashing outside.

Then, he sat in the darkness, looking out at the sea's changing shapes, colours and mood, framed perfectly by the black silhouette of the cave's mouth, and he imagined: this is what God must feel like, witness to it all... with more scars.

16

KIELDER WATER

PETE AND NARESH sat on the bar stools, firmly fixed. They hadn't moved in hours, even to take a leak. They seemed to be waiting for someone, but were in a different pub to the one John was approaching.

The one John pulled up to, The Pheasant Inn, was a picture-postcard, idyllic old English stronghold. Ivy trailed up and around the walls and the old wooden benches outside were full of farmers and labourers killing time away from responsibility. It sat in the heart of the Northumberland countryside, on Stannersburn, a tributary feeding into the North Tyne River. Low beams of old oak held up a ceiling stained with years of smoke and spills. It was a retreat, a hideaway and the perfect time-free haven.

John sat, watched, thought and he wrote.

His mind spewed out its toxic contents, in another purge, to refocus, willing to expel hard thoughts then close the notebook on the torment. And to clarify, and be sure of his attackers. So that, when he finally had the chance, he wouldn't hesitate, and would take aim, fire and then move on. Quit and sever any connections.

He had no spectators in the pub.

He wrote more about being forced out before the rest of his squad. How he'd suffered what he'd been told was PTSD. He wrote about how he worried, most of all, for those that didn't make it out.

A postman ambled in to the snug, soaked through.

'Another delivery to Plashetts, was it?' the barman asked.

It was a running joke. When the nearby reservoir of Kielder Water was made in the 1970s, they blocked up the valley. Evacuated the village of Plashetts, and just let the valley fill with water. The old village still stands, only now under fifty meters of water. Complete with rows of houses, a village green, a post office. And a pub. All abandoned. Left to the pike, eels and algae. So whenever the postie turned up, inevitably like a lot of folk in that neck of the woods, soaked through, they'd say: been down to deliver a parcel, letter or such and such, to Plashetts?

His response was always the same: 'If I had, I'd have stayed down there. That pub's got a fuck site more life in it than this hole. Smells better too: self-cleaning. A bit fishy though.'

And as usual, like it was the first time they'd heard it, they'd all crack up.

'Pint of best?'

'Aye.'

And so it went on. The only changing fixtures were tourists, and John. And it was out of season for tourists. Although the starry night sky brought some.

'What this fella up to, scribblin' away?' The postie said.

'Dunno. Reporter chasing those deaths likely. Looks a solemn sort.'

'What deaths?'

'You fucking pulling one aren't you? You deliver the fucking news... You ever read it?'

'Depressing, why should I?' and he necked half his pint of dark red ale. Then he winked.

They all knew about the deaths. It was a big county, but everyone knew everything there was to know in it, from village to village. Embellishments weren't needed, it was a bloody show. The stories were even stretching outside its borders, those they daren't cross or bare to find out what lay on the other side.

The tourists and strangers, like John, appearing to them, put them on edge. Scared them that they might catch something that made them leave their strongholds. Farmsteads, peel towers and old cottages passed down generation to generation. And it scared them most, one of them might be the killer—no one knew for sure.

'I'm from Alnwick,' John said, introducing himself and not looking up.

'It might be the same county, but it might as well be another city lad—dunno you from Adam.'

'You know me,' a voice went in the corner. 'I drink in here all the time,' Adam said.

The same old broken record jokes played out every day. They never tired of it. All welcomed the old routine. An escape from what lay outside.

A tractor's engines glugged past the window as massive tyres bumped over the road, then stopped. With the sound of clods of earth flying and dropping and splattering.

'Best get 'em in. He'll be thirsty,' the postie said.

The door opened and a big man, in all directions, walked in.

'Usual,' he said, as loud as he was tall, and testing the old wooden bar with his weight. It creaked in defence of his mass that had compacted the old boards, screws and planks for the fifth time in as many days.

'All ready,' the barman said and lifted a frothy amber pint onto the counter top.

'Lot of police about,' the big man said.

'Aye,' the postie and barman replied.

John kept writing. A double of single malt was put down in front of him.

'I go up and down those fields every day. Hardly need to open my eyes. Today I tested it. Kept them shut.'

'Lucky you didn't drive into the water again.'

'You know I was pissed that time. On your dodgy beer. Had an excuse. This time I had it. Up. Down. No problems. Next time I might even have a nap.'

'Why didn't you?'

'Fucking sirens wasn't it. And some dumb lazy out-of-towners, wanting to know way to the jetty without checking a map. Thought it was off season anyway. What are they doing pissing around looking for the jetty? Didn't even have a boat.'

John looked up. His ears perked and his senses tightened.

'These two. All in black. I thought they were tourists. Anyhow I'd better things to be doing. Maybe they were police.'

'Aye maybe. One of old Charlie's boats went earlier. They probably took that. Thievin' bastards,' the barman said.

'Nah, these were undercovers or something. Right shady and useless looking.'

'Takes one,' Postie said.

'Blow it out yer arse... These lot didn't know their arses from their elbows as per usual. Wanted to ask where to launch from to get out into the middle of the water. Just them in a 4x4 with a load of fertiliser bags in the bag. Fuck that must have stank some.'

'Maybe they needed a wash?' Postie said.

John stood up and questioned the man's huge back: 'What did they look like?'

'Weasley. Like you I expect,' the large man muttered before taking a draining gulp from the glass. They all chuckled. 'All in black, like fucking priests or summat. They weren't no priests though. Pretentious city folk is all.'

'Eyes?'

'Whatcha mean, son? They had 'em. A little small and rodent like on one. Piercing maybe. Like he was looking straight through me, I guess.'

'Snake Eyes,' John said to himself, as his hands wrote it.

'Woman's looked like how you might imagine Mary Queen of Scots before her beheading. Fierce as hell. Unrepentant. Cold hearted bitch with a dark Bob. Not been fucked all season, is all. I've a cow the same in the top field. Right mood on. Needs to loosen up some is all. I've a prize bull could have helped her with that!'

'I'd have given it a go,' said the postie.

'Where's the jetty?' John said, cutting the shit jokes short. He took out his phone to call the police. 'You're gonna need a frogman...' he said into the mobile, 'I think they've dropped a body,' and the pub froze on his words.

Pete and Naresh sat on the bar stools. They hadn't moved in hours.

AS THE OFFICERS looked out over the reservoir, John joined the frogmen, picked up a wetsuit, and a tank, and started getting ready.

'What are you doing, John?'

'Someone's doing this to get at me. They're all messages. There might be a trap down there. Stand your men down. Call it in. I've got a free pass—you know that.'

'Means nothing round here,' the officer said, and went to take the tank from him, hesitating at the sight of the scars and tattoos to John's body, his eyes resting on the 'Who Dares Wins' crest before moving up to the bullet holes. John's body had seen more action than the entire squad around him.

'Let him go under if he wants,' a voice commanded. The fierce female agent from his previous visit to the interrogation room stood staring from the back by the parked cars. He hadn't noticed her. 'You fuck with anything you find, other than to get yourself killed, you're going to stay down there to sleep with pike and eels.'

'Okay... what's your name?'

She didn't answer.

'It'll suit you down there.'

Behind her, two police marksmen stood with their MP5 submachine guns resting across tense forearms.

'Finally realised it's got heavy,' John said. And finished stripping to his pants. And again, another round of strangers saw the full extent of his scarred torso.

The iron lady appeared to wilt, a fraction. A squint at his body was the showing tell, as the scars of his conflicts were laid out in front of her.. She shed an ounce of respect with a knowing nod. This role in life that he was forced to play out, it wasn't an act, and now he was exposed, there was no hiding it

He was for real.

'They were always here; the armed unit. As soon as we knew you were coming up,' she gestured at the van and men.

They all looked out over the water and John zipped up.

'Where will you try, it's a massive reservoir for fuck's sake?' an officer asked.

'The pub,' John pointed to the centre of the huge patch of black water.

PETE AND NARESH sat on bar stools. They hadn't moved in hours.

The pub had stopped serving more than twenty-five years ago and the concrete blocks about their feet meant they couldn't go, even if they were still able to. A pike nibbled at Naresh's cheek, tearing free a chunk of fresh meat, as Pete's eyes stared at the crusty mirror behind the bar, before an eel latched on to his eyeball and started to writhe around to release another prize. The eel kept pulling on the eyeball, determined as a bloodthirsty rat, until it eventually detached the ball from Pete's socket with an unheard 'pop' which would float to the surface on the tiniest trickle of bubbles. The ball held on to its owner for a few seconds, tethered by the optic nerve and blood vessels before snapping free in a cloud of blood, as fluids married with the disturbed silt and mud from the reservoir's bed.

John swam down the underwater road, past a post box, a mud-covered truck and then up to the outside of The Mad Jacobite pub as his torch cut beams through clouds of brown and green murky water. He waited as the hanging sign moved as if above water and being touched by the wind. He imagined lights inside, activity. Life.

He moved up to the green door and forced it open with a push, two shoves and then floated in.

Creatures moved inside the darkness, in and out of focus. Large and small; swimming, curling, pulling and dashing back away from John's presence. John shook and dropped the torch as an eel swam past, dragging along a ball on string which seemed to look at him on the way past.

He picked the torch back up and edged forward again through the silty waters, moving like a man bouncing slowly on the surface of the moon, only this was towards an underwater bar.

With each floating step, his heart pounded, as familiar outlines slowly emerged through the murkiness. With their backs to him the image of each of them came out of the gloom like a black and white polaroid slowly developing before his eyes.

He sat alongside them on a stool.

It was like they'd been waiting for him, and he was late. As if there was an awkward pause, anticipation in one of them speaking to break the ice. Hesitantly, he looked left at the blank lifeless faces. Pete's was first, with his hollow eye sockets looking straight on into an infinity. John followed his stare for a while to try and capture a last thought — the moment they were robbed of the simple life. The moment his life finally polluted theirs.

Then, he leaned forward and looked past Pete to where Naresh sat. The body was still, head tilted away from John just a little in protest. A slight current moved the head to the other side to face John, as if finally acknowledging him. John stared as Naresh's face seemed to smirk back at him, just a little. That look, it was like John had interrupted another of Naresh's daydreams... but there was something else to it... most of all, it was as if he always knew he'd end up in one of John's books.

17

ALNWICK CASTLE

IT WAS THE second Chesterfield he'd sat on in a long week, and it should have been relaxing, but he wasn't getting used to it. What was worse, this one was in a fucking castle—complete with drawbridge, ramparts and a dungeon. Life sized iron statues of soldiers stood on the castle's walls, overlooking the surrounding pastures and the river Aln. And countless staff tended to the grounds and building as if it was stuck in a time more befitting.

He'd walked in through a stone arch, expecting to hear the sounds of spears, swords and jousting inside, and for someone to walk past at any moment with a hawk on their arm dangling a tether of meat. The metal soldiers on the walls overhead were a medieval ploy into fooling the Scots that there were twice as many soldiers inside the battlements. Whether or not it totally worked was debatable. The castle was still in the borderlands of England, not Scotland, so some things had, and the border remained fixed in place after all those years of fighting.

Today, it was just a massive mansion and gardens, with no one to frighten off. But for unseen killers on the loose.

Sometimes the castle and grounds were even open to the hoi polloi of the general public, like John. By appointment to the Duke. With half an approval of the police, whose sporadic road blocks, cars checks and interviews and churned up sweet fuck all so far. They played too polite and knew the only way past the killing was for John to draw fire, and for them to pick a moment to put it out.

Some hoped to put John out too.

The officers at the front had ignored him until he was past them, then the venom flew.

John passed through the blackening stone barbican to the side with a tall arch and stone crest overhead. He wanted to reinforce the warning the Duke had already received—to check to see if it was too late. He knew people like this, of high adopted stature, were used to threats and rarely listened.

The leather sofa swallowed him whole. A tray of tea lay in front as a high ceiling and regal intimidation shone down on him from all angles.

'It's quite something, John. All these people you knew, liked and loved that keep dying.

Isn't it?' the Duke started.

'The killer is killing. It's what they do.'

'That sounds cold,' the Duke said, puzzled.

'We do what we do to cope.'

'Did you love or care about any of these people? Are you capable of emotions? And of that one: love?'

'These people died years ago in their own heads. Long forgotten. The killer is just making sure.'

'Jesus... That's quite a coping mechanism, John,' he paused, and filled his cup from a China teapot.

John shook his head.

'It's a killing spree, all in your name and honour, John. Raw book material,' the Duke looked from the chair opposite whilst flicking through a copy of the local newspaper; The Gazette.

'Thanks for seeing me,' John got to the point.

'What makes you think whoever's doing this has desires on little old me,' the eccentric old man quipped.

John dropped the scrap of paper with coordinates on it to the coffee table between them. As he did it, he felt the eyes in the old oil paintings high up on the walls focus in on him with suspicion. Eyes that turned slowly beneath golden mouldings bolstered by eras of history, now coming to life to judge John and this evil chaos in his wings.

'The Scots didn't make it over these walls all those years ago. What's some crazy vendetta ridden maniac going to do now,

John? Seriously... Besides, the killer, could be me,' he winked. Then his other eye twitched as if to imply a madness.

'It's not you... And who says they're crazy? Anyway, *you* let *me* in. What's to stop them just ringing the doorbell as well?'

'True... True enough, John, and a lot of people. The police even... seem to think this killer, or killers, only exist because you do...'

The Duke dropped the newspaper and took a sip from his tea again; made up of a teaspoon of Early Grey and half a spoon of Lapsang Souchong. He seemed to savour the layers of taste. Then paused, contemplating another return comment, whilst John was on the back foot. His family hadn't got and stayed where they were by not kicking people when they were down. He saw true strength in obliterating weakness.

He took his time to savour the tea's smoky taste yet again.

Then, he charged back like a knight on horseback running at a pauper, 'I was sorry to hear the news, John.'

'Thanks.'

'I'm genuine, John. I knew her, your mother...'

John looked at the ageing eccentric. People like this weren't used to touching mortals. His mother... or him.

'A strong woman. Determined. Harder than most around these parts. You must know what that means, John?'

'It means she did what she had to do. Then some more.'

'You're saying it was just... a survival,' the Duke asked. 'From what I've heard and read, you seem to do a lot of that yourself. Don't make it easy on yourself, do you? Maybe she rubbed off on you more than you care to admit?'

'Not sure it's all that unusual. For a mother, alone, to struggle to survive. It's all about that survival from the point of labour, and from then on. If the father's jumped ship, then it starts even sooner.'

'Quite.' He looked into John, clearly knowing more about him than he was letting on. 'Were you...close, John?'

'I'm not sure I understand the question.'

'Not many around these parts do, John. You're nothing special. It comes with the weather and sweeping hills. They're soaked in blood.'

John looked past the Duke and out the window and imagined: 'It's like a scene from a film—how many films *have* they filmed here?'

The castle had been used by Hollywood so much he could smell the dollars behind the Persian rugs and down the back of the leather sofas. The waiters, servants, or whatever the Duke called them to ease his conscience might as well have been bringing around cans of Coke.

The Duke ignored John's veering focus, how it flipped from introspection to being absorbed by the scenery.

'I thought my father hugged me once,' the Duke re-started. 'Turned out he was having a heart attack; had collapsed into me on a grouse shoot. It's about as close as we ever got.' The Duke tapped the mahogany table, giggling to himself. 'He didn't even die then, otherwise I would have said goodbye having believed his last gesture was to show some degree of affection—and he couldn't have had that. Could he, John? A show of weakness in the classes that have none, outward showing anyway.'

'You could be shitting your pants right now. Knowing killers have you and this place marked. And you wouldn't let it show, would you?'

'Something like that, John… But, the point I was actually making was that you're not the first walking abortion around here. My parents probably wanted a daughter. And yours too. If they wanted anything at all.'

'They were of a generation.'

'Yes, John. A generation. Leave school at sixteen and get a job, a degree or get pregnant.'

The giant Persian looking rug, with a plethora of jarring colourways, beneath John's feet made him dizzy. Almost as much as the displaced wealth around him that had been collected by one family over multiple generations. The man's attempts to suggest everyone was the same. Him and John, it didn't wash.

Before John could try to re-establish the distance between them, the Duke started up again: 'Have you heard of Jack Hall, John?'

'No.'

'Was also known as Mad Jack, or Crazy Jack.'

John shook his head, still hypnotised by the grand backdrop to their conversation. Everywhere he looked was library walls, paintings, cathedral-like ceilings and a sense of being close to a deity. He wasn't sure if the Duke was trying to drag John up to his level, with his words, or explain himself down to John's level; 'we're all human,' and all that shit.

'Mad Jack Hall was a Scottish Jacobite leader in the 16' to 1700s. Owned a lot of land and ended up Justice of the Peace in this county: my county, Northumberland.'

John breathed out. Tried not to sound totally bored.

The Duke had some ambling point to make. Something he considered more relevant than the killers in the county carving and boxing people up for their entertainment.

'Mad Jack Hall owned Otterburn Tower in Redesdale. In fact his initials are still carved over a doorway today. Why don't you check it out some time, pay a visit, before it's knocked down? Touch the carvings from one generation to another.'

'Why does this apply to me?'

'It's your generations, John.'

'I don't figure.'

'He was a member of the Clan Hall, John…'

'So?'

'Your clan, John… I believe. I've done my research. Your family tree is relevant here. Your grandfather believed it too.'

'Sounds a stretch, given how we all grew up.'

'It's true, John.'

'Tell it to the third-hand dilapidated Mondeo outside. Or my shirt with dried in blood from last week,' he touched a sleeve.

'Mad Jack. That's why I knew your mother, and grandfather. Some time ago, they tried to get me to endorse a begging letter they'd written to the Queen, you see?'

John spat out his tea, 'Bollocks.'

'True, John, I'm afraid. You see, they saw fit to try to reclaim Otterburn Tower as your family's.'

'Cheeky.'

'Yes, John. I should have had *them* beheaded,' he joked.

'It's a far stretch to swallow that shit, *Sir*.'

'Maybe, John... but it happened.'

'Really? Did you know, I grew up in a one-bed flat with an outside toilet and electricity on a meter that took 50ps. She rarely put any in it. Her barmaid's wages didn't stretch that far after fags and booze. And you're saying she could just walk in here any time and take a slice of this,' he opened his hands, 'from you?'

'Funny, isn't it. Not exactly like that, John. Close though.'

'We all suffered.'

'The real funny thing is, John, is just that. You and them still suffering, after all this time.'

'Why?

'You see your family, in Mad Jack's time, sided all those years ago against the crown. And funny that they should start all those generations, as being so high up in society, in the classes, and generation after generation they've worked their way... all the way... down. Where they belong.' He pointed at John.

John went to stand to leave.

'Sorry, John. I meant no offence. Just a little verbal joust between a couple of knights whose crests have passed a few times on the battlefield.'

John stared down at the man. His words were heavy— transcended the point of his visit. Touched history. Heritage. Survival at all odds.

'All I was saying was... this Mad Jack Hall. He was like you, John.'

'How so,' John sat.

'Disobeying orders, doing what he believed was right. Regardless of missions, words from the King,' the Duke's eyes looked serious. Narrowing. 'Do you know what they did to him, John? T'was quite harsh really, considering Mad Jack had defended the Borders, with and against the Reivers. He'd kept a peace of sorts for so very long… His only crime in the end was to side with the wrong royal. Wrong side of the wall if you like.'

'A hero now is he?'

'Not quite… But, like I said, he did take the wrong side, in the Jacobean uprising though, John… Such a silly boy. Was quite a big deal at the time,' he smirked.

'What did they do to him?'

'He was beheaded for high treason, John.

'Fits.'

'Yes. After being hung drawn and quartered. They made an example of his cadaver. A bit harsh, maybe. Apparently, he had a fiery temper. Was passionate and indiscreet. Any similarities? Remind you of anyone?'

'Quite a handful,' John looked at his own hands, tensing; needing to release the pressure in his tendons that was building. A tension way older than the blood of these dukes and lords.

A Viking blood.

He was unsure if he was being consoled or wound up, as his temper veered between simmering rage and respect, in a stranger's knowledge of John's buried family's history.

'Would you like to meet him, John?'

John looked confused. Fact and fiction spun in the room and in his head.

The Duke stood and raised his hands, 'Look…'

Behind John, high on the wall was a giant painting of a man. Fierce. Strong. The painter had captured arrogance, pride and other flaws as well. John hated him instantly.

He must be family.

'He was also known as Crazy… *John*. Funny that. Isn't it? *John*,' the Duke said.

John stared into the painting right down into the detail of the canvas threads.

'What do you think? What would he have made of you being dismissed from service—killers chasing you over his old patch?'

John felt the Duke smirking; on his side a little. His little joke, at showing a long connection between his family and John's, the underdogs and the Percys of Northumberland.

'How long have you been doing what you believe is right, rather than what you're told to? At all costs?' The Duke looked into him.

'There's been deaths at all these locations, and more. Some random strangers and others the killer believes have some connection to me,' John firmly re-shifted back to the case in point he'd entered with. 'I don't know, now, which you are to me, or to the killer. Or, will be in the end.'

The Duke's eyebrows raised.

'Just how connected to me are you...? Are the killers targeting you for it?' John pointed to the bit of paper on the table.

'No one knows what I told you but me, and those in your family that are dead, one soon to be buried. Suits for me to have kept it that way,' he took out an envelope with a wax seal and put it on the table. 'She never got that begging letter, John. The Queen has more important issues to deal with than a traitor's family wanting a tower back. It was always mine to give or take anyway.'

John shrugged.

'I'm a fan of your family. But I don't want to lose my head doing it,' he reached into his pocket and took out an old heavily patinated key. 'Take it, John. It's yours; Otterburn Tower. Long overdue. If you ever consider coming home. Now you'll have one.'

'Why?'

'Like I said, a home. If you want to belong. My family has been in this castle for more than 700 years. What do we want with another one? Besides, it needs work,' he smiled.

'Have you heard a thing I've said. There's a killer in the county,' John picked up and held out the coordinates again.

The Duke looked amused. As if a child was offering him a pencil drawing of a unicorn. 'There's a drawbridge. A moat, albeit dry,' he tilted his head. 'Ramparts... Now, there's armed police too. Generations of ill-wishers and heathens haven't gotten close to us inside these walls. What makes these killers of yours, whatever side they're on, any different?'

'If it's who I think it is. They aren't on any side. They're like wild dogs; wolves. It's just a way of passing the time for them. They study pain. Their own and any new ways of inflicting it on others they can think up.' He let the melodrama of the words hang in the air.

'How do you do it, all this, John? Without the uniform?'

'It itched anyway. Didn't fit.'

'*They* won't get close, John.'

The air between them stilled further. The Duke's refusal of vulnerability having grown up with a castle around him was understandable. John tried to pick words with the gravity to pull the Duke back down to earth and to smell the blood. Then, he didn't have to.

'They won't ever... get close, John.'

John looked over the Duke's shoulder, focusing in on something.

'*They* already have,' John said, looking at a crate in the corner and slowly raising a hand to point.

It was so out of place, why hadn't he noticed it before? Somehow the crudely nailed together wooden box with familiar red smears down its sides had blended in with the rest of the chests, futons and ornate collectables. Like a trojan horse sneaking past the castle walls—only this wooden decoy was filled with death.

'What?' the Duke said, slowly turning in disbelief as the light from the giant casement windows reflected in an unmistakable pool that had formed under the box.

18

ALNMOUTH LINKS

THE BOY CAUGHT her up in the end on that beach. His mother had slowed enough, and he'd kept going until he made it... legs and lungs burning. But, when she turned and saw him; panting, tired, overwhelmed and happy to finally be there with her, she screamed—like a wild banshee. The yell hurt both their ears. She shook the heavens and parted the waves with her ferocious screams that seemed would never stop.

What was this image that tore at her eyeballs, again?

What had he brought down on them?

Couldn't he just... go? Be normal like the other children?

He'd pulled something along with him, and it had made her more frightened than what he usually carried behind that empty stare of his.

He brought with him, Death.

He had a spine with a skull, and a manic look full of glee with it.

More than ever, pain and suffering would surely follow.

Bones of his 'new toy' were so brittle and dry, so old and decaying... that the skull had been battered from the friction of the boy dragging it the length of the beach, behind him over the rocks and sand.

She knew something wasn't quite right about him. He was a killer. Always was. They all said it: '...this one's not quite right, is he?' Confirmation: she was right to send him away at every opportunity. Far, far away. 'What's that look in his eyes? ...Bit weird isn't it?' And whenever he returned, she was right to keep moving away. Never let him catch up again; always be busy.

When she fully realised the macabre plaything he had with him, and took it all in, the screams ceased.

All energy was diverted into creating division. Between her and the boy. Like the graveyard that had been separated from the village in that old storm.

She ran as fast as she could away from him, again. This time, he didn't bother following. He looked down at his macabre trophy, then, he turned to the waters and walked slowly towards the waves that beckoned him. Wanting him to go fully into the sea, forever. Finally, going home. Towards true love.

As he neared the edge of the waves, they seemed to move away from him as well. Even the sea's tides were repelled now. Inching away. Her waters retreated from him and all the death that followed, lingering in his steps.

The boy was the Devil.

JOHN SNAPPED UPRIGHT in the sands. Awake. His dream ebbed away as the sea's tide moved out. A lucidity grew, and it occurred to him to welcome these nightmares that he was having more and more; full of dispossessed family ties and the demons that trailed behind them like seaweed strands. The visions were a welcome break from the war echoes that had gripped him the last ten years. They stretched and awakened a new murky symphony of his brainwaves.

The full sound of the sea broke into his consciousness and gave him hope.

The dream was just that. A mind's torments looking for conclusions where there were none. Overhead birds circled, swooped and played. On the water's edge, a seal flopped, halfway out of the water. It saw John and hesitated. It waited. Then, rather than retreat back into the waves it continued out and up the shore with a shake of its whiskers and a laughing bark.

He smiled. The first full one since last being with Cherry.

For a moment, he forgot there were killers on the loose.

The sun shattered through clouds to wash a new day with a change; brightening optimism approached. Time to bury the past and move on.

He sat in the dunes and waited for a call to ruin it all.

Then, it came...

19

NORTH TO SOUTH

THE SHARP SPIKY tufts of Marram grass tickled and dug into his back, and his feet sank in the drift of sand beneath him. The sea had moved firmly from calm positivity, and now looked as changeable as ever. An angry crumpled blanket, before rolling up and throwing walls of waves to shore.

The call came—he knew one would. He wouldn't have had money on that particular one... but still it came, another voice from the past to shatter solace:

'John?'

'Yes.'

'It's about your brother...' The voice on the line sounded like a pirate, all the way from Bristol.

Silence.

'You there, John?'

When he saw Pat Lynch's number come up he knew it would be about Jimi, his estranged brother. Jimi hadn't shown face leading up to the funeral, so far. John had half expected that from him, but hoped he would surprise him. With a few days to go until s*he* was buried forever, he half hoped Jimi would show up, for some sort of sense of loyalty and solidarity... He had that in him. They both did. An iron moral compass. And the loyalty. It had gotten them both into trouble and hurt. There wasn't going to be much family to speak of when the big day came. Someone had to toss soil, say a few words and John, with Jimi, would do more together than only one of them alone, if at all.

'I guess he's not coming... I only *just* did,' John said into his mobile.

'He's got himself into a tight spot,' Pat said. Skirting around the obvious, funeral-sized elephant in the room and getting to his own issues at hand.

'He wouldn't thank you. Not for getting me involved, Pat. He's never felt the need to have my back...'

'He's a fucking ox, John, I know. But sometimes the ox needs to keep its head down when the abattoir gates open.'

They had always fought their own battles. Different weapons. Different enemies too. Until John crossed from the battlefields onto the streets. Then the lines had blurred.

'This is different, John.'

'How so?'

'It's the London mob: The South Bank Cricketers. They didn't realise who he was. That he was your brother. Still don't. Or if they do, they don't give a fuck.'

'Can't he just stay the fuck out of it?'

'They aren't giving him any choice.'

'How so? I've never found him that bothered about looking the other way with my shit.'

'They're trying to take his bar in Weston… Got his son wrapped up in it too. Your nephew, Jack.'

John's brother Jimi had named his son Jack, who was now also estranged from both of them. Staying with family tradition Jimi had gotten someone knocked up and jumped ship when things got tough. Jack, a name variation of John—had kept them connected in a tenuous but heartfelt gesture. Now, with what John had learned from the Duke about their ancestor Mad Jack Hall, the name carried even extra weight; a doomed family heirloom.

He sat bolt upright, feeling protective of the boy he'd hardly met. The lad was meant to be going to college and making something of his life, not getting dragged into a load of gangster shit that would taint his career prospects, for life, if he survived.

'They're going in heavier now, 'til they make their point, John. It'll be real heavy handed soon. That's why I'm calling. It's gone rotten. It's going South, John.'

'He wouldn't like that. Someone trying it on for his bar. The Hell's Belles is all he's got now,' John said. He knew the bar was a retirement gift *to* Jimi, *from* Jimi. For a hard life's graft in the building trade. He'd done time for one of Pat's crew and Pat now sponsored this retirement with a little monthly cash as a thanks. Enough to keep a modest, simple pleasure seeking, working man like Jimi in Jacky D. 'I've got my own shit to deal with, Pat. Why don't you sort it yourself?'

'I know about the funeral, I'm real sorry, John. But...'

'There's more to *it*, Pat. *It* follows me these days. I've brought all hellfire down on the North East. It came with me all the way from Manchester. I'm not sure it won't just follow me back down the other way: North to South.'

'What? Who?'

'Killers, and killing. It's all around me. I think it's someone from my past again. It smells like China Bob's work. And someone else. It's real dark, Pat.'

'That's interesting. That evil cunt's out, is he?'

'I'll only make it worse, Pat, if I come down. Can't you deal with them all yourself down there? You're the real gangster on the line.'

'That's debatable, John. After all you've done. Sent ripples up and down the country by cutting the head of the trade... kicking *Mr Big* off that tower block. You know it wouldn't do any good. I don't tread on their toes, John. My Bristol crew and South London, that Cricketers lot, have always kept out of each other's shit. Besides, it's not really them that's the problem anyway. As you know. It's their psycho head... The Cricketers' main man.'

'Oh...' John listened as the stars aligned and the dots joined. Maybe he would make the trip, after all.

'You know who I'm talking about, John?'

'Ballard... Max Ballard.'

'Yes, John. The one and bastard only. In fact, isn't he China Bob's financer, or was before you neutered him?'

Max Ballard used to be as close as China Bob could get to a main employer.

And was still Ballard's go to man for inflicting pure evil, and Ballard had plenty of targets... Both deserving and for the sheer bloody mindedness of it. A way of thinking they both shared. To keep the balance of pain in the world at such levels that people like Max Ballard and Snake Eyes, or China Bob, were comfortably accustomed to.

Regardless of Pat's desire to topple a rival and use John to do it. John now saw his own opportunity to return a blow to China Bob. If he was involved, it may even distract the focus away from his homelands' victims.

A sleight of hand. A distraction from home. Pulling the rat out into the open for the Priest stick to clobber it. It would also pull the game back into open gang warfare, where the dead and dying were deserved. Rather than all these semi-innocent bystanders that had been falling back in John's home town.

If anything happened to, or threatened Max Ballard, all connections to him via criminal tendrils, would gather about him—John was sure of it.

Time to send some ripples the other way, he thought.

'I'll come to Weston, Pat... Stay clear. I don't have time to fuck about. I'll be in and out in a night.'

'THANKS,' PAT SAID. He'd missed John being around. Pat's band of wild loveable pirate rogues had been knocking over banks, the establishment, and the upper classes for years when John first appeared on the Bristol scene. They soon saw him as an ally. Taking down the less moral crews that stood against them and clearing the path for Pat's crew. But just as they were getting used to John's criminal's-criminal take-downs, he left for Manchester. He seemed drawn there. Rather than accepting his Witness Protection, he shed it altogether and raced head on towards what he was meant to be protected from.

Next Pat heard, John had toppled a Greater Manchester gang lord, ending up an unwilling leader over all of them. He had some crooked police endorsement too. With all that, Pat knew John was ideal to retire Ballard. The blood ties to his brother only sealed the deal.

It could have been the perfect set up to get Max Ballard out of action. As it happened Pat was innocent-ish. It's just the way their crazy criminal lives had coalesced and morphed together.

Yes, Pat felt guilty at pulling John away from a family funeral. But if he didn't let him know about his brother being up to his neck—there'd be another one fairly soon, maybe two if his nephew fell too.

A nasty piece of work Max Ballard was—not to be fucked with, unless you were going all out. John would. Ballard would casually glass you whilst fucking your wife as your daughters watched, knowing they were next. John's brother was as disposable as a used Rubber-Johnny to Ballard: a real brutal bastard. And long overdue a retirement trip to meet his dead wife.

Pat knew that if Max Ballard was capable of feeling fear, he would at the sight or mention of John. Now that John's brother was under threat by the South Bank Cricketers—and Max himself—Pat saw a way to retire Ballard from the scene for good. Serves him right for not joining the dots, Pat thought. Jimi and John: brothers. And Jack: a son and a nephew to them.

When the call was done, Pat gloated and quietly muttered to himself: 'Goodnight, Max—say hello to your dead wife when you see her.'

Then he reached behind the counter of the bar he was in and helped himself to a refill of Scrumpy.

'Max Ballard—Wanker!' a parrot called from a cage in the corner of the pub. 'Thief. Thief! Stealin' cider.'

'Shut it, Polly. Or I'll have you stuffed,' he joked. He loved that bird; the most colourful, flea-bitten spy and eavesdropper on his crew. Took less cleaning up after it than the rest too.

JOHN WENT STRAIGHT to the station, he didn't pack a bag, he was going to be in and out of Weston. As he'd told Pat: no time to fuck around. The seven-hour train journey was long enough, and left plenty of time to prepare mind and body. He sat in the train seat and looked at a half bottle of Jameson whiskey in front of him.

Things would go back to black before they got light again. Before the deaths stopped.

Would they ever stop?

He wanted to get this done without his brother finding out. The relationship, or lack thereof, wouldn't survive John getting involved. Jimi fought his own battles—his pride wouldn't take it. But Max Ballard was different, wouldn't be put back in his place. He'd kill or die before backing down.

He knew Jimi had done time, was tough enough... For family, John would go beyond the call of duty. Loyalty and blood-bond meant something to John if not his brother. If it meant taking down one of China Bob's employers—all the better.

MAX BALLARD HAD fallen out with one of his trainee drivers on the drive cross-country from London to Weston. He spooked him up for most of the journey with wind-ups that the boy had fantasised over fucking his own sister. Max loved a wind up. Sicker the better. It just got better and better as the boy squirmed around and sweated. Like there might have been some truth in it—incestuous little prick.

Ballard thought he was on form and up for whatever lay in store at the end of the road.

The lad was so distracted, he'd over shot the bridge junction and rather than taking the M5 down to Weston they'd ended up, bang smack—in fucking Wales. Boyos a plenty. Leeks and sheep. Ballard was fuming when he woke to the sound of all those extra consonants. Fuming to the extent steam seemed to hiss from his pores.

Max Ballard had the patience of a half-spent fuse and they'd taken what felt like a decade to get out of London, down the M4 corridor and had nearly shat themselves after a dodgy bacon bap en-route. No, Ballard did not have time to waste. He had some inbred yokel fuckwit heads to bash together in Weston—time was very much of the essence.

Tick-fucking-tock.

So, Max dragged the lad from the car, hog-tied him and put him in the boot. Then, Ballard finished the driving off himself, pulling over a few times to hammer home the disappointment into the lad's eyes and teeth with iron fists. He turned the radio up to drown out the tears and whimpers from the back—Ballard was easily bored and broke up the rest of the dull-assed journey nicely, taking it out on the boy's once pretty face.

He smiled for the rest of the journey as the boy shook with fear and pissed himself in the back. Everything was falling into place. Ballard just needed that fucker Jimi, on fire, cut up and dangling from the suspension bridge and he could relax back into his old routine.

When Ballard pulled up to the rundown seaside shit-hole resort, complete with Victorian pier and angry over-sized gulls, he was soon beckoned into a cafe for a tete-a-tete with Pat Lynch.

He left the boy in the boot to finish with later, and went in.

The diner was a desperately tired and torn fake Americana, with a grease patina to the chrome and coffee jugs and fag burns to the chequered floor. The red vinyl banquette booths were held together with black carpet tape and the lights had a yellow tint from grease and smoke that would never lift.

Pat Lynch and Max Ballard sat and verbally jousted in gangster subtexts, warnings and windups as Booker T. & the MG's provided the soundtrack. A downtrodden, greasy spoon, hollow-eyed crisis of a mid-aged woman splashed coffee from a dented pot, as it caught reflections of the scene like a broken circus mirror.

Pat meant to tell Ballard about Jimi, that he was John Black's brother and to see the look on Ballard's face drop at the mention of the Devil being involved.

Max wasn't easy to scare and he barely listened to Pat. The coffee wasn't as bad as his expectations and the music made him feel like he was Pacino, and Pat was a lesser image of De Niro, in the film Heat.

Max took in the seaside resort through the window—he was falling for the rotten-beat charm of the place and wanted Jimi's bar more than ever.

The whole, once thriving, resort was down on its knees. It made him think: rather than just taking over Jimi's bar here, he'd have it all: pier, donkey rides, penny slots, the whole fucking shit show. And, that would be his own end of life wind down before meeting *her*, his wife again.

A gangster's paradise in the South West by his own design.

He couldn't stand cider. Gave him a slack arse. But, fuck it. Ballard loved a bit of rum every now and again. They were all descendants of pirates and slave traders over here as far as he was concerned, and Max Ballard, in his own eyes, was fucking Black Beard himself: King Pirate. Hadn't done any slave trading, but could start somewhere... The boy tied up in the boot was hardly free right now.

The conversation between Pat and Max went nowhere.

Max felt a moment's weakness, and gestured to his crew outside that had been there quite some time, to let the lad out the boot, to finally set him on his limping way.

A stalemate between Pat and Max: Max threatened to shatter their long-standing relationship and virtual boundaries between their turfs by moving over to the West Country. To take over Weston.

That's when Pat knew he had to call Jimi's brother, John.

Ballard needed to retire. By his own volition or not.

JOHN WALKED UP the cobbled rainy backstreet to Jimi's bar. Jimi wasn't home. He knew that Max had muscled in by then and Jimi had gone to temporary hiding, before doing something he'd regret.

The street was in the darkness, but for a couple of old Victorian lamps flickering feebly.

He drained the last from the whiskey bottle and dropped it in an overflowing bin.

Jimi had taken over the small live music bar and renamed it The Hell's Belles after his love of ACDC and his new ferocious co-owners, an ex-stripper and a burlesque titty twister he'd met in Bristol: Bettie and Tammy.

It was dead until Jimi, his guitar, and the girls had taken over.

He didn't have to queue to get in or wait to be served. Now Ballard had dominated it, it was dead again.

The bell rang on the door and John walked calmly up to the bar and sat on a stool.

Max had his back to him adjusting some bottles behind the bar. Customer service wasn't Max's strong point. The place was empty.

John opened his palms and stretched them halfway across the counter top in an ostentatious show of submission. Like he was waiting to be cuffed.

Max Ballard could feel a dark presence behind him.

He didn't scare easily. He wasn't used to it and suppressed it with thoughts of his dead wife—the ultimate distraction, in any situation. She used to be a dragon. And was still the only thing to fear.

'Drink?' he turned and poured it from a tap without looking up, or waiting for an answer.

When their eyes met, Max knew... The storm everyone had been talking about, that he'd ignored, was here.

He'd heard everything about him, John Black was the Devil to the underworld; not great to those up top either.

He reached for the handgun taped under the counter.

John's submissive looking hands and open reaching palms were a ruse; positioning himself for a strike he knew he'd have to take. The one he'd decided he was going to make seven hours ago on a train.

John grabbed the gun, kept it in Ballard's grip and put his own fingers behind the trigger guard, so Max couldn't squeeze. Then he tightened his grip until Ballard's anger turned to fear with the cracking of his index bones.

There they were: those retiring bloodshot eyes. 'Goodnight, Max. Say hello to your dead wife when you see her again.'

John met Ballard's ex-driver outside. It was Ballard's turn to be hogtied.

They delivered Ballard on a boat to the island where Jimi was held up. Picked up a surprise package on the journey across too, an overboard, a woman cast afloat, discarded or lost. So, John left her safe, with a note for Jimi saying: Pat's debt is paid up.

The note suggested that was it, and there was no more financial backing from Pat's Bristol gang going to Jimi.

A short, sharp, and eventful trip.

John left and was on the last train back up North. He didn't spare a thought for his brother. And when the call came from Pat to thank him, he didn't pick up. His mind was on China Bob's snake eyes, and knowing he'd cut one of Bob's life lines. Ballard wouldn't be paying his way any more than Pat would be his brother's—although that remained to be seen. Pat and Jimi were tight as thieves. Just ask the parrot in the Bristol Boozer where they'd met and drank together before Jimi moved to Weston.

JIMI KNEW IT was John's work really—with Pat's sponsorship, or not. HE wouldn't thank him for it. He felt it though.

Jimi still wouldn't see him at the funeral. They weren't that close. Even less to their own mother. You can share the violence, take a beating and deal one out for one another. Fuck, you could share the same womb—doesn't mean you have to see eye to fucking eye. Not in a world that had hated them so much.

Jimi was impressed, even a little proud, he didn't know how John had done it all; rescue the girl, appease Pat and retire Max all in one sitting. Fuck, he might even play his favourite, *Back in Black*, as an encore on the first night back on stage in The Hell's Belles. It was John's favourite of the ACDC tracks Jimi's used to crank out. That aside, it fitted the occasion anyway.

Max was buried from influence.

20

TEACHING HIGHSMITH

HE WAS NEVER any good at killing but he'd gotten used to it. He'd always written, it was other people that had to get used to that. At school, ironically, not least of all.

At his middle school they tried to suppress his words from seeing the light of day. Ms Highsmith was the worst. She kept him schtum. Like his words stung all their eyes to witness and pierced eardrums to hear. Like it was her duty to protect the children and prevent John from exercising his dark inner whims, and letting them out into the world that wasn't prepared for the likes of him.

Hard, biting, dirty-real words of little consequence to a middle-class teacher's world.

His writing came from a rundown council estate, and her eyes and ears were fixed in a detached rose adorned cottage down a quaint country lane. Spaniels lapping at her heels.

He was always chased by rabid dogs filled with hate.

Later in his life, after the killing, and then choosing not to when ordered to... he was shot himself; burned, in flames... Since the forces he'd written it out. Heavy with PTSD from childhood and later... war.

He had to write.

The therapist told him what he already knew: if he didn't open the tap, let the thoughts flow like a bleeding wound, he'd capsize under the weight he carried. This was the same as a child. Baggage to let go, throw from the train and lighten the load before the next stop.

It wasn't his responsibility to fix. Let go of it all. Only in later years did he have the help of others that loved him enough to let it out.

On the train back up North from Weston he was writing hard, to do just that: let it go. Between each stroke and brain dump he remembered the origins of that first story. The one where his emotions flew, and with it he shed the restraints of judgement to do so.

Since closing the doors of the classrooms in his past, he'd always carried a notebook.

Some teachers teach. Some box children into pockets of their assumed future societal acceptance of them, and then they nail down the lid with red pen and certificates.

John burned his school books and the certificates that came after. They were worth as little as the faces that bore witness to the judgement, and the older ones that prescribed them.

THAT FIRST STORY, the one that broke him free... It was born in a cold summer in the mid '80s in a rural village middle school in deepest Northumberland:

Ms Highsmith's classes had him disheartened, humiliated and without free thoughts to express. One day he snapped and took the lead back from her. John wasn't alone—most of the kids felt the same. John just went over the edge first.

Normally the last to put his hand up. That day, he was the first. His arm, mind and hand flowed with new confidence.

She'd ruled over the little kids with an iron fist. The other teachers in the small country village joked she could get a centimetre below the knuckles with a cane, or a steel rule. It was no joke.

Most didn't test her; John often did.

He would flick the school tadpoles against the side of their tank until they split open; hanging there by their slimy entrails. Sometimes they flew out the tank and hung by their innards from her classroom walls, baking in the sun. Other times he sandwiched them between the pages of her marking books.

Trudy was first to ask Ms Highsmith if John could read his story out. Then 'Runner' urged her too. The kids all called him

'Runner' or 'The Runs' because he farted and lost one-time in morning assembly during the 'Lord's Prayer'.

They all chuckled—he did too.

'...but deliver us from evil. For thine is the kingdom, the power and the glory, for ever and ever. Amen.'

Runner cried, the little podgy boy was unable to hold it any longer, the seal was broken, and he felt the trickles down his leg, before the main expulsion. As the smell hit them, the rest of the kids laughed so hard they damn near shat too.

The teachers wouldn't let John write back then, not from the guts and heart—caging up his emotions. A simmering monster. Something to be done in secret.

Ms Highsmith kept at John with things he didn't know the answer to; over and over until his rage tore behind his eyes to be released, and he burned red-faced. They all thought it was embarrassment... then, the story came to mind. He knew he had to get it out, then read it out for everyone. To shut her up. For good.

His torrid emotions came—written out for all to witness.

He started his tale, standing and speaking meekly at the front of the class. Ms Highsmith sat by him, cross-legged, in judgment. She looked at the marking book on her lap, red pen poised at the ready. She already had his mark to mind—a clear 'F'.

She had to pander to his lesson rules... He held class that day:

'Jack felt different in English class that day...' he started his story, using the John variation namesake—Jack. Unaware his brother would later use it to name a son.

He continued mumbling into the page.

'Speak up, boy!' she barked, and he could see her top lip quiver. She noticed him eyeing her mid-life lip hairs and her eye twitched angrily. Her mind's eye was already moving towards the bottom drawer, which held her favourite ruler to use on them.

He quivered out each of the starting lines. Then he found a flow, getting closer to the glory of it all:

'He was disconnected, isolated, sick of school and his pretend friends,' the story went on. 'Jack no longer felt part of anything...like a cog in a wheel going nowhere.'

'Is this actually going anywhere...?' she impatiently sneered, and then winked at the class—who stared coldly back. Not the response she'd expected, demanded.

They all felt the power shifting with his words. They knew where he was taking her and were scared what reaction would be the result.

'Jack knew where his teacher lived. The next time she put him on the spot and humiliated him, he'd go there—put *her* on the spot,' he said quietly, almost in a lover's whisper. 'Jack would get an Uzi... no... wait, not an Uzi—where the fuck would I—he—get an Uzi?!'

She froze in the space the words had created at the front of the class.

'A knife instead,' he said, winking at her this time. 'Yes... a shiny razor-sharp Bowie knife.'

By the last of his lines, she was looking past the walls; out into a distance to save her from the uncomfortableness he'd created between him, her and the full class.

Her hands shook on the desk as she tried to grasp onto a wilting domain.

She was on the ropes, but he continued reading his story: 'Jack had lost touch. Jack was a psychopath. She'd made him that way. And who was he to question *her* authority? So *he* paid *her* a final visit at *her* home. That chintz, quaint little rose covered cottage down that stony little lane...' he paused. 'It would be her final lesson,' he finished.

Silence. For a minute.

'That's okay John... I suppose,' she muttered,

He folded the sheets of A4 away as she still managed to judge him.

'Really?' he asked.

'I'm not sure of some of the words you've used. Trifling at best. Also, to listen to, yes, so very trifling... a torrent of trivial waffle, young man.'

'Like?' he cut in.

'The word: psychopath. I think you mean: sociopath,' she criticised, boiling his blood again. But as he looked out at the empathy in the faces across the whole class, he simmered back down. And returned to her and her hairy top lip. She must know they all felt the same. Wished her gone.

'Why?' he quivered through gritted teeth, re-enraged by her defiant face.

'A psychopath... is without empathy. Plans out what they mean to achieve. Cold blooded. Like a snake.'

'That so?'

'Whereas, a sociopath knows it's wrong and hurtful but does it anyway... more hot-headed. Less calculating.'

The look he was giving her evolved into the deepest of stares. Like he was channelling someone a hundred times his age.

'I DID mean psychopath,' he said, and then he jumped at her.

The whole class jumped too. Some fell from their seats and toppled the small wooden desks.

Without a home. He was sent back to the boarding wing where he stayed. To a beating.

And that was Ms Highsmith's last class.

JOHN LOOKED OUT of the train window and smiled, remembering that first use of stories to purge his life. The memory made good where it once haunted him. Now, he wrote his mind's eye down and they couldn't stop him.

He was drinking less these days. Wrote more.

Although, a recent taste of whisky had reignited a thirst. He closed his notebook, stood and walked to the train buffet car.

His past severed, yet more darkness to purge.

Would it ever let him go?

He opened another can on the fold down table and remembered where it turned from the self-prescribed writing to the establishment ordered killing in his life. In his past as a repressed, bitter schooling had pushed him from his need to self-express, he'd then looked to the army. Eventually cast into the SAS.

His gran had said, before he left for service, 'You'll have to kill and be killed. Is that really what you want? To Kill? You really want to sign your life over to that?'

He thought too long on the question, and that it had made her uncomfortable when he told her what he was planning.

She could see the boy, barely late teens, internally deliberating over the answer to give her. Honest. Or, to tell her what she wanted to hear. He hadn't fully decided.

There was no hope, whichever path he took. It was written on her face. He'd spent his formative years executing his favourite toys with an air rifle to release some hidden inner turmoil. Without him having to say it, she had realised that he needed to move on to bigger, more tangible stand-ins, for those dark times—ones that would actually bleed for him. Die for him. Take his demons away, be buried with their bodies as he took the life from them.

'But they'll be bad people, right? That I'm asked to kill…?' He said it as if they all deserved what was coming to them. Like he'd already targets in his head to paint over those he saw down his sights.

So, that remained his lingering response. A question for her, on the fence of morality.

His gran was clearly hurt by how someone so young could become so defeatist in the search of love and happiness, instead of looking to self-destruction and hate.

'There is another way,' she had said.

'There's no other way,' he replied, as he turned to leave.

He had already signed up. Submitted to the Northumberland Fusiliers the day before. He never told her. But she knew if not then, it would be someday soon.

Years later, after he'd killed in service, he saw her again. She was frail, in her last moments. Fractions of time lent to her to be on Earth. A sudden illness had struck her down and all those faith-filled Sundays, the moderate drinking, no smoking and easy, long-term committed loving relationships now grated on her—feeling pointless in the face of death. Now she wished she'd gone all 'hell for leather'. Now she knew it was to end the way it was. Regardless of how she'd lived her life.

'Is anyone, ever, really actually happy?' she'd asked, detached from all previous belief and faith. No longer trying to convert him.

He nodded slowly. Finally, it seemed, she actually understood him.

She looked away, perhaps ashamed at the time it had taken. Now too late.

Looking at her with sympathy, even he was in complete disbelief that life could punish the good willed so easily. The moderate and kind hearted: shattered, broke and dying with the beasts. With such a curse to go ahead of your time. Even worse leaving you so lucid at the end, aware as it slips away.

She turned and smiled, 'Finally, we're on the same page.'

Not long after that meeting, she was gone, and her ashes scattered on the crag they used to walk together, as heather, bird song and yellow hues of light caressed the serene hills that carried her spirit beyond the happiness she thought was so elusive in her last days.

Outside the train, a countryscape morphed from grey to green and back again. Then the trees to fields and back again. Soon he'd be back to Northern England for this, the latest funeral.

What was left of family couldn't stop him. He now wrote, freely. He wrote more than he drank, so he liked to think, and he drank much more than he had killed, recently...

21

THE FUNERAL

JOHN DIDN'T NOTICE her at first. When he did, she was unavoidable and he couldn't notice anything else in the room. She was a medusa; a siren calling him to smash on the rocks.

He'd been in this situation before. Without his mother's coffin to lean on.

She was the only person in the dark back room of the pub, bound up in themselves, looking out of place. Except for him, doing exactly the same. Both like they shouldn't be there.

The rest of the funeral-goers drank and shouted as they let go of their loss, like pulling splinters from swollen angry sores, they waited for the built up resentments to reveal and expunge themselves, along with any remaining respect for family ties.

It was a warm up act before the inevitable 'Who owned what?', 'Who was due what?' and 'Who loved *her* more? Or less?'. As the unavoidable fights and squabbles brewed, any minor inheritance would be smashed out in confused bitter family layers, as chips on shoulders and repressed emotions crashed into each other.

John and the stranger remained disconnected from the room and its issues. And that's what drew them together most of all.

She absentmindedly prodded the buffet table's offerings like they were off and disgusted her. Lancing one lump here and nudging another there. Rolling a king prawn on to its side. She glared and prodded away like the chicken wings and mini-bites were roadkill to be flicked out of her way, eventually resigning herself to drink through it.

They were on the same page.

A distant half-cousin maybe? He had a few.

He moved alongside her. She seemed to John, the only other person there not dying or dead already. She must be from the city, any city. She didn't come with the resigned defeat and pretence of happiness that shrouded the others.

'Look,' he said. 'The living dead, all about us. They'll need to dig a bigger hole.'

An awkward silence.

Then she smirked, unable to contain it any longer… the bait was nibbled.

'Death's waiting room,' she replied. Didn't look up. 'Don't know what the fuck I'm doing here,' she muttered, coldly, still without looking up to acknowledge him.

'How did you know her? Are we related? Were you friends,' he asked.

She didn't answer. Instead, she skewered a battered bit of seafood on a stick like she was fencing a bull. It was done in a way angrier than the moment justified—the action carried the weight of something on her mind, something beyond the funeral. She sniffed at the nondescript scampi-like clod and threw it to the table in disgust. 'Some coastal village and fishing port this is... This shit's from Iceland Supermarket in town.'

'Times are hard. The normal host and provider is in the box.'

She shrugged, couldn't care less.

He looked at her quizzically. 'So… who'll be catching the next ride out?' He looked as innocent and casual as he could, as he steered the dialogue back to who she might be, and who she knew in the room.

It didn't matter. She ignored his presence and only just caught his words. Like his syllables were irritating bugs in the air, buzzing past her jet-black hair.

'That bitch in the stupid hat, or maybe what's in the box is still twitching and they've made a mistake?' she bluntly snapped over the rim of a glass she'd picked up without a care, as she continued the mindless minesweeping she'd started four drinks ago.

In the background a fat farmer with a beard turned from a shorter, younger version of himself—without the beard—that he was bad mouthing the family to. He looked around for his double rum and coke he'd lost. 'I'm sure I put it down here on the fruit machine.'

'No, that one's definitely dead. And the bitch in the hat. She's indestructible. A force of nature,' John said to the mystery woman.

'Fuck 'em. Fuck. Them. All,' she staccatoed, staring ahead.

John squinted at her. Such rage. Almost as much as him: they *must* be related.

'They don't know what life is or they wouldn't be here. This whole fucking region's a depressing graveyard of content, and that's matched only with an undying unease with itself that stops them leaving. All fuck ups. They've made a prison of their lives. And now they'll die in it. So be it. RIP.' And she tipped a glass at the coffin.

Definitely related, he thought. She must have moved away and has been dragged back here by the funeral, just like him. His guard dropped, it all felt so familiar.

In those eyes John saw a mirror looking back. An image of himself. Much more than a reflection of the room. She was channelling death and life, and the lack thereof altogether with each of the disgruntled words carried on her venomous breath. There was a depth of unsaid heavy loads and an irritation in her. The woman seemed stone-like with a black molten core. Unmoved even in the presence of a lost loved one.

John's loss.

Even that seemed to irritate her. She held a skull full of hate. Brimming with it. Her stone-cold blankness, like a robot free of care and emotion, other than that hate looking out through beady dead eyes, under that hard, straight fringe.

He nodded. Cold-hearted-bitch. She *is* one of the family.

'There's room in the box for two—just a waste of timber otherwise, maybe it is *her* time,' he conceded, thinking of the woman in the ridiculous hat in the corner.

'Fancy going?' she whispered. At first he wondered what she meant—did she mean to die? Then she pointed to the door in the other room. He could see she was trying to appear social.

Trying to be human as her china mask cracked, revealing something vaguely resembling a smile. A pulse. Empathy. Again it was familiar ground to John and it warmed him to see it in someone else.

'I said my goodbyes long ago,' he said. 'Why not?'

NINA WAS DISGUSTED he didn't recognise her. Yes, prison had been harsh and the club lights were never on when they had worked together back then, but still. As if she couldn't hate and despise him more.

She did now.

With him following her, like a lamb to the slaughter, with each step down the village street, the last nail had long since gone into his coffin—now she would burn it too. And with it, his empire and all that mattered to him, to the ground.

Finally, she would take over the realm that was meant to be hers.

She'd take back the mantle he'd claimed for himself in Manchester. She'd done her time. Boxed in. Fucked into hell by dirt hungry black dogs in uniform. Now he would do his remaining time, in agony.

SHE WALKED OUT ahead of him, past the makeshift funeral wake in the back room of the pub, and into the main front bar. It was heaving, full of second tier visitors who wanted to pay respects without getting too close to the immediate family. Knowing the family were a ticking time bomb that could go off at any minute.

It was her shape that did it.

As she descended the steps outside in front of him, her silhouette spoke... He felt, he remembered, something. He was unsure where or why. She slinked as she walked with that tight black dress; like a woman sized raven. It was a hard-edged sensuality. He was sure it'd be hypnotising to the most committed fool with a dick. Some women too.

Or was it just another ghost?

'Did you know there's a passageway from the pub at the bottom of the hill, that goes under the estuary, all the way to the small chapel over by Cross Hill?' she said as they walked. 'It's by the pool table of the pub at the bottom,' she pointed to the end of the street with street lamps, a butcher's shop on one side, tea shop on the other and Cross Hill and the sea estuary framed perfectly by the buildings at the end.

'I think I heard something about it. Isn't it the old village graveyard? Got cut off when the river changed direction...'

She wasn't listening to him. His words meant nothing to her.

'You can lift up the shitty Lino and see the hatch,' she said. 'A passageway to the past. Burrowing past skulls, skeletons, generations of dead.'

Rain started without warning, full blast, driving horizontally at them like small stones. They had to shout to be heard.

'Not been told of a hatch or tunnel,' he yelled. He didn't get nervous much. But something about her grew darker with each dampening second they were together.

What was their connection, or relation?

The door to the pub creaked open. And they shut it and the savage weather outside. It was empty. Everyone they knew was at the wake. The rest were in the Sun Inn waiting to cross the road when the time was right, and gate crash the food and drinks later.

'Two triple whiskeys,' she ordered for them both and they took a seat by the pool table.

'You aren't wasting time,' John said.

She said nothing. Looked at the table.

A dragon unfolded its wings. Stretched. Made ready to breath fire.

The patch of Lino flooring called out as they savoured the moment's silence and, the ominous air between them. They both liked it. Uncertainty. Mystery. A non-linear path.

'Ever wonder what would have come of all those wasted fucks?' she asked suddenly.

His eyes widened. Cold hearted and dirty talking. She was hard to ignore.

Now she had his full attention. Now he was entranced.

'What?'

'All those one night stands, glances and passes in the street. As eyes met and potential futures were played out in seconds. Fantasies. In imaginations passing by each other but not lived out. Ever wonder what any of them would have actually played out like? Rather than the one you settled for?'

'Settled?'

'Yes... settled.'

'What makes you think I've got a...?'

'Of course you fucking have,' she cut him short and grinned. It was a half-vicious and half-sweet thing.

'I don't understand?' But he did. She was a hard talker. No small talk.

'I asked you if you wanted to leave, and come here, didn't I? You agreed, admittedly. If you'd asked first, I'd have said you were the one on the lookout, single, or playing away... As it happened, I asked. And you went for it. Straight away. Still.'

'So?'

'So, therefore you were with the confidence of someone already taken, but were quick enough to answer that it's not set in stone. You might stray yet.'

'Maybe I just wanted a drink. To escape. Was bored a little.'

'Just one of these past exploits and flames...' She ignored him again. Stayed on track. 'Take one. For example, a girl at school you kissed playing murder in the dark when you were ten. Or, another one you fingered at the back of the bus when you were fifteen...'

His eyes narrowed. If they weren't related, she'd done some research.

'Take one. Then play it out, the whole sad journey, the whole sorry love affair. Right to the bitter end. Right up to this point in time.'

'What of it?'

'Now, just imagine it.'

'What?'

'All those wasted little fucks you could have been having instead.'

John's face puzzled.

'Sad, isn't it? How we can't have it all.'

'If you say so.'

'I do... And that's how I know this isn't by design. It isn't heaven or a pathway to it. Any of it.'

'What isn't by design?' John asked and his voice wavered.

'Now... pick one.'

She waited. As if he was actually picking a lost love, that could have been played out, in his head.

He wasn't. Instead, he was trying to place the woman opposite. His mind wandered. Could she be connected to the killings? It can't be a coincidence. That this dark mind which matched his happened to be in the area at the same time.

'It doesn't matter which one. You see. You'll always see the other paths for the potential to fill the void of whichever one you're stuck in.'

'Maybe,' he said. Maybe she was flirting? He was trying to justify why he took her bait and why they should make something of it.

'Definitely... You'll always take up the offer, no matter how in love you are, of following that girl in the tight black dress. In order to leave the family funeral. Because, you're a fucking man. In love. But still a fucking sad sack of a man.'

'Who said I was in love?'

'Only a man who doesn't talk, or try to sell himself is. Ironic isn't it. Makes him more attractive if he appears to listen. Do they ever, really, though?'

He looked at her stilling trying to figure her out. A nagging sensation that they had some kind of history beyond vague family grew.

The points in time when it mattered most, the history, when he was gone from his homelands, were mangled through drink, terrors and flashbacks. Deciphering this back catalogue was a game of spherical Tetris in his head—the greatest of hangovers to re-piece together. Futile. Finding her image amongst all this was impossible.

'A hatch,' he said, changing the subject, whilst his brain continued to analyse her. He gestured at the rectangular section of vinyl on the floor. It was a different faded dirty colour to the rest, patched carelessly repeatedly over the years, without hiding fully what was behind it. No one had ever thought to cover the hatch's position from sight all together.

'When the river changed course, cutting the villagers off from their graveyard, some of them clubbed together. Dug out the tunnel,' she explained.

'To stay connected to their dead.'

'Some people don't like the division, still, even though they've lost family ties to who's actually buried there. At one point in the 70s they built the wall at the base of Cross Hill to stop the bones, skulls and carcasses coming out in another round of shifting sands.'

'I heard that.'

'You'd have been a small boy then, wouldn't you? Running along the sands with death behind you? A spine and a skull.'

He stared. His mind joined a recent dream to the words she spoke.

He puzzled at her in his head but kept a poker face.

Then came flashes of the club in Manchester he worked the door of. Faces in a crowd. A bloody dress. A young girl dying, then dead. Her bloody white slip of a dress sprayed from the inside as one leg left the stage and another reached the dance floor below.

Overhead, an unsympathetic DJ played on.

She was that DJ.

'There's plenty of paper articles on it. The Bones falling out, John.'

He couldn't remember her using his name until then. It didn't sound natural. Her lips and face made shapes, like when people talk of injuries. Wincing, knowing they'd forget all about it if they didn't have to keep saying the words out loud.

An injury: John.

She kept going, 'Once, a young boy, maybe around your age, was digging at the base of that hill with the cross. His mother was sunbathing with her friends, or about as many rays as you can catch with the North Pole around the corner here, not sure if it's real sun... Anyway, John, they shouted out for him, thinking he was lost—that little boy.'

His mind ached. He felt trespassed, as she walked through his dream.

'They kept screaming out for him more and more on that beach. No response. Lost. When he appeared and they saw what he had found and was dragging through the sand, they screamed 'til their throats burned even more. Probably wished he'd just stayed lost, John, rather than bring all that death trailing behind him.

His head throbbed. Ached.

'Apparently you could hear it six miles away in Amble. Those screams. They sent the birds flying with their banshee shouts... and then he came back, quite innocently. Running, skipping along. Was it you, John? Pulling that spine and skull through the sands behind you?'

He looked puzzled, non-committal. She'd thrown him a spinner, a curve ball. And rather than attempting to swing, he stood back from the plate. Closed his eyes wishing the growing pain in his head would stop. Wishing she'd get out of his head.

'They were horrified weren't they, the mother and her friends?' She'd decided it was John, the little boy, and projected him fully into the event. 'You never looked happier, did you? With your new dead play-thing?'

One of John's eyes twitched, the dream and memory she'd danced around fitted perfectly, 'I think I heard something,' he played it down.

The woman was at him with something, sharpening knives, firing tracer shots as she spoke, testing her range to his emotional triggers. Since war, he'd slowly got used to the other battlefields people played and fought on. This was no different.

He felt it, and knew now, there would be blood.

'The tunnel would have long since filled up, flooded or crashed in,' he said, changing the subject back to the square patch on the floor.

'Maybe,' she said and took a long draw from her glass. 'But aren't you curious. Just a little,' and with a sleight of hand and magician's smoothness, she moved the glasses, ashtray and table matts around.

Her eyes held him entranced.

The action of her hands seemed irrelevant at first, then he remembered, it wasn't the first time she'd done it as she'd been distracting him with those heavy hard words.

ANOTHER ROUND WAS finished that he couldn't remember agreeing to, as the barman slowly bled out behind the counter.

'Last orders,' a woman whispered in his ear. He struggled to battle the headache and a dreamlike state taking over him. Vision blurred.

He saw double. Then, he couldn't feel his feet anymore. But realised he was standing, then walking... Lifting a hatch. Going in.

Darkness.

Then came more whispered words, unsympathetic and cold:

'Do you ever stop dragging death behind you everywhere you go, little boy?'

22

RESIGNED TO LOVE

THE THIRSTY OLD SOW was normally full of coppers, some bent, others just about getting there; slightly tainted. Old gilded frames and ageing flock paper covered the walls, not a straight line among them. The police pretty much unofficially owned the place as far as they were concerned. But the ex-cons and the Madam who ran it had other ideas. As far as they were concerned the pigs that filled it were the cancer within and they were the cure. One dirty pint and spit in a sandwich at a time.

Eddie made sure they had the place to themselves for as long as they could get away with. Eddie relished the prospect, jumped at the chance when she'd suggested it. Knowing it was as near to an actual date as he was going to get with Cherry before she left. 'You know what it'll mean if you do this?' Eddie had sat opposite her on the small circular table all afternoon trying to listen objectively. It was *hard*, and in all the wrong ways, he joked to himself. As usual, he was thinking as seedily as hell and didn't care less. A few drinks down, maybe he'd try it on anyway. What's to lose?

He'd always had desires on her when they were on the cases together, and he didn't want her to leave his unit. And not for John Black, for shit's sake. The man was on the wrong side of the law, Eddie thought. Regardless of what he'd been branded recently: writer, undercover loose canon...

'You sure, Pet. Is this really what you want?' He felt anger, as he did his best sympathetic act. Desperately wanting to smack some sense into her. And, the rest.

An ex-burlesque titty twister to the filthy rich, and once a hard-nosed street Madam, now turned fierce landlady, glared from the pub counter. She'd taken an instant dislike to him ever since he started coming in. Something didn't sit right with her about him. He seemed more rotten than the rest, and a rotten copper was worse than most.

'Yes,' Cherry said.

'You sure?' he said again. He wasn't going to let her leave without squirming a little for him. 'Come on. Of all the ways your life could go.' He thought of himself... He did that a lot. 'You had to decide it's with him.' He thought of John: hated him, wanted him dead.

It had played on his mind for a long time: Cherry's distractions and fascinations with John. A month ago, when Cherry interrupted him as Eddie was about to ask her out... she went on to talk about John's latest book, some criminal takedown—and some other shit, and it had stopped him sleeping. He lay awake that night tossing about, sweating. Eventually, the sweating stopped and the scheming started; he'd get rid of him, have Cherry to himself. John Black would disappear as quick as he'd appeared.

'Pet, come on... Really?'

'IT IS. What I *really* want. *Yes*, Eddie.' She hated when he called her Pet. And most of the times in between. She'd never been that fond of him. Like the landlady, something about the man just wasn't right—she could sense it. The middle-aged tired-looking man in an unwashed, creased Oxford Blue button-down shirt carried the air of lost self-respect, yet he still demanded it from others. And, most of all there was that seedy persona that lingered about him.

'You know it's all gone bad up there. As soon as John arrived back in his hometown the place went to the fucking dogs,' Eddie smirked and winced all at once. It was an evil combination and hard to pull off. The only true thing she would have said he was good at.

IT WAS AFTER the third sleepless night; Eddie had been doing some of his darkest thinking, plotting and research. When, the day after, he'd learned of Nina and China Bob's release dates, it all fell into place, giving him some deadlines to work to. It formed a beautifully crafted end piece for John Black in Eddie's head. China Bob wouldn't need any persuasion, maybe Nina neither, but he'd wanted to make sure and decided to pay her a visit or two inside. He'd enjoyed fucking her round to his way of thinking.

He wouldn't control either of them, when they were loose, and didn't need to. He just let them know where John would be and that he'd be disarmed, in every sense, at a funeral. Fuck, it was poetic as hell, Eddie thought. And, if Cherry wasn't going to be with him, and was going to choose John Black after all, she could meet the mixed up, fucked up, pair of savages as well, and it'd be goodnight sweetheart.

When Eddie started visiting Nina in prison, to make sure the rot had set in, he hammered it into her. She got to wear the cherry red wig too, same as the rest he preyed on. Although Nina was older than the rest, he still let her wear the wig when he gave it to her... It was her privilege.

He told her each time, 'John asked me to pay you these little visits, I've a little something he wanted me to give you.' And then he'd kneel her down, put the wig on and make her swallow him whole, until she gagged.

Nina had never once blamed Eddie himself. All the time, it was only ever John. For putting her in there and at the mercy of everyone that visited her cell. She never questioned the identity of any of the others who visited her cell either. It was like she only saw John's face.

She'd told him that she'd started off thinking she and John could have ruled it all as king and queen of the underworld. By the end she only thought of ways to make him hurt.

She was bleeding by Eddie's last visit. Neither of them seemed to care. Both evil. Going through some mechanical ritualistic motions together. Attacking John in their heads and bodies.

'Seriously...' Eddie went on at Cherry in the pub. He very nearly told her, stopped short of saying: 'Look at what you could have had'. He couldn't control his hands which were patting his chest, mirroring his thoughts anyway.

SHE DESPISED THE man more than ever. She worked hard at her poker face, but felt sure it was cracking. He must know how much she hated him by now. Why was he drawing this out?

She knew that Eddie loved badmouthing John to her. Without the sense to realise that she would be more wary of John if Eddie did ever take the time to approve of him somehow, and say something positive. Ultimately, she guessed that by talking him down, he was as close to influencing her emotions he was ever going to get. He couldn't make her squirm with pleasure so he would with resentment instead.

Cherry knew Eddie was full of it. Everything came out of him like an, 'I told you so'. And he'd been full of them all day... 'I'm the better man, look at the state of John's life.' That kind of shit. Cherry saw his true colours. Despite hating him more than ever, she needed him onside. It wasn't the time to be burning bridges whilst begging for severance pay, and to keep your pension intact.

'If all that badness can happen up there, it'll happen anywhere—he's just got too many enemies. That really the life you want? Shit chasing you around like that?'

THE LANDLADY CRASHED a glass ashtray onto the table between them, interrupting his flow.

Eddie scowled. He'd never liked her. She was crooked as hell as far as Eddie was concerned. He knew she used to look after street girls. He preferred a cheaper, younger, more broken sort... He knew she could smell it on him the way only people who've worked the trade can.

Cherry looked at Eddie and the landlady's stern confidence—commanding the space around them. The landlady ignored them both, scraped the old empty ashtray across the table and walked away.

Cherry's face puzzled. Eddie was way too bothered by such a small innocuous action.

'Do you…?' Eddie continued, as if they'd been talking some top-secret shit and had been interrupted by an office junior, '…always want to be looking over your shoulder?' In his head, he smirked again and thought: I'm the real enemy. He'll be dead before you get up there.

'Is it any worse than this?' she said, looking around the grotty boozer. 'A character from either of our pasts could come through those doors any second with a chip on their shoulders, and we could be put under, opened up with a machete, machine gun or petrol bomb. Fuck it, Ed.'

He hated when she called him Ed.

'It happens all the time, Ed, in fact… I'm probably safer with *him*. *He* does have enemies. *He* also has friends on both sides of the fence too. You know that.'

Not me, Eddie thought, and if you go to him, you'll fucking die too. Stupid bitch.

THE BARMAID LOOKED out at them both from the counter. She sure as hell hated Eddie as well, with all her might, but was unsure of Cherry just yet. She had to be wary. It didn't pay to trust the police in her business. They might have been crooked cops, but there were even crookeder villains running the pub.

'So do we… you know… have friends on both sides,' Eddie chipped back in. The battle was lost but he kept moaning on for his own release. 'In fact, some think he is our biggest insider, on the *other* side. And that's what makes him most prone to be taken out.'

'Who said he's to be taken out.'

'Sorry, figure of speech. I'm talking shit, Pet,' he wasn't though. Eddie meant every word. 'You go then. Settle for what you want, if it is him.'

'I'm settling for what I deserve, Eddie. And it is him. It's John.'

'Then, we'll have to take your badge, and...' he paused for some last controlling effect. 'I'm going to have to get a lot more drinks in.' He smiled.

She didn't.

He wanted to take her dress too, as well as the badge, and to take her out back and fuck some real sense in to her. He'd always thought about doing it to her, and never did anything about it... Not ever with her, or any of the other ones strong enough to tell him to 'fuck off and die'. That's why he wanted them all so much. The forbidden fruits from an unclimbable tree.

CHERRY DOMINATED EDDIE'S fantasies, and the young ones he paid to look like her didn't do it for him. But he kept at it. Paying. And doing it to them. Over and over again.

He insisted the young girls wore a cherry red wig he took along with him each time in his pocket. He pulled it onto their heads rough, hurting them as he did it. The sex, if you can call it that, got harder too; full of resentment and bitterness as he got drunker and drunker before meeting the girls each time. Angrier and angrier at himself as he channelled feelings for her out and into them with each hammered stroke.

Eventually, one of the girls' pimps was to stick a joiner's bradawl spike deep into his ear as he was about to come. The girl rolled out from under, gave him a kick and the man that had stabbed him laughed as Eddie faded out on the floor. They just saw another rotten police pig who'd stopped paying, tipped off to them by a local landlady.

He had started asking for protection money rather than paying for a service. With that, and all the creepy shit with the red wig — he wasn't worth it to them anymore. A worthless piece of corrupt pig shit. He didn't know anything they didn't know anyway. He wasn't much of an insider anymore. He'd gotten distracted with something, or someone, lately. He'd lost the edge and thirst to get them anything really meaty information wise.

In the end all they saw was a dying failed bent copper.

And all he saw... was a faux image of Cherry, the last one that got away. Fading out to nothing as he bled out on an abandoned factory floor.

It was the same factory he always insisted they all meet him at. The girls. And the same one John Black once told Eddie how he felt about Cherry in, after they'd found a dead street girl wrapped in a polythene sheet.

Eddie's sheet.

It was Eddie's first and last murder victim, made up to look like her. He'd accidentally strangled her mid act, and disposed of her body like a tainted sandwich, or the condoms he would throw by a kids' playground on the way home.

'I KNOW,' Cherry said, and put her badge on the pub table in agreement. I've been thinking of leaving for a while. He's an added extra, and I love him.'

He cringed. Felt sick. What the fuck has love got to do with anything. He was immune.

'We know he walks a fine line between one side and the other. Gangster, police, informant... Writer even,' Eddie tried to turn back on to topic. Away from the 'L' word.

She nodded and he stood up to get more drinks.

'If he was *just* a writer, we could maybe make it work. But then he'd have no fucking material, would he?' Eddie said, and walked off. He let out a mini-laugh then choked it back. There was no space for humour in the room. They all harboured demons. The bar staff included.

Other than them. The place was empty, but felt full of love and hate.

She smiled. Damn it, she hated having to try and get along with Ed. And she knew he knew it too.

Their time slot overran. They couldn't keep the punters at bay forever and the pub around them grew full of off duty police, some retired detectives and a handful of informants.

THE LANDLADY OF The Thirsty Old Sow didn't mind the filth too much. They always paid, and there was rarely any trouble that they knew of. Except that dirty bastard who was sat in the bar with the woman with the deep red hair—he had a taste for the teen barmaids.

'Not this time,' the landlady whispered in the chef's ear as he went to add his usual dose

of bodily fluids to the chip butties. 'I don't know what it is with her, that girl that's sat with him. Something's different—I think she needs a break. Give that dirty cunt both barrels though—blow a throat oyster or two over *his...*'

'Will do, boss,' the chef grinned and re-started gurgling, sniffing and coughing in preparation.

'I think that bastard she's with had something to do with Penny disappearing.'

And he did.

With a throat growl and gurgle, the chef summoned up a glob of phlegm, let it dangle to show her, then let it drop into a chip filled bap, ketchupped it to cover the evidence, and sealed it shut with his dirty hands.

'Aww, a real beauty. A real greasy one. I was saving it for that prick PC Armstrong—I

owe him one after the shit with the scabby dog, a fire I didn't start, and the nurse's uniform with those strap-on tits I wasn't wearing... Honest, nowt to do with me...' The chef loved telling the story. It had all happened, and more.

She always laughed knowing it was all true and she loved the way he kept telling it, like a cheeky school boy.

The chef had done time. All the bar staff had, and the punters knew it. Why any of them trusted the food—who knows. The bent coppers thought the bent criminals cancelled each other out—like they had a mutual respect. Most of the coppers had caught, first hand, and put the staff away in some shady past lives. It was a power play; a modern-day master and slave thing; them ending up working in that favourite police boozer.

Now released, both sides of the law had them trapped, to keep an eye on—and vice versa.

It was the only sure way of not getting accused of anything as far as the ex-con staff were concerned. The irony being, the bar and kitchen staff knew it was the perfect alibi: *'Sorry officer, I was working that night in The Thirsty Old Sow. Didn't you see me? I was nowhere near the cashpoint that got lifted out the wall with a forklift. I was pulling pints at the time. Honest Gov.'*

The landlady delivered the food to the table. Eddie didn't look up. Not even a glimmer of thanks. Cherry did though, and mouthed 'thank you'.

The landlady walked away smiling, proud—another small victory.

EDDIE STOOD UP again from the small padded stool opposite Cherry, looked deep into her eyes both in lust and sympathy. 'If you go, they won't let you back in, Cherry. You know that, right? Sorry, Love. I feel like I'm going on a bit.' But she knew he wasn't sorry.

She hated being called 'Love'.

'I know, Ed… And make it a double while you're at the bar…' If she was going to drink through it, dull his words before leaving. She needed a hard drink.

'Triple more-like. I need something to take the taste of that sarnie away,' he said, rubbing his mouth. 'Food's not getting any better in here is it?'

'Mine was okay,' she said, and looked over to the landlady at the bar, who cast her a knowing look.

Cherry's gaze moved from the comfort of the landlady's eyes, to Eddie leaning on the bar. She was sure she could see strands of dark red hair poking out from his back pocket, like a wig. The landlady looked back at Cherry, saw a look of disgust on her face... Then, she looked back at Ed, who was oblivious to the landlady now putting the drinks down in front of him.

He was texting on a cheater's, dealer's or side-line phone. The landlady could spot them a mile off. He'd had four rounds before Cherry had walked in and was too drunk, distracted and arrogant to hide it now. He didn't notice her looking at his fingers and the screen of the phone.

The landlady joined Cherry in looking disgusted. She saw Ed's full text as his clumsy hard and greasy fingers stabbed away, setting up another fix of pretend-Cherry before they even parted ways:

A young one. Younger than the last.
Usual place. Redcliff Back Tower. Top Floor.
I want this ride 'on the house'.
Or, I take her and you in. And the protection ends.

He wouldn't live to sign off Cherry's severance pay, and she'd wasted what was left of the day humouring him. The drinks she'd shared with him, and the words she'd said to get him to see and understand, had ensured that spike would pierce his brain all the more.

Eddie fumbled the phone back into his pocket. 'What are you looking at, bitch?' he glared at the landlady, who looked at him like a grandmother might view dogshit on a child's shoe.

She said nothing. Just stared, her inner disgust gnawing at her to make the call she knew now she was going to make.

His mask had slipped. But, so had hers. He was just too drunk and distracted with Cherry to notice.

Normally the landlady left *them*, the pigs, to sort out any trouble amongst themselves. This *one* was different, when the penny dropped, and she realised what he was up with the girls, she'd decided to make sure he got stuck in the ear with something sharp and rusty.

23

THE CROWS OVER CROSS HILL

JOHN WOKE AND the woman was gone. His mind was more of a mess than normal. More polluted than normal. And he had long since lost track of what normal was.

The last he could remember was salty sea water dripping from the ceiling to his face and lips as he was being ushered along in the darkness.

A skinny dark figure, different from the one that had put him there, now crouched down and ran bolt croppers over a stone in front of a chair John was tied to. Real slow, each stroke like the cuts and hacks John was about to endure. The shape before him savoured the preparation as though longing for the moment the dulled blades would meet John's cold shivering flesh.

He was fully exposed to the North Sea winds and his captor kept pouring water on him to make sure it was working.

Evil snake's eyes stared at and through him.

'Dulling and blunting them for you. Want you to feel it. ALL of it,' he muttered, stood, and then looked disapprovingly at John's lack of full lucidity before breaking a vial under his nose. 'Snap to, soldier boy. The war's not over yet,' he sneered.

Small patches of steam rose from John's shivering, naked body. Then the figure picked up another ice cold bucket of water and threw it over him, and invigorated the steam that rose instantly as his body started to shake violently, uncontrollably, in shock.

The figure in front shook too. Excited. Like a child in front of a free pick and mix. He didn't quite know where to start first. To yank off a nipple, tear off an ear or to crush through tendons.

First, he had to taunt his victim. John had to know what was to happen to him: 'You'll feel it because you'll know it's there. The damage happening to your body. Senses dimmed by the chills, heightened by your poppered-up brain as it imagines everything that I'm doing to its feeble shell. I thought of dissecting you, slowly, drugged up... but still knowing the torture. Instead, I've gone for a brutal, less refined approach. Like your winning blow over me when we last met, John.'

John tried to look. He tried to see through the colours, cold and pain... John tried to see the demon.

'Only it wasn't a fucking blow was it, John? You tried to pull my fucking testicles off, John.'

Inside John's skull, adrenaline raced and buried his fears. It was automatic. He didn't need to sober fully for the training to kick in. As North Sea air battled the outside of his skull his training and experience bolstered his inner core. Acid had spiked his drink and now his heart pounded with the poppers. He saw the demon's true form: China Bob. A shape from his past. A spectre he was sure he'd never see again. Now with those glistening snake eyes.

He tried to mouth a response.

The replies stayed internal, flashing in front of tired, blurred eyes. Full of colours, shapes and silhouettes and further shifting forms. In his head and eyes a flock of crows were murmurating about his mind and with each flap of wings, they cast down shadows, blood and unburied the past and crushed present love. He saw rotten faces. Sliced eyes. Crushed hands he should have set free.

His inner dialogue struggled to address his captor:
You were out to kill me, Bob. I didn't stand...
a chance.
I was...
a cornered animal.
I did what I had to, to survive, at the time.
Now you have me. Put it to rest and leave them all out of it.

Bob nodded as if knowing John was trying to speak, to save himself. To save the others. He saw John's torment, trying to justify to himself everything in his life that had brought him to these torturous last few moments.

'Wondrously intimate isn't it, John? Way more connected than to anyone you've ever hoped for before. And I am the last face you'll see, ever... This is all it was for, these precious moments together. You and I. A true soldier's embrace. All that was ever good for you, John. You can't protect yourself now. And you can't ever protect *them*,' he smiled.

His face changed for a moment. Agreeingly. A sympathy. As if conceding John and him were warriors, caught on the wrong side.

Then, it snapped back to hell... 'Whatever, John. This is the way it goes. For my own enlightenment. You can't protect your loves. I've taken every one of them from this shit-hole coastal Northern cesspool. Everyone you did, could, and would have loved. Because, you chose to hide *her* away, to distance *her* from yourself, to protect *her*. It won't work. When she hears what's happened to you, she'll come to you... They always do, don't they, John.'

He let it hang in the air, knowing in those comments came John's true torture. That Cherry was to suffer again, because of him, after he was gone.

John's memory was tainted by the drugs forced upon him. And the alcohol taken voluntarily beforehand.

'Not the first time you've been here is it,' Bob glanced at the marks, holes and burns on John's torso.

John wavered side to side on the chair. Looked like he might fall.

The image in front of him split into three, then four. Magentas, cyans and yellow copies of his tormentor danced apart then together again. A crow's call brought an element of him back to his bonds, the chair and those bolt croppers as Bob propped him back up, before taking his first bite with them. Slicing and tearing through the side of John's ear.

Then his shoulder.

Thigh.

The tip of an ice-cold toe.

'Stay too. We're tougher than that...' He whispered in a jilted lover's tone. Disappointed in John's blank reaction and over familiarity to the pain.

Bob stood, realising his efforts weren't working. He remained casual, like he'd delivered a slap or a thrown glass of wine and the true punishment was to follow.

'Been here before too,' he said, opening the blades and resting them around John's cock and balls. 'I owe you one, John. And I always... follow through... on my debts.'

Bob had alluded to the bar fight in which John had met him previously. He'd thought Bob was gone for good after that. That time, Bob had John on the centre of a dirty dance floor in Bristol, a smashed glass about his head as the shards dug into his knee caps. The whole room was sure he was done for, and was on a knife edge waiting for Bob to deliver a final blow over John; broken, defeated. John had bypassed Bob's fine-tuned martial arts training, short circuited all of his pre-programmed fighting expectations, and had simply reached up yanked between his legs. It was down and dirty. But John had been dragged through wars, nothing was a clean cut game. And the players either won, or they ended up dead.

Up until now it had seemed a lifetime away. John had forgotten. China Bob had not. The poised bolt croppers were a savage reminder.

'When I take this snip... I think I'll leave you here to bleed out, John. Like your lovers, discarded about these verdant and hardened hills and slopes you call home,' he let the words hang like poetry in the air. He waited for it to harden some resonance within his foe. 'You thought you could protect your love, John. By keeping her in Manchester, Bristol or wherever the fuck... I've preyed on your pasts. *Has, could* and *would have beens* are here, John. And the best bit. She'll be here too, to save you. Cherry, won't she? And I'll have her too. Fucked up, cut up, battered within an inch of her own sanity then buried arse out for days. And then when she's lost, I'll take all that's left, as much as I like. Then, when she's tainted past even my ill tastes, then, and only then, I'll let the animals have what *they* want. Eating, gnawing at the exposed flesh of hers that I'll leave poking out for them to feast on from her box. And then... I'll bury her as she still tries to breathe her last breath.'

John snapped awake. Enough to feel his whole world that he tried to protect, all that was worth going on for, all that he tried to keep as far away from himself as possible. He felt it as clear as ice water; all of it, in threat.

He thought of his past exes, their pains at his expense.

Black butterflies carrying memories, reason and distress fluttered about his head. His past partners, already tortured souls, beyond repair. That's how they'd gravitated together in the first place. Now the darkness overshadowed them all; past, present and future. Everything. All of them. No more.

Bob's snake eyes glinted as his hands tensed and his muscles readied on the bolt croppers, charged to bring down the final curtain. Like a boy over a giant egg holding a hammer.

John's face sobered. Eyes blackened. He saw a Viking warrior. A goddess before him.

The birds stopped. The sea stilled.

Silence.

Then a massive crescendo of cawing, waves, screeches and calls.

Bob's eyes narrowed, confused. He felt a presence about him. In the walls, the air and the sea outside. Most of all, in the doorway behind him.

A blast rang out.

Ringing. So much ringing.

Bob crumpled to the floor, a hole through his torso framed John's perfect apparition, Cherry. The one he tried to protect and keep away.

THEY STUMBLED OUT of the tiny old chapel by Cross Hill. John's clothes hanging off him like he'd been pulled from a prison camp seconds before his execution. Her muscles ached to create their distance from the scene, to skirt the shoreline back to that main blown out central sand dune. The one she'd parked behind. The same dune John used to play as a child, sliding down the giant sugary sands on a tea tray as if he was sledging in the height of winter. The same dune the troops in WWII used to line their targets up, shooting at pretend cut out Nazis. That same dune John would collect the empty 303 rifle shells as the sands turned to expose history's forgotten relics many years later. Ley lines of time converged on that central main dune. It drew them closer. She wasn't sure she had the strength to carry him, though she found it. And even though he still saw triples and quadruples of everything, and the demon's image that had cut and hacked at him, his frozen limbs wobbled like jelly, and kept moving him on.

Regardless of everything that had attacked them and their purpose, together, they forced on through.

The sea mist thickened on the shoreline up ahead as their feet broke fresh sand.

A shot rang out.

A shape emerged fifty yards ahead through the spray.

The sea, again, seemed to calm in recognition of malaise. It stilled, as the gulls feigned respect, for a moment.

Cherry fell, slumping as if her strings had been severed. Blood as black as the nights that chased them started to pool about her stomach.

John froze as his brain tried to piece together a polluted jigsaw in his head. It swirled, moved, reorganised and slotted cells and meaning into place.

Another shot.

A trickle went down his head.

A primal visceral instinct took control. His eyes blackened over as he threw himself down. He looked at Cherry, her eyes closing. Weakening streams of air came from her mouth and nose as her body gasped to hang on.

John lay still and watched the silhouette slowly approaching through the mist.

'Don't send a man to do a woman's fucking job...' A voice yelled. 'Your patch is mine, John. Manchester, Bristol the lot of it. My feeble half-brother warmed you up. Now it's for me to do it. To finish you.'

John spied over Cherry's thigh as another shot ran out and kicked up sand across her back and into his eyes. He touched his head where the second bullet had grazed him, then looked back at Cherry. She used her left hand to open her coat showing John the holster.

Looking through blurred eyes from the blood, elements, emotion and LSD, John watched Bob's so self-titled half-sister approach slowly to finish them. It was a black human sized raven: the woman from the pub, who'd pushed him down the tunnel.

His heart skipped a beat or two then went into overdrive. Automatic reflex, training, and a pure animal instinct to survive.

He drove his hand to the Glock and pulled it towards himself leaving a trail in the sand. It felt heavy, like lifting the whole beach up as he rested it on Cherry's thigh and he took aim.

He saw three, then four outlines, silhouettes, coloured bodies moving towards him. When they merged into three, he took aim at the centre one and concentrated. The weight of everyone he'd ever loved was in the mass of the cold trigger.

'Kill that bitch,' Cherry managed to get out.

He squeezed.

Crack.

Cherry's thigh shifted with the recoil and the birds overhead scattered.

The shape kept advancing. Untouchable.

John fired a quick two and three at the remaining advancing demon's shapes who still jerked towards them like an old stop frame animation, the sand adding interference.

Crack. CRACK.

And *it* was down in the sand.

They both lay bleeding out as the crows circled overhead... preparing to mourn both their passing. And then the gulls gathered, less respectful — when the time was right, their eyes would be a fresh watery snack.

They both coughed blood. For now, still alive. Just.

He leaned, rolled off and dragged himself up and close to her face. 'Why didn't you bring back up?'

'They don't like fraternising... with... the other side. Made me quit...' she coughed. 'When I wouldn't leave... you...'

'You should have stayed away,' he said.

'I told them... I was going to ask you... to mar...'

CRACK. A gun shot rang out from the shape ahead. Now it was up off the sand and kneeling to take aim at them again, silhouetted by a morning sun that glared through the sea fret. The sinister form, a reaper, still approached them. It was a dark heap, dragging itself along the sand. Firing idly. Sand, blood, and seaweed flew.

He jumped back to his prone spot. Looking down the sights, he saw only one shape this time.

Crack. An explosion of crimson, skull and matter haloed the beast in front. And its body collapsed for good into the lapping tide.

John fell to the sand alongside Cherry. Their blood pooled together. He stared into her. He willed to transfer any life force he could. He wished they'd never met... Sure of these being the last shared moments, together. Sobered by the shots still ringing in his ears. Echoing life's harsh climax over them both.

Cherry's smashed phone lay by her open coat: lost to hope.

Now, unable to finish her sentence, Cherry's arm stretched in front of her into the damp, flat sand. A shaking finger outstretched further. It slowly moved and shook more, drawing two overlapping rings... and then a question mark.

He doubted what he saw, maybe it was the drugs?

'Well... if you think you can't do any better?' he struggled out. In the face of their joint deaths, and eventual peace together.

'I'm dying,' she shrugged slightly with a slight twitch of a smile. Not without a sense of humour, despite bleeding out with him. She strained, nodded, head sinking deeper into the sands.

'We all settle for the love…' he paused wheezing for air, '…that we think we deserve.'

She smiled, finger at rest on the dot of her sand question mark. Then her arm collapsed back into her pooling blood.

Her arm moved slowly back up and around him as the sea lapped at their feet. The birds returned. Nature's pausing respite short lived. Both as sure as the birds that mourned them that they would drain there and die.

A big red dog appeared over the dunes. Then a huge black one joined it; both hell dogs, drooling and lapping over their prize as a murder of crows shuffled into position on the crest of *that* main dune—time's rolling exhibition and centrepiece. It readied shifting sands, churning, welcoming another era to burn through overhead.

The sea winds wrapped their bodies in a blanket made of sand. Together. Forever.

117 metres back up the beach, a WWII concrete tank block lay lazily to one side. A large cast cube, twisted in the sand with gnarly pitted and weathered sides trapping grains of sand, pieces of fishing net and seeds that waited to try and take root—if the sea gave her permission. Seaweed and shells gathered at the base like it was a nautical shrine. In amongst the matter lay the skeleton of a sea bird that had died at sea, been forgotten, and had washed ashore alone. By its left leg lay an old bullet casing. Another war relic regurgitated by the sands of time. Its dead wings spread open like an angel's. Its right wing held John's mobile phone, dropped as they'd struggled.

The screen was black, lifeless; blank.

The sharp grasses waved in the breeze as the sirens screamed in the background. The dogs' owner called it in.

Overhead birds spotted the carcass of their fallen comrade, the washed-up skeleton by the tank block. They cried as they circled slowly dropping lower in concentric circles getting closer and closer to the beach below. The group of birds walked a slow parade, in line, towards the dead bird's carcass as the phone in its wings vibrated, then it lit up, then faded away.

The birds all stopped, to attention. Waiting for their time to restart their approach.

Droplets settled on the phone's screen as it relit with a message:

You finished yet, John? That book idea… I long for it to sing, lover,
with burning notes touched by sea air, hope and fury.
Or, you better be dead.
M. Pamplemousse X

Season 1965-66

Football League Division 1

Date	Venue	Opponents	Score H.T.	F.T.
21st August	A	Leicester	1.0	3.1
28th August	H	Sheffield United	0.0	0.1
1st September	A	Sheffield United	0.0	0.0
4th September	A	Blackpool	1.2	3.2
6th September	A	West Ham	4.0	5.1
11th September	H	Fulham	1.0	2.1
15th September	H	West Ham	0.1	1.1
18th September	A	Tottenham	0.1	1.2
25th September	H	Everton	1.0	5.0
2nd October	H	Aston Villa	1.0	3.1
9th October	A	Manchester United	0.1	0.2
16th October	H	Newcastle	2.0	2.0
23rd October	A	West Bromwich A.	0.1	0.3
30th October	H	Nottingham Forest	0.0	4.0
6th November	A	Sheffield Wednesday	0.0	2.0
13th November	H	Northampton Town	3.0	5.0
17th November	H	Blackburn Rovers	3.0	5.2
20th November	A	Stoke City	0.0	0.0
27th November	H	Burnley	1.0	2.1
4th December	A	Chelsea	0.0	1.0
11th December	H	Arsenal	1.1	4.2
18th December	A	Newcastle	0.0	0.0
27th December	H	Leeds United	0.1	0.1
28th December	A	Leeds United	1.0	1.0
1st January	H	Manchester United	1.1	2.1
8th January	A	Arsenal	0.0	1.0
15th January	H	West Bromwich A.	2.2	2.2
29th January	H	Leicester	0.0	1.0
5th February	A	Blackburn Rovers	1.2	1.4
12th February	H	Sunderland	0.0	4.0
19th February	H	Blackpool	1.2	1.4
26th February	A	Fulham	0.1	0.2
12th March	H	Tottenham	0.0	1.0
19th March	A	Everton	0.0	0.0
26th March	A	Aston Villa	1.0	3.0
6th April	H	Sheffield Wednesday	1.0	1.0
9th April	A	Northampton Town	0.0	0.0
11th April	A	Sunderland	2.2	2.2

16th April	H	Stoke City	1.0	2.0
23rd April	A	Burnley	0.1	0.2
30th April	H	Chelsea	0.0	2.1
10th May	A	Nottingham Forest	0.0	1.1

CHARITY SHIELD

| 14th August | A | Manchester United | 1.1 | 2.2 |

FA CUP

| 22nd January | H | Chelsea | 1.1 | 1.2 |

EUROPEAN CUP WINNERS CUP

29th September	A	Juventus	0.0	0.1
13th October	H	Juventus	2.0	2.0
1st December	H	Liege	1.0	3.1
15th December	A	Liege	0.1	2.1
1st January	A	Honved	0.0	0.0
8th March	H	Honved	1.0	2.0
14th April	A	Celtic	0.0	0.1
19th April	H	Celtic	0.0	2.0
5th May	N*	Borussia Dortmund	0.0	1.2

* at Hampden Park, Glasgow

Season 1966-67

Football League Division 1

Date	Venue	Opponents	Score	
			H.T.	F.T.
20th August	H	Leicester	2.2	3.2
24th August	A	Manchester City	1.1	1.2
27th August	A	Everton	0.1	1.3
30th August	H	Manchester City	2.0	3.2
3rd September	A	West Ham	0.1	1.1
5th September	A	Blackpool	1.1	2.1
10th September	H	Sheffield Wednesday	1.1	1.1
17th September	A	Southampton	1.0	2.1
24th September	H	Sunderland	1.1	2.2
1st October	A	Aston Villa	1.1	3.2
8th October	H	Fulham	2.2	2.2
15th October	A	Nottingham Forest	1.1	1.1
29th October	A	Stoke City	0.1	0.2
5th November	H	Nottingham Forest	1.0	4.0

9th November	H	Burnley	1.0	2.0
12th November	A	Newcastle	1.0	2.0
19th November	H	Leeds	1.0	5.0
26th November	A	West Bromwich A	0.1	1.2
3rd December	H	Sheffield United	0.0	1.0
10th December	A	Manchester United	2.2	2.2
24th December	A	Chelsea	2.0	2.1
26th December	H	Chelsea	0.0	2.1
31st December	H	Everton	0.0	0.0
7th January	H	West Ham	2.0	2.0
14th January	A	Sheffield Wednesday	1.0	1.0
18th January	A	Leicester	0.0	1.2
21st January	H	Southampton	2.1	2.1
4th February	A	Sunderland	2.1	2.2
11th February	H	Aston Villa	1.0	1.0
25th February	A	Fulham	0.1	2.2
4th March	H	Stoke City	1.0	2.1
18th March	A	Burnley	0.0	0.1
25th March	H	Manchester United	0.0	0.0
27th March	H	Arsenal	0.0	0.0
28th March	A	Arsenal	0.0	1.1
1st April	A	Tottenham	1.0	1.2
7th April	H	Newcastle	0.0	3.1
22nd April	H	West Bromwich	0.0	0.1
28th April	A	Sheffield United	0.0	1.0
3rd May	A	Leeds United	1.0	1.2
6th May	H	Tottenham	0.0	0.0
13th May	H	Blackpool	1.3	1.3

CHARITY SHIELD

13th August	A	Everton	0.0	1.0

EUROPEAN CUP

28th September	H	Petrolul Ploesti	0.0	2.0
12th October	A	Petrolul Ploesti	0.1	1.3
19th October	N*	Petrolul Ploesti	2.0	2.0
7th December	A	Ajax	0.4	1.5
14th December	H	Ajax	0.0	2.2

FA CUP

28th January	A	Watford	0.0	0.0
1st February	H	Watford	2.0	3.1
18th February	H	Aston Villa	0.0	1.0
11th March	A	Everton	0.1	0.1

* at Brussels

Season 1967-68

Football League Division 1

Date	Venue	Opponents	Score H.T.	Score F.T.
19th August	A	Manchester City	0.0	0.0
22nd August	H	Arsenal	1.0	2.0
26th August	H	Newcastle	3.0	6.0
28th August	A	Arsenal	0.1	0.2
2nd September	A	West Bromwich A	1.0	2.0
5th September	A	Nottingham Forest	0.0	1.0
9th September	H	Chelsea	1.0	3.1
16th September	A	Southampton	0.1	0.1
23rd September	H	Everton	0.0	1.0
30th September	H	Stoke City	1.1	2.1
7th October	A	Leicester	1.0	1.2
14th October	H	West Ham	2.0	3.1
24th October	A	Burnley	0.1	1.1
28th October	H	Sheffield Wednesday	1.0	1.0
4th November	A	Tottenham	0.1	1.1
11th November	H	Manchester United	0.2	1.2
18th November	A	Sunderland	1.1	1.1
25th November	H	Wolves	1.0	2.1
2nd December	A	Fulham	0.0	1.1
9th December	H	Leeds	2.0	2.0
16th December	H	Manchester City	0.0	1.1
23rd December	A	Newcastle	1.1	1.1
26th December	A	Coventry	1.1	1.1
30th December	H	Coventry	1.0	1.0
6th January	H	West Bromwich A	1.1	4.1
20th January	H	Southampton	0.0	2.0
3rd February	A	Everton	0.1	0.1
12th February	A	Chelsea	0.1	1.3
24th February	H	Leicester	0.1	3.1
2nd March	A	Wolves	0.1	1.1
16th March	H	Burnley	1.1	3.2
23rd March	A	Sheffield Wednesday	1.0	2.1
6th April	A	Manchester United	2.1	2.1
12th April	H	Sheffield United	1.1	1.2
13th April	H	Sunderland	1.1	2.1
15th April	A	Sheffield United	1.1	1.1
20th April	A	West Ham	0.1	0.1

27th April	H	Fulham	2.1	4.1
29th April	H	Tottenham	1.1	1.1
4th May	A	Leeds	0.1	2.1
11th May	H	Nottingham Forest	3.1	6.1
15th May	A	Stoke City	0.0	1.2

LEAGUE CUP

13th September	H	Bolton Wanderers	0.1	1.1
27th September	A	Bolton Wanderers	1.1	2.3

FAIRS CUP

19th September	A	Malmo	1.0	2.0
4th October	H	Malmo	2.0	2.1
7th November	H	Munich 1860	3.0	8.0
14th November	A	Munich 1860	1.1	1.2
28th November	A	Ferencvaros	0.1	0.1
9th January	H	Ferencvaros	0.1	0.1

FA CUP

27th January	A	Bournemouth	0.0	0.0
30th January	H	Bournemouth	2.0	4.1
17th February	A	Walsall	0.0	0.0
19th February	H	Walsall	3.0	5.2
9th March	A	Tottenham	0.0	1.1
12th March	H	Tottenham	1.0	2.1
30th March	A	West Bromwich A	0.0	0.0
8th April	H	West Bromwich A	1.0	1.1
18th April	N*	West Bromwich A	1.1	1.2

* at Maine Road

Season 1968-69

Football League Division 1

Date	Venue	Opponents	Score	
			H.T.	F.T.
10th August	H	Manchester City	1.1	2.1
14th August	A	Southampton	0.1	0.2
17th August	A	Arsenal	0.1	1.1
20th August	H	Stoke City	0.1	2.1
24th August	H	Sunderland	3.0	4.1
27th August	A	Everton	0.0	0.0

31st August	A	Leeds United	0.1	0.1
7th September	H	Queens Park Rangers	1.0	2.0
14th September	A	Ipswich Town	0.0	2.0
21st September	H	Leicester	4.0	4.0
28th September	A	Wolves	3.0	6.0
5th October	A	Burnley	2.0	4.0
8th October	H	Everton	0.0	1.1
12th October	H	Manchester United	1.0	2.0
19th Octber	A	Tottenham	1.1	1.2
26th October	H	Newcastle	1.1	2.1
2nd November	A	West Bromwich A	0.0	0.0
9th November	H	Chelsea	2.1	2.1
16th November	A	Sheffield Wednesday	1.0	2.1
23rd November	H	Coventry City	1.0	2.0
30th November	A	Nottingham Forest	1.0	1.0
3rd December	H	Southampton	1.0	1.0
7th December	H	West Ham	1.0	2.0
14th December	A	Manchester United	0.0	0.1
21st December	H	Tottenham	0.0	1.0
26th December	H	Burnley	1.1	1.1
11th January	H	West Bromwich A.	0.0	1.0
18th January	A	Chelsea	0.0	2.1
1st February	H	Sheffield Wednesday	0.0	1.0
15th February	H	Nottingham Forest	0.1	0.2
22nd February	A	West Ham	0.1	1.1
15th March	A	Sunderland	1.0	2.0
29th March	A	Queens Park Rangers	1.0	2.1
31st March	H	Arsenal	0.1	1.1
5th April	H	Wolves	1.0	1.0
7th April	A	Stoke City	0.0	0.0
12th April	A	Leicester	1.0	2.1
19th April	H	Ipswich Town	2.0	4.0
26th April	A	Coventry City	0.0	0.0
28th April	H	Leeds United	0.0	0.0
12th May	A	Manchester City	0.0	0.1
17th May	A	Newcastle	0.1	1.1

LEAGUE CUP

4th September	H	Sheffield United	0.0	4.0
28th September	H	Swansea	0.0	2.0
15th October	A	Arsenal	0.1	1.2

FA CUP

4th January	H	Doncaster Rovers	0.0	2.0
25th January	H	Burnley	2.1	2.1

| 1st March | A | Leicester | 0.0 | 0.0 |
| 3rd March | H | Leicester | 0.1 | 0.1 |

FAIRS CUP

| 18th September | A | Bilbao | 0.2 | 1.2 |
| 2nd October | H | Bilbao | 0.1 | 2.1† |

† Bilbao won on toss of disk after extra time.

Season 1969-70

Football League Division 1

Date	Venue	Opponents	Score	
			H.T.	F.T.
9th August	H	Chelsea	1.0	4.1
12th August	H	Manchester City	1.0	3.2
16th August	A	Tottenham	2.0	2.0
20th August	A	Manchester City	1.0	2.0
23rd August	H	Burnley	1.0	3.3
27th August	A	Crystal Palace	1.0	3.1
30th August	A	Sheffield Wednesday	1.1	1.1
6th September	H	Coventry City	1.1	2.1
9th September	H	Sunderland	2.0	2.0
13th September	A	Manchester United	0.0	0.1
20th September	H	Stoke City	2.1	3.1
27th September	A	West Bromwich A.	1.1	2.2
4th October	H	Nottingham Forest	0.1	1.1
7th October	H	Tottenham	0.0	0.0
11th October	A	Newcastle	0.0	0.1
18th October	A	Ipswich	1.1	2.2
25th October	H	Southampton	1.0	4.1
1st November	A	Derby County	0.2	0.4
8th November	H	Wolves	0.0	0.0
15th November	H	West Ham	1.0	2.0
22nd November	A	Leeds United	1.1	1.1
29th November	H	Arsenal	0.1	0.1
6th December	A	Everton	0.0	3.0
13th December	H	Manchester United	1.1	1.4
26th December	A	Burnley	3.0	5.1
10th January	A	Stoke City	1.0	2.0
17th January	H	West Bromwich A.	0.0	1.1
31st January	A	Nottingham Forest	0.1	0.1
16th February	H	Newcastle	0.0	0.0

28th February	H	Derby County	0.1	0.2
3rd March	A	Coventry City	1.1	3.2
7th March	H	Leeds United	0.0	0.0
11th March	A	Southampton	1.0	1.0
14th March	A	Arsenal	0.1	1.2
16th March	H	Sheffield Wednesday	0.0	3.0
21st March	H	Everton	0.1	0.2
24th March	H	Ipswich Town	2.0	2.0
28th March	A	West Ham	0.1	0.1
30th March	A	Wolves	1.0	1.0
3rd April	H	Crystal Palace	1.0	3.0
14th April	A	Sunderland	0.0	1.0
18th April	A	Chelsea	1.1	1.2

LEAGUE CUP

3rd September	A	Watford	1.0	2.1
24th September	A	Manchester City	1.1	2.3

FAIRS CUP

16th September	H	Dundalk	5.0	10.0
30th September	A	Dundalk	2.0	4.0
12th November	A	Setubal	0.0	0.1
26th November	H	Setubal	0.1	3.2

FA CUP

7th January	A	Coventry City	1.1	1.1
12th January	H	Coventry City	1.0	3.0
24th January	H	Wrexham	0.1	3.1
7th February	H	Leicester	0.0	0.0
11th February	A	Leicester	0.0	2.0
21st February	A	Watford	0.0	0.1

Season 1970-71

Football League Division 1

Date	Venue	Opponents	Score	
			H.T.	F.T.
15th August	A	Burnley	1.1	2.1
17th August	A	Blackpool	0.0	0.0
22nd August	H	Huddersfield	2.0	4.0

25th August	H	Crystal Palace	1.0	1.1
29th August	A	West Bromwich A.	1.0	1.1
5th September	H	Manchester United	1.1	1.1
12th September	A	Newcastle	0.0	0.0
19th September	H	Nottingham Forest	2.0	3.0
26th September	A	Southampton	0.0	0.1
3rd October	H	Chelsea	1.0	1.0
10th October	A	Tottenham	0.0	0.1
17th October	H	Burnley	1.0	2.0
24th October	A	Ipswich Town	1.0	0.1
31st October	H	Wolves	0.0	2.0
7th November	A	Derby County	0.0	0.0
14th November	H	Coventry City	0.0	0.0
21st November	H	Everton	0.0	3.2
28th November	A	Arsenal	0.0	0.2
5th December	H	Leeds United	0.0	1.1
12th December	A	West Ham	2.1	2.1
19th December	A	Huddersfield Town	0.0	0.0
26th December	H	Stoke City	0.0	0.0
9th January	H	Blackpool	1.1	2.2
12th January	H	Manchester City	0.0	0.0
16th January	A	Crystal Palace	0.0	0.1
30th January	H	Arsenal	1.0	2.0
6th February	A	Leeds United	1.0	1.0
16th February	H	West Ham	0.0	1.0
20th February	A	Everton	0.0	0.0
27th February	A	Wolves	0.1	0.1
13th March	A	Coventry City	0.1	1.0
20th March	H	Derby County	1.0	2.0
29th March	H	Ipswich Town	1.0	2.1
2nd April	H	West Bromwich A.	0.0	1.1
6th April	H	Newcastle	1.1	1.1
10th April	A	Stoke City	1.0	1.0
12th April	A	Chelsea	0.1	0.1
17th April	H	Tottenham	0.0	0.0
19th April	A	Manchester United	1.0	2.0
24th April	A	Nottingham Forest	0.0	1.0
26th April	A	Manchester City	2.1	2.2
1st May	H	Southampton	1.0	1.0

LEAGUE CUP

8th September	A	Mansfield Town	0.0	0.0
22nd September	H	Mansfield Town	1.1	3.2†
5th October	A	Swindon Town	0.0	0.2

FAIRS CUP

Date	Venue	Opponents	H.T.	F.T.
18th September	H	Ferencvaros	1.0	1.0
29th September	A	Ferencvaros	0.0	1.1
21st October	H	Dinamo Bucharest	0.0	3.0
4th November	A	Dinamo Bucharest	0.1	1.1
9th December	A	Hibernian	0.0	1.0
22nd December	H	Hibernian	1.0	2.0
10th March	H	Bayern Munich	1.0	3.0
24th March	A	Bayern Munich	0.0	1.1
14th April	H	Leeds United	0.0	0.1
28th April	A	Leeds United	0.0	0.0

FA CUP

Date	Venue	Opponents	H.T.	F.T.
2nd January	H	Aldershot	1.0	1.0
23rd January	H	Swansea	0.0	3.0
13th February	H	Southampton	1.0	1.0
6th March	H	Tottenham	0.0	0.0
16th March	A	Tottenham	1.0	1.0
27th March	N	Everton	0.1	2.1
8th May	N	Arsenal‡	0.0	1.2

* at Old Trafford   † after extra time   ‡ at Wembley – after extra time

Season 1971-72

Football League Division 1

Date	Venue	Opponents	Score H.T.	F.T.
14th August	H	Nottingham Forest	2.1	3.1
17th August	H	Wolves	2.1	3.2
21st August	A	Newcastle	1.2	2.3
24th August	A	Crystal Palace	0.0	1.0
28th August	H	Leicester	2.2	3.2
1st September	A	Manchester City	0.0	0.1
4th September	A	Tottenham	0.1	0.2
11th September	H	Southampton	1.0	1.0
18th September	A	Leeds United	0.0	0.1
25th September	H	Manchester United	2.0	2.2
2nd October	A	Stoke City	0.0	0.0
9th October	H	Chelsea	0.0	0.0
16th October	A	Nottingham Forest	1.1	3.2

23rd October	H	Huddersfield Town	0.0	2.0
30th October	A	Sheffield United	0.1	1.1
6th November	H	Arsenal	1.1	3.2
13th November	A	Everton	0.0	0.1
20th November	A	Coventry City	0.0	2.0
27th November	H	West Ham	0.0	1.0
4th December	A	Ipswich Town	0.0	0.0
11th December	H	Derby County	2.1	3.2
18th December	H	Tottenham	0.0	0.0
27th December	A	West Bromwich A.	0.1	0.1
1st January	H	Leeds United	0.0	0.2
8th January	A	Leicester	0.1	0.1
22nd January	A	Wolves	0.0	0.0
29th January	H	Crystal Palace	1.0	4.1
12th February	A	Huddersfield Town	0.0	1.0
19th February	H	Sheffield United	1.0	2.0
26th February	H	Manchester City	1.0	3.0
4th March	H	Everton	1.0	4.0
11th March	A	Chelsea	0.0	0.0
18th March	H	Newcastle	3.0	5.0
25th March	A	Southampton	0.0	1.0
28th March	H	Stoke City	1.1	2.1
1st April	H	West Bromwich A.	1.0	2.0
3rd April	A	Manchester United	0.0	3.0
8th April	H	Coventry City	1.0	3.1
15th April	A	West Ham	1.0	2.0
22nd April	H	Ipswich Town	1.0	2.0
1st May	A	Derby County	0.0	0.1
8th May	A	Arsenal	0.0	0.0

LEAGUE CUP

7th September	H	Hull City	2.0	3.0
5th October	H	Southampton	0.0	1.0
27th October	A	West Ham	1.1	1.2

EUROPEAN CUP WINNERS CUP

14th September	A	Servette	0.1	1.2
27th September	H	Servette	1.0	2.0
20th October	H	Bayern Munich	0.0	0.0
3rd November	A	Bayern Munich	1.2	1.3

FA CUP

15th January	A	Oxford United	0.0	3.0
5th February	H	Leeds United	0.0	0.0
9th February	A	Leeds United	0.1	0.2

Season 1972-73

Football League Division 1

Date	Venue	Opponents	Score H.T.	F.T.
12th August	H	Manchester City	1.0	2.0
15th August	H	Manchester United	2.0	2.0
19th August	A	Crystal Palace	0.1	1.1
23rd August	A	Chelsea	2.1	2.1
26th August	H	West Ham	1.2	3.2
30th August	A	Leicester	2.2	2.3
2nd September	A	Derby County	1.0	1.2
9th September	H	Wolves	1.0	4.2
16th September	A	Arsenal	0.0	0.0
23rd September	H	Sheffield United	3.0	5.0
30th September	A	Leeds United	1.1	2.1
7th October	H	Everton	0.0	1.0
14th October	A	Southampton	1.0	1.1
21st October	H	Stoke City	0.1	2.1
28th October	A	Norwich City	1.0	1.1
4th November	H	Chelsea	1.0	3.1
11th November	A	Manchester United	0.1	0.2
18th November	H	Newcastle	2.1	3.2
25th November	A	Tottenham	2.0	2.1
2nd December	H	Birmingham City	2.3	4.3
9th December	A	West Bromwich A.	1.0	1.1
16th December	A	Ipswich Town	1.0	1.1
23rd December	H	Coventry City	2.0	2.0
26th December	A	Sheffield United	1.0	3.0
30th December	H	Crystal Palace	0.0	1.0
6th January	A	West Ham	0.0	1.0
20th January	H	Derby County	1.1	1.1
27th January	A	Wolves	1.1	1.2
10th February	H	Arsenal	0.0	0.2
17th February	A	Manchester City	0.1	1.1
24th February	H	Ipswich Town	0.0	2.1
3rd March	A	Everton	0.0	2.0
10th March	H	Southampton	2.1	3.2
17th March	A	Stoke City	0.0	1.0
24th March	H	Norwich City	0.0	3.1
31st March	H	Tottenham	0.1	1.1
7th April	A	Birmingham City	0.1	1.2

14th April	H	West Bromwich A.	1.0	0.1
17th April	A	Coventry City	1.0	2.1
21st April	A	Newcastle	1.1	1.2
23rd April	H	Leeds United	0.0	2.0
28th April	H	Leicester City	0.0	0.0

LEAGUE CUP

5th September	A	Carlisle United	1.0	1.1
19th September	H	Carlisle United	2.0	5.1
3rd October	A	West Bromwich A.	0.0	1.1
10th October	H	West Bromwich A.	0.0	2.1†
31st October	H	Leeds United	1.1	2.2
22nd November	A	Leeds United	0.0	1.0
4th December	H	Tottenham	0.0	1.1
6th December	A	Tottenham	0.3	1.3

FA CUP

13th January	A	Burnley	0.0	0.0
16th January	H	Burnley	1.0	3.0
3rd February	H	Manchester City	0.0	0.0
7th February	A	Manchester City	0.1	0.2

UEFA CUP

12th September	H	Eintracht Frankfurt	1.0	2.0
26th September	A	Eintracht Frankfurt	0.0	0.0
24th October	H	AEK Athens	2.0	3.0
7th November	A	AEK Athens	2.1	3.1
29th November	A	Dynamo Berlin	0.0	0.0
13th December	H	Dynamo Berlin	2.1	3.1
7th March	H	Dynamo Dresden	1.0	2.0
21st March	A	Dynamo Dresden	0.0	1.0
10th April	H	Tottenham	1.0	1.0
25th April	A	Tottenham	0.0	1.2
9th May	H	Borussia Moenchengladbach		*
10th May	H	Borussia Moenchengladbach	2.0	3.0
23rd May	A	Borussia Moenchengladbach	0.2	0.2

* 27 mins. Abandoned   † after extra time

Shanks for the Memory

Season 1973-74

Football League Division 1

Date	Venue	Opponents	H.T.	F.T.
25th August	H	Stoke City	1.0	1.0
28th August	A	Coventry City	0.0	0.1
1st September	A	Leicester City	0.0	1.1
4th September	A	Derby County	1.0	2.0
8th September	H	Chelsea	1.0	1.0
12th September	A	Derby County	1.2	1.3
15th September	A	Birmingham City	0.0	1.1
22nd September	A	Tottenham	1.1	3.2
29th September	A	Manchester United	0.0	0.0
6th October	H	Newcastle	1.0	2.1
13th October	A	Southampton	0.1	0.1
20th October	A	Leeds United	0.1	0.1
27th October	H	Sheffield United	1.0	1.0
3rd November	A	Arsenal	0.0	2.0
10th November	H	Wolves	1.0	1.0
17th November	H	Ipswich Town	3.1	4.2
24th November	A	Queens Park Rangers	1.0	2.2
1st December	H	West Ham	1.0	1.0
8th December	A	Everton	0.0	1.0
15th December	A	Norwich	1.1	1.1
22nd December	H	Manchester United	1.0	2.0
26th December	A	Burnley	0.1	1.2
29th December	A	Chelsea	1.0	1.0
1st January	H	Leicester	0.1	1.1
12th January	H	Birmingham City	2.1	3.2
19th January	A	Stoke City	0.0	1.1
2nd February	H	Norwich City	0.0	1.0
5th February	H	Coventry City	1.0	2.1
23rd February	A	Newcastle	0.0	0.0
26th February	H	Southampton	0.0	1.0
2nd March	H	Burnley	0.0	1.0
16th March	H	Leeds United	0.0	1.0
23rd March	A	Wolves	1.0	1.0
6th April	H	Queens Park Rangers	2.0	2.1
8th April	A	Sheffield United	0.0	0.1
12th April	A	Manchester City	1.0	1.1

13th April	A	Ipswich Town	0.1	1.1
16th April	H	Manchester City	4.0	4.0
20th April	H	Everton	0.0	0.0
27th April	A	West Ham	0.1	2.2
2nd May	H	Arsenal	0.0	0.1
8th May	A	Tottenham	0.0	1.1

EUROPEAN CUP

19th September	A	Jeunesse Esche	1.0	1.1
3rd October	H	Jeunesse Esche	0.0	2.0
24th October	A	Red Star Belgrade	0.1	1.2
6th November	H	Red Star Belgrade	0.0	1.2

LEAGUE CUP

8th October	A	West Ham	1.1	2.2
27th October	H	West Ham	1.0	1.0
21st November	A	Sunderland	1.0	2.0
27th November	A	Hull City	0.0	0.0
4th December	H	Hull City	2.0	3.1
19th December	A	Wolves	0.0	0.1

FA CUP

5th January	H	Doncaster Rovers	1.2	2.2
8th January	A	Doncaster Rovers	1.0	2.0
26th January	H	Carlisle United	0.0	0.0
29th January	A	Carlisle United	0.0	2.0
16th February	H	Ipswich Town	1.0	2.0
9th March	A	Bristol City	0.0	1.0
30th March	N*	Leicester	0.0	0.0
3rd April	N**	Leicester	0.0	3.1
4th May	N***	Newcastle	0.0	3.0

1974 CHARITY SHIELD

| | N*** | Leeds United | 1.0 | 1.1† |

N* at Old Trafford   N** at Villa Park   *** at Wembley   † Liverpool won on penalties

Printed in Great Britain
by Amazon

ABOUT THE AUTHOR

John's work has appeared online and in print for the likes of Red Dog Press, Close to the Bone, Bristol Noir, Storgy Magazine, Litro Magazine, Punk Noir Magazine, Necro Magazine and Deadman's Tome.

He grew up on the coast in rural Northumberland, a region steeped with a history of battles, Vikings, wars and struggles. These tales and myths fascinated him as a child, and then as an adult. In the mid to late nineties, he studied in Salford enjoying the bands, music, clubs and general urban industrial-ness of Greater Manchester, including the club scene and the infamous Hacienda. He was also there when the IRA bomb went off in 1996

John now lives in Bristol with his wife and daughters, where he has been since the late nineties. He is a professional designer, artist and writer as well as a proud husband, father, brother and son

He is the founder, curator and editor-in-chief of Bristol Noir, an online magazine showcasing the best new and established indie crime noir writers.

AUTHOR'S NOTE

If you've read this far it might surprise you to know, I love all of the places I write about. They're very much, and always, in my heart and mind.

The next Black Viking Thriller (VIKING: The Jungle Turned Black) is based in Borneo and Malaysia. Mainly, it is set on the beautiful island of Pangkor Laut. This is where we spent our honeymoon. Until pirates took over the island, kidnapped my wife, and I had to awaken the darkness inside to try and rescue her.*

Like I said, I love the places I write about. But, like all the best love affairs, it's complicated.

Only the island truly knows what happened.